Dele
Weds
Destiny

Dele Weds Destiny

Tomi Obaro

R A N D O M   H O U S E
L A R G E   P R I N T

Copyright © 2022 by Oluwatomilola Obaro

All rights reserved.
Published in the United States of America by Random House Large Print in association with Alfred A. Knopf, a division of Penguin Random House LLC, New York.

Cover illustration based on an image
by robin.ph / Shutterstock
Cover design: Linda Huang

The Library of Congress has established a Cataloging-in-Publication record for this title.

ISBN: 978-0-593-60784-8

www.penguinrandomhouse.com/large-print-format-books

FIRST LARGE PRINT EDITION

Printed in the United States of America

1st Printing

This Large Print edition published in accord with the standards of the N.A.V.H.

To my parents,
Dami and Kamiye

Prologue

In the photo they are eating something out of frame, pounded yam, perhaps, or maybe eba. They hadn't bothered to take off their graduation robes; they were ravenous, tired from the heat; their bottoms sore from the plastic chairs they had sat in for hours; their feet swollen from the high-heeled shoes they had worn for the ceremony. Funmi sits on the left. She had pinned a yellow flower to her graduation cap so her loose, bouncy curls, courtesy of Mama Fatima's hair rollers and not, as many people seemed to think, a biological gift from her late Lebanese mother, frame her face just so. Enitan sits in the middle, her hand hiding her laugh. She had gotten her hair relaxed as well, but the results were not as striking. She was glad that her graduation cap added volume to what was now chin-length, lackluster hair. She had worn powder to mute the impact of her shiny forehead and to cover the smattering of acne that dotted her cheeks. Zainab sits on Enitan's right-hand side. She wears a tight black scarf that pulls back the hair around her face, and she has twisted the ends of the scarf into a low knot at the nape of her neck so it looks like a sophisticated chignon.

Zainab and Funmi were the striking beauties of the trio—"Coke and Fanta" people would joke when they would see the three of them walking together on campus. That Enitan never got a nickname was a slight she was used to. "You attract beauty," a boy had told her once, but he had meant this quite literally; she attracted beauty only in the sense that she herself was not beautiful but her two best friends were.

Enitan had wanted to mark their graduation with some sort of pageantry; she was the unabashed sentimentalist of the group, prone to easy tears. She procured a candle used when there was no light and had stuck it in the swallow since they had no cake. Funmi had rolled her eyes at first, saying it was childish, but then Zainab lit the candle and they all erupted into peals of laughter, their shoulders juddering, their stomachs aching from the strain of giggling so hard. The photo hadn't captured that moment, though, only the aftermath, when Zainab had taken the candle out and they were all eating greedily with their hands, slurping ogbono soup off their fingers.

Though well acquainted with unexpected

sorrow, they were still so excitable that day, drunk with the potential they believe they have—at nineteen, twenty-one, and twenty-two, their lives stretch out before them, vast and expansive. They feel fortunate—they are fortunate.

One of them marries a good man and has four sons, four tall, dark sons with cheekbones sharp as cutlasses and milk-white teeth. She will be surrounded by so much steady and abiding affection, so unlike the love she coveted from the romance novels she read voraciously in school, with their dramatic declarations and epic back-and-forth. But then there's tragedy—the usual, ordinary, ruthlessly unromantic kind. Three strokes and just like that she has an incapacitated husband, and the looming, imminent prospect of life without him. It is so hard to think of what she will be when he leaves her. She has been wife, then mother for so long.

Meanwhile, the one who brought the three of them together suddenly leaves the country, less than a year after this photo is taken, opting to marry the first man who ever really looks at her. She had never known what it felt like to be gazed upon with rapt admiration, to say something and know that she will be listened to. It's an intoxicating feeling—this attention. For a long time, she will think it is enough to sustain her. She is wrong.

And one of them will become quite rich, as in she-has-an-apartment-in-London, shops-at-Harrods rich, as in she-also-has-a-house-in-Lekki-and-a-sprawling-compound-in-her-husband's-village rich. As in tinted-black-SUV-windows rich and walk-in-closet-full-of-brand-name-shoes-she-seldom-wears rich, as in drivers-and-servants-and-what-her-husband-does-is-ill-defined-and-definitely-involves-bribery, but-she-prefers-not-to-think-about-it rich.

These three women are essentially sisters, though Funmi would chafe at the sickly sweetness of such a term. Their love has the makings of an ancient habit; it is automatic and unyielding. And though their unexpected separation so shortly after graduation tests their friendship, they remain steadfastly in each other's lives. And now they are going to be reunited, for the first time since this photo was printed and handed out to each of them, a few days after their college graduation ceremony in Zaria, Kaduna.

Part I

Lagos, December 2015

CHAPTER I

Enitan

"I THINK THEY'VE LOST OUR LUGGAGE," ENITAN announced to Remi. They both watched the only item left on the carousel—a haggard, haphazardly taped Ghana-Must-Go bag—make yet another turn.

"Well," Remi said, and then she looked at her mother and they both began giggling, the unfettered, unhinged laughter of the exhausted. Their journey from New York to Lagos had been a chaotic one. Remi was supposed to have spent the night with her mother in Enitan's new apartment in Jamaica, Queens, where Enitan now lived since she had moved out of the family's two-bedroom Park Slope apartment. But Remi had decided to take the train to Queens instead that morning, slowing them down considerably.

Even when she and Remi had finally managed to get a car, they had had to endure a two-hour-long wait to get through security at JFK because everyone, it seemed, was desperate to go somewhere warm two weeks before Christmas. Then they had another three-hour wait when they got to Heathrow because their flight to Lagos had been delayed. Now, at last, they had arrived, tired, hungry, and apparently without luggage.

Still, it was good that Enitan and Remi were laughing together. That Remi had even agreed to come had been somewhat unexpected. Since Enitan and Charles had announced their intention to separate, Remi, nineteen years old, had reverted back to a younger, more beleaguered self; her eyes had rapidly filled with tears when they had sat her down and first told her the news. They had not expected her to take it so hard. In truth the divorce had been a long time coming. Remi's departure for college had clarified that yes, this man Enitan had abruptly and dramatically left Nigeria for, while she loved him and always would in the familial sense (he was the father of her child after all), he was no longer someone she could envision spending the rest of her life with—certainly not as husband and wife. In many ways, it felt like a miracle that they had been together as long as they had. Sometimes Enitan wondered if, were it not for her utter literal dependence on him those first few years in the U.S., and the shared deep sense of mutual obligation toward the other—he for taking her away from everything she had ever known; her for doing so without complaint and even excitement—their marriage would have lasted as long as it had.

But to Remi, who was nineteen but a young nineteen, Enitan thought, a naïve nineteen, her mother was a traitor; she was breaking up their beautiful, close-knit family that had always prompted smiles from neighbors who thought that Enitan's presence in the neighborhood belied the persistent and aggressive whitening of the area. Just that morning, as Enitan kept refreshing the ride-hailing app hoping for a car to magically appear, Remi had rolled her eyes and sighed melodramatically and then suggested they take the bus so Enitan could save money for the divorce. Enitan had told Remi to cut it out and Remi had rolled her eyes again and so Enitan had slapped her reflexively. They had both stared at each other in shock. Remi began to cry. Enitan said she was sorry and then their car had come.

So yes, laughter was good and suggested momentary forgiveness, which Enitan appreciated. In general Remi had always been bad at holding grudges. And Enitan was grateful that Remi had given up a ski trip with her boyfriend's family over the winter break to attend the wedding of a girl she had only met twice. Once, when Remi was a baby and Destiny a docile five-year-old, dutifully holding on to the handle of the pram in which Remi had been lying in Washington Square Park; the second time as surly adolescents, when Funmi had come with her daughter on another occasion to the city and they had gotten breakfast at the Waldorf Astoria. Charles had insisted on paying the bill, and Enitan had felt so embarrassed she barely spoke to him on the train ride home.

She hoped that the trip would be good. Charles was going to be spending the holiday with his sisters and their children in that giant house in Newport—that last vestige of family wealth—so if Remi was feeling guilty or traitorous there was no need for that. In fact, before Enitan had finally decided to go to the wedding, Charles, ever the gentleman, had invited Enitan to join him there for Christmas. Everything had been amicable considering, but the thought of being in that drafty house—probably built by slaves, Enitan suspected—seeing the secret, knowing smiles from his sisters, who had never liked her, and all their bratty children—loud and entitled in that uniquely white American way—made her say no. Enitan genuinely would have preferred to stay in her apartment. Alone for the first time in two decades that first night, she had climbed onto the twin bed in her narrow bedroom and cried like she hadn't cried in years. Not since her mother's funeral five years ago. Which, incidentally, was the last time she had been home.

"So, what do we do now?" Remi asked. Enitan moved a strand of hair from Remi's face. Remi automatically flinched at the gesture, and they looked at each other then, the memory of the slap still fresh.

"I wish I had some water," Remi said, stepping away slightly from her mother.

"We should be able to buy some. I have to break these bills anyway," said Enitan. "But let's sort out this luggage situation first." It was hot, stiflingly so; the overhead fans didn't appear to be doing much. The bright fluorescent lights only seemed to make the hall hotter. Fellow passengers coming from abroad were quickly shedding layers in the humidity as sinewy luggage boys finessed trolleys stacked with suitcases. Cranky toddlers cried in harried mothers' arms, a phalanx of drivers with signs for clients stood near one side while oyinbo businessmen, dressed in cargo shorts and boots as if they were going on a safari, marched toward them.

"Wrong side of the continent," Enitan wanted to mutter to them.

She checked her watch—still set to New York time. It was 3:04 p.m. there, which meant it was 8:04 p.m. here. Funmi had told Enitan that Sunday, her driver, would be coming to meet them.

"We'll report the luggage missing and then we can find Sunday and head to the house," Enitan said. She scanned the crowds looking for a uni- formed official. She spotted one walking without evident purpose, a walkie-talkie attached to his belt loop.

"Excuse me!"

He didn't seem to hear her. She rolled her shoulders back. She tried to channel the aggression that felt so necessary when traveling in Nigeria. As soon as the plane had slowed to a crawl on the runway, the clicking of unbuckling seat belts began even as one of the flight attendants asked, at increasing volume, for passengers to remain seated. Her pleas were futile as men, always men, sprung out of their seats ignoring her. Enitan and Remi had exchanged a meaningful eye roll after the man in front of them leaped from his seat with alarming alacrity, opening the overhead bin to retrieve a dilapidated carry-on. That competitiveness, a singular, almost-myopic self-centeredness, that dog-eat-dog mentality, permeated every interaction with a stranger in Lagos. It was why Enitan had always hated visiting Lagos as a child. She felt unprepared, caught off guard by the demands of the city. Abeokuta was so much more tranquil in comparison.

At dinner parties with Charles's acquaintances, whenever talk turned to cities and the inevitable, slightly ostentatious comparisons of the ones his guests—fellow failed or struggling artists who had lived in Prague or Berlin or what have you— had visited, Charles would tell them that Lagos was like the New York of Africa. She knew he was just trying to draw a point of comparison for them but she still inherently chafed at the phrase, which she hated because it made Africa sound like one massive country, something a lot of Americans irritatingly seemed to believe, if not literally, then in essence. The other reason was because, if anything, Lagos was what New York wished it was at its grittiest. Lagosians were desperate in a way New Yorkers would never be. When failing meant actual starvation, the hustling became boundless. Of course, long term, these gripes didn't really matter. As Remi never failed to periodically remind Enitan, both cities were going to sink into the ocean one day.

"Our luggage has not arrived," Enitan told the officer, tipping her head up at him in an imperious manner. She watched the officer look at the both of them, his gaze lingering on Remi, who shifted under his eyes. The stares were going to be inevitable on this trip. She was mixed ("half-caste" as they said here at home, though Enitan had learned the hard way that this was not the appropriate term in the U.S.) and tall, with a mass of red curls and freckles. No one ever assumed that the short, skinny woman, with closely cropped hair and a complexion the warm brown of a coconut husk, standing alongside Remi was her mother. Enitan had begrudgingly accepted this fact.

The officer smiled, revealing a prominent gap between his front teeth. He leaned in conspiratorially.

"You are from America?" He was still looking at Remi, smiling. Remi reddened and looked at Enitan quickly before answering.

"Yes?" she said, making it sound like a question. She always sounded less sure of herself when she was anxious. Enitan had given Remi a lecture during their layover in London about not divulging more information than necessary to strangers while they were in Nigeria.

"You know there are kidnappings. You don't want to give anybody any reason to think you have a lot of money."

Remi had rolled her eyes. "Please, Mom. You're being ridiculous. Didn't you say yourself that kidnappings are happening on the roads? Aren't we going to be in Lagos the whole time? And as soon as people look at me, they're going to know I'm not from here, so who are we trying to fool?"

Enitan had been quiet. Remi was right of course. Enitan wanted to scare Remi into being vigilant; she was distressingly lacking in street smarts, a naturally trusting person. She had been the kind of child who would engage strangers in conversation on the subway and would say hello and goodbye as a toddler to passersby when Enitan took her on walks in the park in the middle of the day, sleep-deprived and depressed and often mistaken for the nanny.

Enitan knew her anxiety was slightly unreasonable. But traveling to Nigeria fueled her paranoia.

Just the thought of going home made her deeply apprehensive and anxious—on a molecular level. The stress of it. Now that her mother was dead, there had been no strong incentive to ever go back. Not until now.

"Don't worry, fine gehl, we will get your luggage for you in no time," said the official, and though he did not lick his lips, he looked like he would have had Enitan not been standing there. Enitan cleared her throat and mustered up her strongest glare. The official's smile weakened. "Please, follow me," he instructed them. "We will go to the computer and should be able to locate your boxes." He led them away from the carousels to a booth and asked for their passports and boarding passes. He held Remi's passport up, squinting.

"Is this the same person? This small pikin?" And he smiled again at Remi and winked. This man. Enitan had had enough.

"Please, tell us where our luggage is!"

The official now eyed Enitan warily.

"No problem, no problem." He began typing on a keyboard—hen pecks, not the QWERTY style Enitan had learned to do on Charles's old typewriter when she had first arrived in New York, unable to work legally and utterly bored. To save paper, she would reuse the same sheet over and over again so at the end of her self-guided lesson superimposed lines of **see the quick lazy fox run** filled the page.

"It looks like your luggage didn't make the flight," the official said.

He printed out a paper and handed it to Enitan. "Your boxes will be coming on this flight tomorrow. You should be able to pick them up here at that time."

He smiled again at Remi.

"Welcome to Nigeria."

THEY WALKED BACK INTO the arrival hall, this time studying the signs the drivers were holding up more closely. Sunday should be here by now. She spotted him at the far end of the line.

"Sunday," Enitan said when she saw him. "How far?" They had met before briefly. Five years ago, he had picked her up from the airport and had driven her to Abeokuta the following morning—courtesy of Funmi.

"This is my daughter, Remi," Enitan said.

Remi smiled and stuck out her hand. "So nice to meet you, Uncle Sunday."

Sunday looked bewildered. He took Remi's hand tentatively, while looking at Enitan as if for permission.

All Remi's life, Enitan had told her that calling adults by their first names was rude. Mister or Ms. sufficed, though Enitan still thought those honorifics sounded so formal, so distant. They were fine for white people Enitan didn't know. Charles told Enitan he thought it would be odd for Remi to call their friends "uncle" or "aunty" if they weren't related. Enitan had fought this battle and won for a while when Remi was young, but by the time she turned eleven, Remi had abandoned the habit. She had decided it was awkward after her friends would stare at her quizzically when she told them the Indian woman with the Trinidadian accent who sometimes picked her up from school was Aunty Maya. Remi hadn't revived the practice until now.

Enitan smiled at Sunday and he took her carry-on. Then he looked behind them as if he expected the rest of their luggage to suddenly appear.

"Madam, na all your bag be dis? Where the remaining?"

"They didn't make it," Enitan said. "Don't worry, we will get them tomorrow. Let's go."

They followed Sunday out of the hall and into the humid night air. The streetlights cast a soft lambent glow and illuminated the hordes of flying insects hovering near each lamppost. Enitan used her knuckles to knead her lower back slowly. She had had to pick up extra shifts at the nursing home in order to accrue the ten days of vacation she was taking and to start saving up for the divorce. The dull ache there was a reminder that her body was no longer cut out for such labor. As annoying as standing around and waiting for their missing luggage had been, it was preferable to sitting at the moment. And judging from the long line of traffic right in front of the airport, they would be sitting for a long time.

A zealous young man speed walked past them commandeering a luggage trolley loaded with precariously positioned suitcases. A fashionably dressed young woman wearing Dolce & Gabbana sunglasses, her phone glued to her ear, followed slowly after him.

Sunday led them to where the SUV was parked and loaded their carry-ons into the trunk. They settled into the car and immediately drove into the snaky line of traffic, succumbing to a snail's pace.

Sunday put on the air-conditioning and switched on the CD player. "God will make a way when there seems to be no way," boomed out of the speakers. Enitan recognized the cloying baritone. It was Don Moen, the American praise and worship leader whom her mother had loved so much, especially after she had gotten heavily involved in the Celestial Church and renounced all secular music. She had played Moen's music ad nauseam.

Remi smiled. "This is Grandma's music." Enitan smiled back and squeezed her daughter's hand.

Enitan's mother, Sharon, had visited them in New York on two different occasions, and she and Remi had shared a bedroom. Her eyesight was failing, so Charles bought her a portable CD and tape player. Enitan had scavenged around Fulton Market, looking for Agatha Moses or Midnight Crew—Christian acts that at least sang songs in Yorùbá and Igbo with percussion sections that you could dance to. But her mother favored the rhythmless Americans, singing along with the machine in her bedroom until late into the evening. Charles had found it amusing, as he generally found all religious expression to be, until the upstairs neighbors began to complain. But Enitan didn't have the heart to confront her mother about the noise. Her presence in New York had been a hard-fought détente. Enitan did not want to disturb this fragile peace. And Remi loved her grandmother. The hardness Sharon had acquired in her later years melted in Remi's presence. She taught Remi how to roll meat pies and how to cut plantain in oblong ovals. She and Remi went on walks together; Remi always so talkative, asking so many questions and Sharon happy to answer them all.

Those were perhaps Enitan's favorite memories of her mother. Obtaining Sharon's forgiveness had been such a difficult experience. When Enitan had finally gathered the courage to call her after she and Charles had eloped, the first thing Sharon had screamed into the phone was "Is he even a Christian?" He was not. Not Muslim either. Just nothing. At the time, Enitan had found this thrilling.

As the synth-laden keys began to transition into another song, Enitan knew she couldn't listen to this music much longer.

"Please, can you put on the radio?" she asked Sunday. He nodded and fiddled with the sound system until a pop song started playing.

The singer sang in Yorùbá. Remi hummed along. Enitan looked at her daughter.

"You know this song?"

Remi pretended to look annoyed. "Yes, it's a huge song, Mom. Afrobeats is global now."

"Afrobeats? This isn't Afrobeat. That's Fela."

"Afrobeats," Remi said, emphasizing the plurality of the word. "It's a totally different genre," she added, but they had finally started moving and so her voice trailed off as they began speeding toward the bridge. Enitan looked out her own window. The city sprawled before them, a maze of scattered objects indiscriminately placed together: flyover bridges, yellow Keke NAPEPs and fearless okada drivers negotiating space on the roads, weary office workers trudging to car parks, snack and newspaper vendors weaving into traffic, illuminated billboards for Milo hot chocolate and mobile phone service providers featuring cheery brown families. She looked over at Remi, whose face was plastered to the window. This was Remi's first time in Nigeria, and Enitan was surprised at how suddenly and urgently she wanted Remi to love the country. As if she hadn't left Nigeria voluntarily for a whole raft of reasons.

"Is that Makoko?" Remi asked. Enitan looked out Remi's window and saw the telltale maze of wooden huts floating above the fetid water—a few canoes with kerosene lamps illuminating the stillness of the ocean. A structural feat, both of human ingenuity and of cruelty.

"Yes."

They sat in silence as another upbeat pop song played: "I'm looking for my Johnny," sang the artist. After two hours, the car finally slowed in front of a gate. A uniformed security guard, his AK-47 resting loosely in his right hand, waved them through. The SUV eased over a cobblestoned path. The car's headlights briefly shone on a man circling around the perimeter, huffing and puffing, wearing a tight T-shirt that clung to his convex stomach and shiny gym shorts. Behind him a woman in a long flowing buba and denim jeans was walking a tiny dog.

Sunday turned down the street and drove past imposing houses barricaded by cement walls with barbed wire festooned on top. He stopped at a yellow gate and honked the horn. The gate slowly opened forward and then back. Sunday rolled into the courtyard. There were two SUVs parked outside. The headlights from Sunday's car shone onto the house's exterior, which was an intimidating bulwark of cream brick with a coral stucco roof.

Purple bougainvillea lined the walls and there were banana trees planted around the perimeter of the courtyard.

"Wow," Remi said, opening the car door and stepping out. "Beautiful." Enitan also got out of the car and stretched. They both watched the front door open.

"Enitan, is that you?"

CHAPTER 2

Zainab

TAKING A BUS FROM KADUNA TO LAGOS HAD been a mistake. Hamza hadn't wanted Zainab to do it, but she felt uneasy about flying ever since that plane crash killed all those schoolchildren coming home for the Easter holiday. She also didn't feel right about spending so much money. Since Ahmed had retired from the polytechnic, they were dependent on the minuscule payments from his pension, which, given the constant threats of strikes at the university, were now often late or nonexistent. The middle child, Hamza, and his family had moved back into their flat presumably so Zainab could help with the children. His wife's last pregnancy had been a grueling one and taking care of three children under five was a challenge. But they all knew, even Ahmed, though he was no longer capable of expressing it, that it was easier to care for him when there were more adults around. It was too demanding for Zainab to do it alone anymore.

The irony of Zainab, the only one of "the trio," as they had dubbed themselves back in university, who had not read nursing in school, now relegated to caretaking for her husband was not lost on her. She was content to do it, because she loved her husband and hated to see him suffer. It was hard, though. The demands were difficult. The stroke had left him completely paralyzed on his left side, so he needed help with everything. Getting out of bed in the morning. Eating breakfast. He could only eat soft foods—so she was constantly making moin moin, blending beans and pepper and stuffing them into little foil packets with a soft-boiled egg, heating them over water and then storing them in the freezer, defrosting when she had to.

He couldn't really talk anymore; the stroke had rendered his speech mostly unintelligible and his mouth partially open at all times. But it was the sponge baths he found most humiliating. Those were the moments when Ahmed seemed the angriest. Though he couldn't talk, he could shake, and he would violently, purposefully it seemed, going out of his way to avoid being bathed by her. It made him feel helpless and childish. And there was nothing like seeing that once sinewy body, now shrunken because of all the food he could no longer eat, his penis hanging limply between his legs. He was only fifty-five.

Zainab had received the invitation in the mail.

Funmi had also texted the WhatsApp group the children had helped set up for them. Funmi was by far the most prolific user of the group. She was always sending video clips without context or doctored photos of American celebrities wearing traditional clothing that would clog up Zainab's camera feed so that when she wanted to take a video of her youngest granddaughter toddling around in her grandmother's best high heels, there was no storage available. (Though the photo of the Obamas wearing aso-oke had admittedly made Zainab laugh.) And the Bible verses. There were so many Bible verses. Zainab had repeatedly asked Funmi to stop sending them and Funmi would text **Sorry!!!!!** with that many exclamation points but then would quickly forget and start back up again, sending devotionals about wearing the full armor of God and being a virtuous wife and how God had a plan and future for the righteous. They were always typed in bright, ugly fonts in garish colors. What made it doubly strange was that it wasn't as if Funmi was particularly religious. She just sent them because they were sent to her and she was bored and rich. Zainab had once seen Funmi text her "Footprints in the sand" right in front of her when she was visiting Funmi in Lagos. She didn't even blink, just continued talking as a WhatsApp banner lighted up Zainab's phone.

Occasionally, Enitan would send a solitary **lol** in

response to one of Funmi's altered celebrity photos. And Zainab and Funmi had learned through the group chat that Enitan was returning to Nigeria for the first time since she had "absconded" (as Zainab had put it in a letter she had mailed to Enitan's mother in the hopes it be sent to Enitan in America). It had been a simple text:

I'm coming home. My mother is dead.

Zainab had quickly started finalizing plans to fly down to Abeokuta for the burial, but then Ahmed had his second stroke and it just wasn't possible for her to go. She hadn't physically seen Enitan in more than twenty years.

Zainab would have ignored the wedding invitation Funmi texted to the group, as she did most of the things Funmi sent, had Enitan not responded a few minutes later with:

Wow. How time flies. Destiny is getting married. Praise God.

Zainab looked more closely at the text from Funmi now. It was a photo of an invitation:

The honorable Professor Olusegun David Balogun and his wife Architect Elizabeth "Bisi" Balogun and the

esteemed General Olayinka Joseph
Akingbola and his wife Olufunmilayo
Faith Akingbola request your
effervescent presence at the wedding of
their son Dr. Ayodele Esupofo Balogun
to their daughter Dr. Destiny Ifeoluwa
Akingbola on Saturday, the twelfth of
December in the year of our Lord two
thousand and fifteen.

Details to follow.

So it was official. Destiny had called Zainab a few
weeks before the invitation arrived to tell her Dele
had proposed. Zainab and Destiny kept in regular
contact, speaking on the phone once a month; she
was Destiny's godmother after all and Zainab had
no daughters of her own; only sons—four of them,
only two of whom still lived in Kaduna. Zainab
liked to think of herself as an intermediary between
Funmi and Destiny, whose relationship had always
been somewhat strained, primarily because Funmi
was a loud and indomitable woman who did not
have the patience to deal with a personality as shy
and sensitive as Destiny's.

About eight months before Zainab had received
the wedding invitation, she and Destiny had been
having one of their monthly phone calls:

"And do you have any . . . friends?" Zainab had

asked, in a manner that she hoped was subtle but also exact.

"Oh, Aunty" was all Destiny had said at first.

"I'm just curious. No pressure."

"Well," Destiny had replied. "There's someone in my program. He's also Nigerian. I think my parents would really like him."

"And do you like him?"

"I do."

"What do you like about him?"

"He's very confident."

"Is that right?"

"Yes. Aren't you supposed to be attracted to the qualities you don't have? Isn't that a saying some-where?"

Zainab laughed. "I'm not so sure it is. And why do you not have confidence, Destiny? You know you are the most talented photographer I know."

"Oh, Aunty, stop," Destiny said.

"Have you been working on your photography?"

Destiny sighed. "I haven't had any time, not since we started doing rounds. And I have to get used to the lighting here as well. It's always so cloudy."

A pity, Zainab had thought. She liked to think that she had been the one to encourage Destiny to pursue her photography even though she was reading medicine; she started taking it up in ear-nest during the few months she had stayed with Zainab and Ahmed during her gap year between boarding school and university seven years ago now. A creative outlet was a useful thing; she and Destiny had bonded over their love of the arts. And it had been Destiny in whom Zainab had felt comfortable confiding that she had started writing again, after so many years of not doing so.

The next time they had talked, Zainab learned his name: Dele, one of four Nigerians also reading medicine at Destiny's school in London. A Yorùbá man. Funmi and Yinka would be thrilled. And then the wedding invitation came. Zainab had been surprised at the speed with which it all appeared to be happening; Destiny was only twenty-four. "Dele says we'll have a better chance of being placed at the same hospital if we marry now," Destiny had explained to her.

Of course Zainab planned to attend the wedding, but then two weeks before she was set to go to Lagos, Ahmed caught pneumonia and had to be hospitalized. Two days after he had been released, she sat at the dining room table, holding the invitation in her hands. It had come in a velvet envelope and it smelled faintly of dust and pepper; it had been sitting on the dining room table for months now, soaking up the scents of their crowded flat. Zainab traced the lines of embossed cursive with her finger. She looked at her phone then, noticing she had a voicemail from Destiny. It was from a couple of days ago, when Zainab and Hamza had been alternating shifts at the hospital, sitting with Ahmed. Zainab listened to the voicemail. It was hard to hear; all she could make out were the inchoate sounds of loud, thumping music, a chest-vibrating bass, and then she heard Destiny say "Aunty," and then the line went dead. It was not like Destiny to call so unexpectedly. She wondered if there was something wrong.

During Zainab's weekly phone conversations with Funmi, Funmi would complain about Destiny's lack of interest in the wedding planning, but to be fair, the extent of Funmi's obsession with the wedding planning would be enough to drive anyone mad.

When Zainab and Ahmed had married, the ceremony **and** reception had been only two hours long. But a wedding thrown by Funmi and Yinka in Lagos? It would be an extravagant and interminable event; a feat of fastidious and immaculate party planning. There would be fog machines and mood lighting, performances from rap stars, so much spraying of dollar bills, maybe even fireworks. Zainab had never been to such a wedding; she only read about them in the society pages. But she knew that this wedding was guaranteed to be a scene; it would probably be written up in the newspapers and on lifestyle sites like BellaNaija. Funmi wouldn't spare any expense for the nuptials of their only child, and Yinka wouldn't stop her.

And while Zainab did worry about Destiny, she had to admit she was excited about leaving Kaduna for the weekend. Funmi's compound in Lekki was massive. It enabled Zainab to pretend that she was fabulously wealthy, at least for a few days. Servants set up the bedrooms so they resembled hotel suites, complete with monogramed towels and custom-packaged soap in the bathrooms. There were even house slippers placed near the bed so your feet wouldn't have to touch the cold tile floor in the morning, made frigid from all the arctic air-conditioning.

It was the thought of that large soft bed, and those down slippers—of the boiled plantain with fish stew she would ask the cook Muyiwa to make her—that motivated Zainab as she sat on the bus, her lower back aching and her left foot numb. Calling it a bus was generous; it was one of those vans made out of rusted metal and held together by prayer. It had one functioning sliding door. If she looked down when the van was moving, she could see the road speeding by through a tiny hole in the floor. She had been sitting in a window seat but had gotten up to let a mother and her two children, a big-eyed, full-cheeked baby and a little boy, sit next to her. Now Zainab sat in the aisle seat, her bag wedged on her lap, her right hand holding on to the row in front of her for dear life whenever the bus made a sudden lane change. The baby was finally asleep, head nestled against the mother's bosom, thumb stuck in his mouth, but while he had been awake, she had enjoyed watching him. He was likely around nine months, a few months younger than her grandchild Jenabou, who could now stand on two feet and wander into rooms she was not supposed to. How quickly children grew!

She had packed a small sleeve of Walkers shortbread for the journey and had offered some to the young boy, making eye contact with his mother as a form of implicit permission. He had accepted it gratefully. The baby boy had watched the exchange and waved one dimpled fist in the air, crying out.

"You want some too?" Zainab asked, and smiled. "But it is too big for you." The baby was insistent. He cried and pointed at the biscuit. She broke off a small piece. "See, too big." The baby began crying in earnest, louder and more prolonged. The mother looked flustered. "Here let me," she said, and she took the piece of biscuit from Zainab's hand. She put it in her mouth and chewed a little. Then she spat out the masticated mass in one hand. "Here," she said to the baby, cupping her palm to the baby's mouth. Flashing pink gums, the baby sucked on the mother's hand greedily.

That had been hours ago. The baby and the boy and the mother were all asleep now; their heads in exactly the same position, leaning toward the left, their mouths slightly ajar. The bus had stopped at three different points; the only city Zainab remembered was Abuja, where she was able to get some meat pies and puff puff from a street vendor, and they all got off the bus to piss at the latrines in the bus park. But that was a long time ago. They should have already been on the outskirts of Lagos by now, but as she looked out the window, straining to see recognizable landmarks amid the darkness, all she saw was the color black. She ignored the small pinprick of alarm she felt deep in her abdomen. A man in front of her said aloud with annoyance, "What is taking so long now? Have we lost our way?" Other passengers hissed. Zainab checked the time on her cellphone: 10:31 p.m. She had been texting Funmi updates periodically for the past two hours. **Running late,** she texted Funmi now. She readjusted herself in her seat and closed her eyes, trying to sleep. They were speeding along and Zainab was dreaming of that bed, when the bus abruptly halted and jolted passengers awake.

"Kidnappers!" somebody yelled and suddenly the bus was alert with movement, with gasps and fumbling; the panic rippled like a wave. They all looked out the windows. Standing in the weak glare from the bus's headlights were seven men holding AK-47s in the air.

"Jesus! Jesus! Jesus!" a woman behind Zainab kept uttering.

"Run them over!"

"Drive through them!"

"Why have you slowed down!" some of the passengers were screaming at the driver. There were no other cars on the road. They had lost their way completely. Zainab looked at the time on her cellphone: 10:53 p.m. There was a missed call from Funmi. The bus came to a complete stop as one of the men walked right in front of the vehicle, waving a flashlight. A rifle hung from his shoulder.

"Security check," he shouted. They were not wearing the uniforms of the soldiers who normally did such checks. The other men in the street had their rifles aimed at the bus.

"Please, abeg, don't let them come onto this bus," the woman behind her whispered. The mother sitting beside Zainab had clutched the boy frantically to her chest. He was whimpering softly, tears falling smoothly down his face. The baby was still sleeping.

"Open the door," the man instructed the driver.

"Please, sir, me I don't want trouble . . ." said the driver.

"Commot from this bus right now!" shouted the man. "Put your hands on your head!" The driver slowly opened the door and got off the vehicle.

The man nodded at one of his associates. They both slid open the bus door and flashed their torches around. The light was white, harsh and unforgiving. One of the men had an empty flour bag. "You will exit the bus in an orderly fashion," said one of them.

"Any valuable for your body: phone, jewelry, earring, money make you drop am." He waved the bag around. "If you do anyhow, we go shoot o."

There was a swallowed murmur of panic.

"Jesus, Jesus, Jesus," muttered the woman behind her. Zainab watched as the other men in the road strategically took position surrounding the bus. One on each corner. The driver stood by the road-side, his hands hanging limply.

"Get up get up get up!" the ringleader shouted. The passengers obeyed frantically, grabbing bags and slipping on shoes they had taken off in an attempt to relax during the long trip. Zainab twisted off the wedding ring on her finger and discreetly put it down her blouse. She took her cellphone and, reaching between her legs, slid it into the back of her underwear, hoping the long, loose dress she was wearing and the wrapper she had tied around her waist would hide it. She wondered fretfully what to do with the notebook she had—foolishly now—brought with her in a naïve belief that she could perhaps write a little this weekend, on the bus or late at night before the trad and the wedding. It had been years since she had felt compelled to put pen to paper, not since her uni days. But there was an inkling of a play in her, one that had possessed her as of late, and she figured that if Buchi Emecheta, a mother of five, could write her novels and Balaraba Ramat Yakubu—a mother, a wife many times over, and a Hausa woman—could write her books too, then so could Zainab. And so she had brought the notebook and two biros. No one would take it, she hoped—why would they, it would not be of value to them. She breathed in deeply. She was grateful now that she had chosen to sit near the back of the bus, so she had enough time to take these precautions.

"Oya oya oya!" the men yelled.

The passengers began to file out of the van in a single line. The robbers stood on either side of the open door. They yanked handbags out of women's arms and shook the contents out. They grabbed wallets from the men and stuffed naira bills into their trouser pockets. "One false move, and we shoot o!" shouted one of the robbers.

Zainab moved ever closer to the open door. Her heart was beating so wildly; she could hear the blood rushing in her ears. She took a deep breath and briefly closed her eyes. Her legs shook involuntarily. She refused to think through the worst possible outcomes. She imagined that bed and those slippers and the call she would make to the house before going to sleep. She would ask Hamza how much Ahmed had eaten. She would see Enitan and Funmi and she would hug them and tell them she loved them and she would make sure to pray with extra diligence at Friday jumat and then she would dance at the traditional ceremony and again at the white wedding on Saturday, dance like she had never danced before because she was alive and she had never realized how beautiful this simple act was, the breathing in and out of air.

"Any money in here?" hissed one of the men, snatching her bag out of her hands and shaking it vigorously. She had packed lightly for the trip; she was only planning to stay for the weekend. The two dresses she was going to wear for the trad and the church wedding tumbled out as well as the note-book. And her wallet. The man rifled through the wallet, pulled out the folded naira she had brought for the trip (25,000 naira total), and dumped the wallet on the ground.

"Go stand with the others," he instructed.

"Please, sir, let me just take this—" She bent to pick up the notebook; he made as if to kick her, but looking up they accidentally made eye contact and she saw that he could not have been more than twenty-three, the age of her youngest son, Musa. He had a long scar that lined one side of his face. "I said go!" he yelled, and Zainab hurried over to the group of passengers by the roadside, clutch-ing the notebook tightly to her chest. Another one of the men stood a few feet away from them all, his gun aimed at their feet. Muffled cries and fur-tive prayers—that was what Zainab barely heard above the thunderous sound of her own heartbeat. The mother, when she had relinquished what she had, hurried over to Zainab, clutching the boy's hand and the baby, who was now awake and crying. The boy buried his face in his mother's skirt. Zainab rubbed the mother's arm. She couldn't think of what to say.

Once all the passengers had exited the bus, the two ringleaders hopped on board and looked through the seats to see if any passengers had hidden anything. Then they jumped from the bus and instructed all the passengers to turn and face the bush. "Are we going to die?" whispered one woman beside Zainab. "Oh, God."

"Shut up!" shouted one man, and a shot rang into the air. Everyone froze after that.

"Lie down on the ground!" Zainab couldn't recognize who was speaking anymore. She quickly adjusted her wrapper, tucking her notebook into the folds, and prayed that she had remembered to turn off her mobile. She got down on the ground and closed her eyes. Dust clung to her chin and forehead. Soft whimpers filled the air. She could hear the men talking quietly to each other now, in Hausa, which surprised Zainab. It would have been a smart decision since they were in Yorùbá land, but most of the passengers could likely understand; they had been coming from Kaduna after all. The robbers were deliberating over what to do with the passengers.

"Should we search them?" one of the men was saying.

"We don't have time; another car could pass by."
She couldn't make out what they said after that.
"Lie down!" shouted one of the men, and then
there was another shot and the unmistakable hiss of
a tire giving out. The screech of a car and a revving
engine and the scuffle of feet. And then another
shot and this time a cry of agony.

CHAPTER 3

Funmi

ALL DAY FUNMI HAD BEEN FIGHTING A
wicked migraine, but she hadn't had time to
rest. The wedding planner had called her in a panic
that morning saying that the alága ìjókòó they had
hired for the traditional had catarrh and so they
had had to scramble to find somebody else suitable;
there was a lot of forwarding of WhatsApp messages with queries for help and lots of phone calls.
They were both aware of the stakes of their request.
Funmi had gone to engagement ceremonies that
had lasted for nine or ten hours because the families
opted not to hire professionals and had blood relatives officiate the ceremony instead, and the aunties
inevitably had no sense of pacing and no sense of
humor; they couldn't tell the jokes that made all the
waiting around for the various proceedings—
the entrance of the families, the dancing, the greet-
ings, the prayers, the reading of the proposal, the
entrance of the groom and of the bride—more

bearable. But they had finally managed to secure someone for tomorrow, thank God. As her reward, Funmi was lying flat on her back in her darkened bedroom, hoping that the two Excedrin she had taken thirty minutes ago would cease the incessant throbbing in her right temple.

No thanks to Destiny, it must be said. Funmi had been quietly hoping that wedding planning would somehow bring them closer together—that it would end the awkward silences and stilted conversation that seemed to define their relationship since Destiny had come home. Destiny had taken the whole month of December off for the wedding, which was the longest amount of time she had spent with her parents since she was seventeen.

The first week of Destiny's stay, the three of them—Funmi, Yinka, and Destiny—would come down for breakfast in the dining room at the same time. Yinka would make an effort to put down his BlackBerry and would ask Destiny questions about her studies; she was about to begin her two-year training as a junior doctor, hopefully in a hospital in London. Destiny would gamely answer the questions he posed to her, but then silence would inevitably descend upon them all, and their attempts to start independent conversations were like straining garri with your bare hands, as Funmi's grandmother used to say. After that first week, Yinka began getting breakfast at the club again, and so Funmi would come downstairs and eat by herself. Funmi would hear Destiny's door tentatively creak open and then shut as she was coming down the stairs, as though Destiny was specifically waiting for a moment when Funmi was not eating to make her own descent, and Funmi had been surprised at the degree of hurt she had felt when she realized her own daughter was avoiding her, though she would never be willing to admit this to Destiny.

As for the wedding planning, Destiny had participated in the major decisions. Before she had come to Lagos, they had already decided that they would throw both the traditional and the church wedding on the same weekend because it would be hard for Destiny to be able to take time off once she began her NHS training, and they had chosen the color rose gold for their aso-ebi. But as far as caterers or musicians or drinks for the cocktail hours, or whether or not to only serve Nigerian cuisine at the church reception or to have English food as well, or what kind of floral centerpieces they should have for the traditional reception—Destiny had had no strong opinions. This is all to say that it is not as if Funmi intended to fully commandeer the wedding planning; it was just that if Destiny did not wish to dive headfirst into the planning, then Funmi would do it, because she enjoyed it, actually. Wedding planning gave purpose to Funmi's days, which had long been rudderless, an endless slew of shopping trips, lunch dates with the wives of Yinka's business associates, charity balls, and benefits. It was hard to admit, but there were moments when Funmi actually missed being a nurse. She missed being so exhausted by the time her shift was over that she did not have time to think or move. These last few months of wedding planning had reinvigorated Funmi.

Funmi had thought that perhaps Destiny would have strong opinions on the photographers and videographers who would capture the proceedings, since she had developed a fondness for photography. When they had spent a few months abroad (New York, Dubai, Beijing) during Destiny's gap year, on the evenings they did not have dinner or an outing planned, Destiny would assiduously edit her photos on her laptop. Her fastidiousness in this work was something that Funmi, who had no creative instincts, approved of in a vague way and mainly because so many other people, particularly Zainab, commented on Destiny's apparent natural talent, and so Funmi felt that she deserved credit for this somehow. But she honestly could not see what was so remarkable about Destiny's portraits of market women and stoic schoolgirls; everybody looked so ordinary. Zainab would say that was the point, but Funmi did not understand.

Destiny had even told Funmi and Yinka that she wanted to study the subject at university, and

Yinka had had to remind her that she was there to read medicine. But when Funmi had presented Destiny with the portfolios of three of the most highly sought-after wedding photographers in Lagos, Destiny had shut down.

"Whichever one you want, Mummy," she had said. They had tried to have a conversation about photographers whom Destiny liked and Destiny had said that Nigerian wedding photographers did too much retouching, which Funmi had found interesting because Funmi privately thought that Destiny's photos were not edited enough, but she held her tongue because Zainab was constantly saying that Funmi was too hard on the girl.

"She's intimidated by you," Zainab would tell Funmi whenever Funmi would call and complain about her relationship with Destiny. Zainab and Destiny had the kind of close relationship Funmi really did want with her daughter and had tried at various times to cultivate. But she and Destiny were different—very different; they just were; it could not be helped.

Funmi was brash, loud, stubborn—qualities she felt she had to have given how she had grown up. Destiny was exceedingly sensitive; as a baby, she had had colic and so would cry and cry and cry, and as a toddler she followed Funmi everywhere, even to the bathroom, one hand in her mouth. But then as a child, she was quiet, so quiet she would be afraid to raise her hand to ask to use the toilet when she was in day school. Funmi had had to pack extra bedsheets for her when she first left for boarding school at eleven, which itself had ignited many bouts of inconsolable crying; Destiny not understanding why her parents would abandon her even though going to boarding school was the norm for people of their social class and, as Funmi had told her, patting her back stiffly as Destiny wailed, growing up, all Funmi had dreamed of was going to boarding school and fleeing her father's house.

The tears made Funmi wonder if she had what it took to raise a girl child; if she maybe lacked the requisite tenderness it seemed to require. She had observed how Enitan and Remi openly bickered the last time she and Destiny had visited them in New York. Even though Funmi was convinced Remi was shockingly rude, she had seen that the flare-ups between Enitan and Remi stemmed from an inherent closeness and intimacy Funmi and Destiny did not have. Funmi watched Remi rest her head against her mother's shoulder when they were sitting on the train—which surely could not have been a particularly comfortable position, as Remi was almost a foot taller than her mother—and Funmi had turned away, feeling strangely embarrassed at the sight of such easy, public closeness.

Funmi opened one eye to check the time: 9:43. Enitan and Remi should be close now. Sunday had called about an hour ago from the car, saying they were stuck in traffic. Funmi let herself lie back for a few more minutes. She had drawn the shades and turned the AC to its lowest setting in the hopes of beating the headache. The house was loud. One of Yinka's brothers was staying with them for the weekend as well, and he had three rambunctious children and a beautiful but meek-mannered wife who did not know how to discipline them.

The most irritating thing about having a migraine was how completely it prevented you from doing anything else, including sleep. Things Funmi usually would have done when she was bored or tired, such as watch TV, or read, or browse wedding sites on her iPad only exacerbated the pain. She just had to lie there and think, which Funmi hated doing. She hated stillness. She hated self-reflection. The headaches seemed to be getting worse as of late, a condition, her doctor had told her, of menopause. She still felt in her spirit that she was no more than thirty, but her body was beginning to betray her. A man's shout suddenly reverberated throughout the house. The men were watching a football game. She looked again at the clock on the dresser. It was 9:53. Enitan really should have arrived by now.

And as if the simple wondering had conjured their arrival, she heard the car pull up outside and the clanking of the gate as it opened. Funmi hastily sat up. Instant regret. The pain pulsed through her right temple. She closed her eyes and waited it out. One two three. Rest. Then she very gingerly reached for the bottle of Excedrin and the glass of water beside her. She unscrewed the lid and popped another one in her mouth. From what rudimentary memories she had of her nursing classes all those years ago, she knew she was treading a fine line, taking her third Excedrin in one hour. But she wanted to welcome Enitan and Remi with the full force of her faculties. She took off the scarf she was wearing and massaged her temples. She had started doing this in an attempt to stimulate growth where her hair had begun thinning. For years Funmi had prided herself on the fact that the long hair that fell down her back a little past her shoulder blades was all her own. Now that was no longer the case. Funmi had taken to wearing wigs to hide the baldness. She was sometimes tempted to cut it all off but knew Yinka would never tolerate the idea.

She turned on the nightstand lamp and got up very slowly, grimacing against the waves of pain radiating from her right temple. When it had subsided, she stood, searching with her feet for her house slippers. She fished around the bed for her bra and put it on, immediately regretting it, as the wire dug into her back fat and her stomach. She stopped in front of the mirror to straighten out the wrinkles in her dress and to retie her headscarf.

She scrutinized her face in the mirror. The

eyeliner she traced onto the top of her eyelids every morning was still miraculously intact. She took an additional moment to center the gold chain she wore with every outfit. Since she last saw Enitan, she had begun to feel more self-conscious about her appearance—a stark contrast from when they were teenagers and Funmi had mainly felt persistent pity. She suspected it had something to do with the way Enitan had aged. She was still so skinny, and outside of Nigeria that carried so much currency. Funmi was still a beautiful woman, she knew, but the twenty pounds she had gained over the past year had been unexpected and unwelcome, and though she had never been skinny, she had always been soft, proportional. Small waist, full breasts, thick thighs, ample bum. Now her waist was conglomerating. But she did not care to dwell! She ran some Vaseline over her lips, slipped her phone into her dress pocket, and then shuffled into the hallway and down the stairs. The men were in the living room, watching the match, gesticulating and shouting at the screen every so often. She walked past the living room and into the foyer and opened the front door.

"Enitan, is that you?"

It was Remi who appeared first, so much taller than Funmi remembered, carrying a backpack that she set down.

"Aunty!" she said, and she hugged her warmly.

"Remi! See how tall you are now." Funmi leaned

back to take her all in. Remi was very fair with lots of freckles. Her red curly hair was piled up into a messy bun and she was wearing jeans and a T-shirt with a sweater tied around her waist.

"Funmi."

Funmi peeked behind Remi to see Enitan standing in the landing, holding her carry-on suitcase.

"Oh, but Sunday should have taken that inside for you!" Funmi peered out into the darkness to see where he had gone.

"Never mind that," Enitan said, leaning in for a hug.

"They lost our luggage. We'll have to get it tomorrow. There's nothing for Sunday to bring in."

"Oh, dear, I'm sorry," Funmi said.

She leaned back to take a look at Enitan's face. It appeared as though she hadn't slept well, which was obviously the case. There were dark circles under her eyes. She also had a mole on her left cheek that hadn't been there before and from which a noticeable strand of hair sprouted. Her hair was still cropped close to her skull. Funmi had been so shocked when she had seen the wedding photos Enitan had mailed to her. Enitan had said in her letter that it was prohibitively expensive to get your hair done in America, so that was why she had cut it.

In the photos, Enitan and Charles stood stiffly outside an imposing white building. "City Hall," it was called. She was wearing a simple belted white dress, white shoes, and a little church hat with a veil. A white ribbon tied under her chin held the hat in place, making her look even more childlike, especially in contrast to Charles, who was much taller than her. He had his arm around her shoulders and wore those thick Coke-bottle glasses that were the fashion then. Such a strange pairing. Funmi had wanted to ask Enitan why he hadn't come with them, but she would ask later.

"Wow, Aunty. Your house is beautiful," Remi said, walking in and looking up at the ceiling. Funmi smiled at her. She loved this house. It had taken five years to complete but it **was** beautiful. The biggest house by square footage on the estate, Yinka had made sure. Six bedrooms; four bathrooms. A garage for three cars. Funmi smiled at her tired guests. "You two must be hungry. I'll have Precious show you to your rooms so you can have your bath, and then we can have dinner. I believe Destiny is still on the premises. You haven't seen her in a few years, right, Remi?"

Remi nodded. "Yeah, it's been a while. Not since I was twelve."

"Unbelievable," said Funmi, shaking her head. "How time flies!" She noticed Enitan looking at her phone.

"Is everything all right?"

Enitan nodded. "Yes, it's just Charles checking

in. I forgot that my phone automatically connects to the Wi-Fi here."

"Send my love to Charles, I wish he could have been here."

"Yes," Enitan said. Remi looked like she was about to say something, but her mother interrupted.

"Where should we take these carry-ons?"

"Hold on, hold on," Funmi said. "Let me call Precious." The only frustrating thing about having such a large house was that she had to phone the maids in order for them to do anything beyond their immediate daily duties. They were all too eager to go off to the servants' quarters to watch Africa Magic on the TV installed there. She took out her cellphone and saw a text from Zainab.

CHAPTER 4

Zainab

IN HINDSIGHT, THE ROBBERS HADN'T DONE AN especially thorough job. Not searching each passenger one by one had been a mistake because as soon as it was clear that they were gone, people began frantically grabbing cellphones out of dress pockets, and from underneath head ties and wrappers. One man even fished his mobile out of his shoes. Other passengers had crowded around the driver, who was clutching his bleeding leg, lying in the middle of the road. Nobody was sure who the robbers had meant to maim, the driver or the vehicle itself.

Zainab reached underneath her wrapper and took out her cellphone. It was slippery with sweat, her own animal fear. Hamza had texted.

Have you arrived?

Not yet, Zainab texted back. She felt calm, her body on autopilot: Do these things and return to some semblance of normalcy. Don't think about the

25,000 naira that was stolen from you. Don't think of how you could have died.

Zainab called Funmi next. She wasn't sure exactly how far away they were from Lagos but surely they must be close. The phone rang and rang and rang but nobody answered.

The mother from before, carrying the baby on one hip and dragging the boy along with her free hand, walked up to Zainab. Zainab smiled at the baby, who was no longer crying but was quiet, contemplative. His older brother had his hands wrapped deeply around his mother's wrapper and his thumb in his mouth.

"Please, can I use your phone?" the mother asked. "Mine is out of credit."

"Of course," said Zainab, and she handed it to her.

The mother dialed a number very slowly with her free hand. She placed the phone to her ear. Zainab could hear it ringing.

An angry male voice answered. The mother began speaking in rapid Hausa, apologizing over and over again.

Zainab couldn't make out what the man said in response, but it was loud and furious. The mother began crying silently and was soon so overcome with sobs that she handed the phone back to Zainab, the man still shouting. The boy looked bewildered; he wound his hand deeper into his mother's dress. Zainab quickly ended the call.

"Let's just drive the bus," yelled one of the men who had gathered around the driver, loud enough that Zainab could hear him speaking clearly. "I can drive it. It's not safe to stay out here in the road."

He walked toward the bus and then climbed into it.

"They left the key!" he announced triumphantly. "They left the key!"

"Thank you, Jesus," said the woman who had been calling on His name during the actual act of robbery. He had delivered in this case.

The mother was still crying silently. Zainab patted her arm.

"Are you all right?" Zainab asked. The mother didn't answer. The passengers began to migrate back toward the bus. A group of men carried the driver, who yelped with every movement. Someone had wrapped up his leg with a head tie that became stained with splotches of blood. The men laid him out on top of the front row of seats.

"Oya, oya!" said the man who had found the key. "Everybody, please," he said, softening his tone a bit, recognizing, as everyone else had begun to, that he sounded as impatient as the robbers. "Please get on this bus so we can leave this godforsaken place."

Zainab put her arms around the mother.

"It's all right, it's all right," she said. "Let's get on the bus." She led her to the queue of passengers who were shuffling on board, slowly but eagerly. Zainab helped the woman and her children to seats close to the front of the bus. The woman allowed Zainab to move her gently toward the window seat. The boy sat down next to his mother, looking bewildered.

"Mummy, stop crying," he said.

She looked at him through her tears and continued wailing.

Zainab sat down in the seat behind them.

The man who had found the key started the ignition and the bus began moving. Palpable relief seemed to radiate throughout the vehicle. A few passengers even cheered.

The bus moved with punishing speed. Some of the male passengers began arguing over how to get back on the main road. Zainab kept her head against the window. The moon had now emerged—white and spectral. She took deep breaths and then closed her eyes. When she next opened them, she could see fires from roadside villages burning in the distance. They were on the right route. She closed her eyes again. She woke when her mobile rang. It was Funmi. Zainab picked up.

"Where are you? I have been calling and calling and calling! Ṣé you lost your way? It's almost midnight. Are you at the bus park now? Should I send Sunday?" The sound of Funmi's voice triggered something in Zainab. Maybe it was the feeling of immense relief washing over her. Or maybe it was exhaustion from all the exertion being terrified required. Or maybe it had been the sight of the mother crying—tears are contagious. Or an impossible-to-calculate combination of all these emotions. Whatever the cause, whatever the reason, Zainab broke into sobs. It caught her off guard. She couldn't stop.

"Zainab? Zainab?" Funmi was saying her name over and over again on the phone, her voice raised in concern. But Zainab couldn't stop. The sobs were trapped in her throat and she had to let them out. The tears stung her eyes but still they kept falling. The mother had stopped crying some time ago. No matter. They were united in their shared, abrupt sadness.

CHAPTER 5

Enitan

THE COOK ASKED THEM WHAT THEY WANTED to eat. His question reminded Enitan that she was hungry, quite hungry, actually, even though it was late, after 11 p.m. After she and Remi had taken their baths, Funmi had insisted they eat something before they slept. It had been some time since Enitan had had a proper home-cooked Nigerian meal so she did not say no. Growing up, Enitan had never been a particularly good or attentive cook and this had irritated her mother to no end.

"How will you find a husband if you can't cook?" Sharon would ask Enitan, exasperated by the jollof rice that was too soggy, the semovita that had too many lumps, the puff puff that were shaped like algae blossoms, not perfectly round and smooth like they were supposed to be. (Never mind that despite Sharon's expert culinary skills, she had no husband to speak of.) When they had money and when Sharon had time, she had loved to cook. The walls of their room and parlor would sweat from the oil and the steam. The sight of Scotch bonnet pepper still reminded Enitan of her mother.

When Sharon had visited them in the U.S., she would make chin chin, splitting the dough into strips using a pasta maker Charles had bought on a foolish whim and never used. She enlisted Remi as her sous chef, letting her roll the dough while she fried. She bagged the chin chin in little ziplock bags that Enitan could slip into her pants pockets and nibble on at work. She rarely had time to eat full meals; the nursing home was so understaffed.

"What are the options you have for us?" Enitan asked the cook, a lean, wiry man with large brown eyes.

"Anything you want, madam," he said deferentially.

"Yes, but what do you have already made? I wouldn't want you to go out of your way."

"We have rice, jollof rice, fried rice, plantain, efo riro—"

Efo. She would love some efo. Even though she knew it would later run right through her. But she associated loose bowel movements with the cleansing effect of being home. Something about the humidity and the stillness and the heat always triggered that gastrointestinal response.

"Do you have yam?"

"Yes."

"Can you make pounded yam for me? You have an electric yam pounder, right?"

The cook nodded. Her stomach grumbled agreeably. She hadn't had real pounded yam—not that disgusting powdered kind—in years. He turned to Remi, looking at her expectantly.

Funmi had left them sitting in the dining room, which was long and narrow with a hutch at the far end, filled with dishes that didn't appear to ever be used. On the walls hung portraits of Yinka, Funmi, and Destiny. The largest portrait was of the three of them. Yinka was the only one who sat, draped in a blindingly white agbada with a red fila parked on top of his head, as he glowered at the camera. Funmi stood behind him, wearing a gold, off-the-shoulder dress that hugged her still-formidably curved body and a giant red gèlè that framed her face like a crown. Destiny, who looked exactly like Yinka, stood beside her. Her hand rested delicately on her dad's shoulder.

"I will have jollof rice, please, thank you so much," said Remi.

"Beef or chicken?"

"Oh, no meat, please," and here Remi turned scarlet. Enitan had forgotten about this. Vegetarianism was the latest trend Remi had picked up from that liberal arts college in Ohio.

"Do you want plantain?"

"Yes, please." Remi nodded eagerly. She loved

plantain. It was the only thing Enitan knew how to make well—not that it required much skill. But she had been horrified at the quality of the plantain they were served at the Caribbean restaurants in Flatbush they would sometimes go to. Always so mushy, it was practically inedible. When she and Charles had just moved into their first apartment, Charles had made a great ceremony of taking her to his favorite Jamaican restaurant, where customers lined up to make their food choices like they were in a school canteen, and the server had placed two shriveled pieces of black, oily plantain on top of her rice and peas (though inexplicably, there were no peas, only beans, in this dish). The plantain had cost an extra three dollars.

Enitan had never ordered plantain from restaurants after that. But Charles said the smell of hot canola oil nauseated him and so she had gradually stopped frying it, only making it on very special occasions, ensuring that she opened all the windows and turned on the ventilation fan and even then, Charles would stare at her with this pained, slightly irritated look in his eyes. The first night alone in her new apartment, she had bought plantain from the Hispanic grocery store and fried it for dinner, and the smell of hot canola oil had lingered for days and days.

"Thank you very much," Remi said. "Please, Uncle, what's your name?"

"Muyiwa," he said.

"Moo-wee-wa," Remi said slowly.

"It's Muyiwa," Enitan said.

Remi tried again. "Thank you, Uncle Moo-ye-wah." Muyiwa smiled and left the room.

"You know you don't have to call every man you meet here uncle," Enitan said when he had gone.

"Every man, or every servant?" Remi responded with a sharpness that caught Enitan off guard.

"You need to watch your tone with me," snapped Enitan. "I'm not sure when you decided to start treating me like your age mate."

Remi glared at her.

"It is up to you to determine how civil you would like this trip to be," Enitan added in a lower tone.

Remi looked down at the table and said slowly, as if she were gritting her teeth, "I'm just pointing out the fact that it is upsetting to see how nice this house is when there are people literally living in boats on the ocean because they can't afford to find adequate housing." She looked up at her mother and in a different, more casual tone, asked, "What does Uncle Yinka do again?"

Enitan actually wasn't sure. It had something to do with real estate. She had decided long ago that it wasn't any of her business. Neither was it Remi's. She appreciated Remi's concern; she really did. She was proud of Remi's empathy and that she had not yet grown inured to all the societal problems that seemed so intractable here. But her pushing could be tiresome. It had honestly been a bit of a relief for Remi to go to college for that reason. Toward the end of her high school years, Remi's politics had begun to take a combative, more demanding tone. She insisted that they only use tote bags when they went shopping, no more plastic, cringing every time Enitan would unceremoniously add a nylon to their growing plastic bag drawer that never shut completely because it was so full. No more buying things on Amazon. No real Christmas tree (even Charles had struggled with that one, as taking a day trip to go to a Christmas tree farm upstate had been a family tradition).

After the police killings of black men on Staten Island and in Ferguson, Remi had wanted the whole family to join the protests in Washington Square Park and later the ones where they would hold up traffic in the road, lie down on the street, and play dead. For what? Enitan had forbid her from going, but Remi had gone with Charles anyway, which had been a powerful referendum on their marriage and a foreshadowing of which parent Remi would choose to eventually align herself with. Remi didn't understand why Enitan was so resistant. "It is quite literally the least we can do," she would say. But it scared Enitan—all this rabble-rousing, these protests. Not because she couldn't understand their anger, the senseless deaths. But Enitan knew what protests could do. She remembered what happened to Damola. The mercilessness of the police forces. For Remi, these protests were thrilling, a prime opportunity to expiate herself of whatever feelings of confusion she had had growing up mixed; over-compensating for her light skin and her red hair and her freckles, a chance to atone for her—how did she put it—privilege. But in real life, injustice was rife and inevitable. Life was fundamentally, cruelly, capriciously unfair. Jacob stole his blessing from Esau. God blessed Jacob anyway.

The poor died young and the rich lived long, healthy, evil lives—with shrines erected for them when they departed. The only solace was to believe in Hell—to really believe that there was a place these wicked people could go, that God would let them roast. Heaven Enitan could take or leave, to be honest. The thought of worshipping God forever and ever scared her. What was forever anyway? But Hell. Please let there be Hell. Some people really deserved it. She was about to respond to Remi when Funmi came into the room. She sat down beside Enitan and whispered in Yorùbá:

"I finally got in touch with Zainab. She said the bus was held up by armed robbers."

"Jesus!"

Remi looked up. "What's wrong?"

"Nothing," Funmi and Enitan both said automatically.

"So is she all right? Where is she now?"

"On her way to Lagos. Apparently, they did not do a very good job. They left the key in the ignition so another passenger is driving them to the bus park. But she was quite upset, of course. I think I will go with Sunday just to calm her down, to make sure she sees a familiar face."

"Of course, of course. Please, let me come with you."

"Are you sure? You should go and rest. You've just traveled and the ceremony is tomorrow. You haven't even eaten." Enitan turned to look at Remi, who was watching them and trying to parse out what they were saying based on the bits of English they dropped into the conversation. Her eyes were narrowed in concentration.

"I can eat later," Enitan told Funmi. Of course she would go. How could she not?

CHAPTER 6

Funmi

Nothing compared to driving in Lagos at night, especially over the bridges. The way the moonlight shimmered over the still water; how even recognizable landmarks transformed into unfamiliar shapes in the darkness, lending a new perspective and strangeness to a city Funmi now felt she knew by heart. She had traveled to other global metropolises of course—London, Paris, Rome, New York, Beijing, but still nothing compared to the feeling of speeding across Eko Bridge when the roads were finally clear of traffic.

Yinka forbade her from driving at night. There had been a rash of armed robberies during traffic stops recently, which were particularly frightening because you got a crystal clear preview of what would happen to you once the men approached your car and yet there was nowhere to escape.

Despite his ban, Funmi would sometimes get up around two or three o'clock in the morning on nights she couldn't sleep. She would sneak downstairs to the garage where the keys to the cars were kept in a locked safe and would take the Lexus and drive it around the estate and then back home again. She even opened and closed the gate herself. It helped that Yinka was a very deep sleeper; **he** would probably sleep through an armed robbery. She found driving at night soothing. She liked the feeling of control. Driving had been one of the few moments of connection she had had with her aunty Buki, who had taught her how to drive stick shift with the rusting Peugeot she bought decades ago. They would circle slowly around the perimeter of the teaching hospital where Aunty Buki had worked. Even now, Funmi missed the precision of driving stick, the way she could calibrate down to the very nanosecond how fast she wanted the car to go, how slowly she wanted the car to stop.

She wished she was driving now, though Sunday was doing a fine job. They were about fifteen minutes away from the bus park. Enitan had been agitated for most of the drive.

"I just can't believe it. Why did she decide to take a bus from Kaduna? Couldn't she have flown?"

Funmi shrugged. "You know how Zainab is. Very proud. I offered to fly her here and she refused."

"Utter stupidity," Enitan said, harshly enough that Funmi stared at her.

"What? It's true now. So reckless. What if she had been kidnapped?"

Funmi sighed. The years Enitan had spent away from Nigeria had gotten to her. The important thing was that Zainab was safe. Perfectly safe. She had sobbed on the phone, yes, but that was just relief.

"You're reading too much news. She's fine. Zainab has been through worse," Funmi said.

Had they not lived through the '87 riots during their uni days? Enitan had forgotten that the persistent threat of violence was just a fact of life in Nigeria. Nigeria unleashed constant reminders of one's mortality: death via traffic accident, a bridge collapse, a plane crash, an especially bad case of malaria, a sloppy blood transfusion, a kidnapping gone wrong, robbery, stress-induced heart attack, food poisoning, an act of black magic, poverty. The ways to die were endless. That's why you had to live, and live ferociously, and often selfishly and exploitatively, but Funmi did not worry herself about these details. Thinking about life's unfairness was a fool's errand. It paralyzed you. It was best to count your blessings and keep it moving.

She and Yinka had been the victims of an armed robbery once when they lived in VGC in the mid-'90s, back when robbers would pay off the police and security guards so they would know not to patrol the houses that day. Thank God nobody had been home. Destiny had been in school at the time. Funmi had gone shopping. She had driven home and the gate that led into the compound was ajar. There was shattered glass on the verandah, the front door had been forced open. Droplets of blood led to the kitchen. The maid had run away as far as her feet could take her; who knows how they would have violated her. Their houseboy was nowhere to be found and later they learned he had been the one who had tipped the thieves off. The robbers took everything. Their televisions, their VCRs, shoes, knives, food. The diesel for the generator but not the generator itself, fortunately, since it was too heavy for them to carry. They had taken her mother's jewelry, which had been most painful. Her mother's wedding ring, the only photo she had had of her parents together, smiling on their wedding day, gone. They moved shortly after that, and Yinka had bought a gun that he kept in a locked desk drawer in their master bedroom. He wore the key on a chain he never took off, not even when he bathed.

Sunday slowly pulled into the bus park, which was still quite busy for this time of night. Cars were picking up their passengers, while some people without transportation were trying to find a driver willing to take them into the city. Zainab was sitting alone on a bench. Looking at her, you would never have thought that she had just experienced a robbery were it not for the noticeable absence of any luggage or a handbag. She was holding something close to her chest though, a notebook of some kind.

As soon as Zainab spotted the car, she stood up and waved. Sunday came to an abrupt halt in front of her. Funmi unbuckled her seat belt and got out of the car and Enitan, in parallel movement, did the same.

The three of them embraced each other at the same time; no need for words, holding on tightly as if they were a football team celebrating after a goal.

When Funmi pulled back, both Enitan and Zainab were still hugging each other, crying.

"Has it really been so long? Kai," Zainab said, holding Enitan at arm's length. "You have not changed one bit. Still so skinny. Only now I am jealous."

"How can you make jokes like this?" said Enitan. "I am just so glad you are all right. I wish you had flown."

Zainab didn't respond; she merely used one sleeve to wipe the tear that was streaming down Enitan's cheek.

How long had it been since they had last been in the same place at the same time? Thirty years or something like it? Funmi could have cried then as well, but she would save her tears for the wedding on Saturday. She had never been one for too much sentimentality.

"Oya, please let us go, Sunday is waiting," Funmi said, not bothering to disguise her impatience. Zainab and Enitan both laughed at that. "Still the same old Funmi fumes," Enitan said.

"Funmi the furious," Zainab added.

"Funmi the fierce," said Enitan.

"It is after midnight," Funmi informed them. "You want me and Sunday to leave both of you here in this bus park?"

Zainab and Enitan laughed again, more jubilantly this time. Funmi turned on her heels in mock anger and Zainab and Enitan followed her. She opened the backseat door and climbed in, gripping onto the roof of the car so she wouldn't lose her balance. Enitan got in after her, fittingly since she was the smallest, now by a significant margin, and then they both helped Zainab climb up into the vehicle. Zainab sighed and shut the door. "Allhamdulillah," she muttered under her breath.

Enitan began to giggle.

Both Funmi and Zainab turned to her. "What is it?" Funmi asked.

"Look at how long it took us to fit inside this car!" Enitan exclaimed. "Haba! When did we become so old?" Zainab started to chuckle and then even Funmi couldn't help joining in. It **was** funny. Every time they thought they were done, one of them would start back up again, until they were in a stomach-aching fit of tears and giggles they couldn't seem to escape.

"Jesus," Funmi said after they had finally appeared to reach a lull. She wiped a tear from her eye. She had forgotten what it was like to laugh that hard, to laugh so freely. She turned to Zainab and Enitan. "I am so glad you are both here."

"Yes, o," Enitan echoed.

Zainab nodded.

"Sunday," Funmi instructed. "Take us home."

CHAPTER 7

Enitan

MOM. MOM. **Mom!**"

Enitan opened her eyes to see Remi's face hovering over her.

"What is it? What is wrong?"

"The toilet isn't flushing."

Enitan blinked a few more times in an attempt to wake herself up. She sat up slowly.

"Is there a bucket?" she asked, fishing around with her feet for the slippers she had pleasantly discovered late last night when she had snuck into the room around two in the morning, Remi already fast asleep.

"Yes."

Enitan found the slippers and stood up.

Remi turned to face her mother grimly. "Just . . . breathe through your mouth," she said.

Enitan laughed. "You're forgetting I am a nurse!"

She walked into the bathroom. It was sparsely furnished, especially in comparison with the rest of the house, which was decorated with a sort of garishness Enitan found off-putting—all plastic shellacked chaise lounges and hutches stuffed with saccharine items. Enitan loved Funmi, but the woman had horrible taste. This bathroom, in comparison, was quite minimal. There was a bathtub with a blue bucket and small plastic bowl inside of it, a small vanity mirror that hung on the wall above the sink, and then the toilet, which was currently filled almost to the brim with brown liquid. The smell was not pleasant but certainly nothing compared to one of her patients, Mrs. Brighton, and her eye-watering stools. A small wastebasket stood next to the toilet. Enitan moved it aside to reach the plunger.

"What did you eat yesterday?" Enitan asked as she filled the bucket with some water from the bathtub faucet and poured it into the toilet bowl.

"Just jollof rice," Remi said. "It was spicier than I expected."

Enitan plunged the toilet a couple of times and then added more water. The toilet made a hacking sound and then the water whooshed away in a whirlpool. A thin shit-encrusted ring lined the bowl.

"We'll have to get some cleaning supplies from one of the maids so it doesn't stain," said Enitan.

"I can do it," said Remi. "I came up to get you. Aunty Funmi says we should come down for breakfast."

"Okay. You can go downstairs. I just need to change and then I can join you."

Remi didn't move.

"What's wrong?"

"It's just a lot of people I don't know down there. I'd rather wait for you."

"Suit yourself. Help me pick out what I should wear."

And then she remembered. They only had their carry-ons. Fortunately, Enitan had packed another dress to wear in the event that she lost her luggage. Her paranoia about airlines' ability to safeguard her valuables had finally been validated. She washed her hands and face, swished some toothpaste in her mouth, and changed.

"We're in the dining room!" Funmi yelled when they reached the base of the staircase. The smell of yam and stew hung in the air and they could hear the sound of cutlery scraping against plates.

Yinka, Funmi, Destiny, and a man who must surely be Dele were all sitting at the dining room table, an ample breakfast spread out before them— scrambled egg omelet and stew, boiled yam, rows of boiled plantain, freshly cut oranges, pineapple, pawpaw and mango, golden brown akara, and some steaming pap in a pewter bowl.

"Good morning," Enitan said, Remi trailing behind her. Dele and Destiny both got up. Destiny looked unchanged from the last time Enitan had seen her, when Destiny was seventeen and just about to start university. She had the same slim yet curvy physique as her mother, with her father's high rounded cheekbones and his coloring, like black coffee. Dele, whom Enitan had only ever seen from photographs, was the same height as Destiny, a very innocuous-looking Yorùbá man. He already had the beginnings of a belly.

"Good morning, Aunty. Thank you so much for coming," Destiny said, and she kneeled down in front of her. Enitan helped her stand up. "There's no need to do all of that." She hugged Destiny. "It's good to see you. We wouldn't have missed this for the world." Dele touched the floor with his hand as well as a sign of respect.

"Aunty, it's a pleasure to meet you. I've heard so much about you," he said. That couldn't possibly be true, but Enitan appreciated the effort he had made to connect.

"Please, come and join us," Funmi said from over at the table.

Enitan and Remi sat down across from Funmi.

"Yinka," Enitan said, nodding at him. Yinka, who had been looking at his BlackBerry, nodded at her and smiled slightly. "You have arrived," he said, and turned back to his phone. He always acted this way around Enitan, as if she wasn't even remotely among his concerns, her presence just barely acknowledged. Even when Yinka would come to

New York with Funmi and Destiny, he would spend most of his days in his hotel room, not bothering to come down for lunch or to go shopping with them.

He was a powerfully built man who had aged gracefully, though, something Enitan had not predicted for him. His lips were thick and pouty, making him look as if he were perpetually posing for a photograph that had yet to be taken. His head was completely shaved, and he wore a thin gold chain around his neck. His most noticeable feature was his voice, which Enitan rarely heard. It was hoarse and raspy, as if he had spent the first half of his life screaming at the top of his lungs for something and now that he had received it, he had no reason to ever raise his voice above a whisper. Funmi had met him during the riots of '87 and, though he was supposed to have been sent by the army to help stop the fighting, Enitan had always wondered to what extent he had been involved in any of the violence. There was something quietly menacing about him, but she could not put her finger on what exactly.

They all sat back down at the table. Enitan spooned some egg and yam onto her plate.

"I thought you didn't like akara," Enitan said as she speared one onto her plate.

Funmi laughed. "For the guests now," she said, shrugging. "And Yinka likes his pap with akara."

Enitan nodded. Then lowering her voice, she asked Funmi, "How is Zainab?"

"She's still sleeping," said Funmi. "She had a long day."

"We heard about the robbery last night," said Dele, piping up from across the table. "It's a shame. This country has really lost its way."

Enitan resisted the urge to roll her eyes. How old was this small boy? He couldn't be older than twenty-six.

"What robbery?" Remi asked.

Funmi looked quickly at Enitan. Then she turned to Remi and said breezily, "There's no cause for alarm. Your aunty Zainab was on a bus that was attacked by armed robbers last night but everyone is fine now. She is safe and sleeping in her room."

"Wow," said Remi. "I had no idea."

Remi's ears were turning red. She was angry, Enitan knew, embarrassed that everyone at the table appeared to know about this horrific event that had happened except for her. She had always hated feeling excluded. Even when she was younger, as a toddler barely speaking in complete sentences, if Charles and Enitan were whispering to each other in her presence, she would climb between them and demand, "Tell me!" She was always insatiably curious, nosy, Enitan would tell her later, always asking questions: Why is that woman so big? Why is Mommy brown and Daddy pink? What is sex? Charles encouraged transparency, never hesitating to answer Remi's questions as honestly as he could even if they were wildly inappropriate. He would always be open with his daughter, Charles would say when he and Enitan argued about this. His family had operated under a cloud of secrecy so thick, it had driven them all to various forms of addiction.

Enitan disagreed with his approach. Her mother had loved to tell her in excruciating detail about the mundane minutiae of her life, like exactly how much money she had in her bank account, or how she wasn't getting her periods because of stress, but would refuse to tell Enitan any actually pertinent information, like who her father was or why she had only met her grandparents once, when she was a baby, and the only way she knew that this meeting had in fact taken place was because there was photographic evidence of it that Enitan had found at the bottom of her mother's underwear drawer. She was her mother's only friend in essence, and such acts of confiding were far too heavy a burden for a child. By keeping Remi in the dark about their financial troubles or in later years, their marital ones, Enitan was giving Remi the blissful, carefree childhood Enitan had never had. At least, that was the reasoning Enitan gave for her parenting approach.

"That's just so awful," Remi said.

"Yes," said Destiny. "Thank God no one was hurt."

"What an instance of government failure," said Remi, her voice rising. "It makes you wonder if there were more steps put in place to address the income inequality in this country, maybe these robbers wouldn't have had to resort to violence like that."

Enitan looked at Remi pointedly. She could tell Remi was purposefully avoiding her gaze.

"So you think it's joblessness that's the problem?" asked Funmi, looking at Remi with a slightly amused expression.

"What else would it be?"

"Let me tell you a story," said Funmi, and she settled into her chair. "Some years ago, we hired a houseboy. A boy from Yinka's village. His job was to cook and clean and we would pay his school fees. We paid him well. He was able to have Sunday mornings off to go to church. When his mother was sick, we paid for his bus ride back to the village. When he got malaria, we paid for his hospital fees. We did not abuse him or mistreat him. Not a hair on his head was harmed. Then one day Yinka and I come back to our house and discover we have been robbed. They have taken everything—our televisions, our jewelry, all the cash we had hidden in the house. They had even taken the diesel for our generator. Our maid had fled the premises. Our houseboy was nowhere to be found. Do you know what happened?"

Remi shook her head.

"He set us up. The houseboy was the one who told the robbers when we wouldn't be home, where all our valuables were hidden. We never saw him again and we moved anyways shortly after that. But tell me, what are you supposed to make of a boy such as this? After everything that we have done for him, providing housing and paying for school fees, paying for his trips home, and still he decides to rob us, to betray us? Some people have jobs and it doesn't matter. There is a wickedness in their hearts that comes from the Devil and no human being can get rid of it."

"But, Aunty, how can you say that?" asked Remi. "You're making so many assumptions already. What if he wanted to make his own money without feeling indebted to your whole family? That's the problem with capitalism, especially as it's practiced here. There are no good choices for anyone."

"So you are in favor of communism, then?" said Dele, with a wry grin.

Remi's face grew redder.

This was about to go badly, Enitan thought. She stood up. She was finished with her yam and egg. "Aren't we supposed to be going to the nail salon?" Enitan asked. "Should I go wake Zainab?" Funmi had mentioned scheduling an appointment for the five of them last night.

Funmi looked at her watch.

"Yes, o," Funmi replied. Remi and Dele were now in a loud, heated argument.

"We need to define our terms," Remi was saying. Yinka was still on his BlackBerry. And Destiny was eating quietly, contributing a "yes" or "correct" whenever Dele would look at her for validation of his assertions.

"Let me go and have my bath quickly and then I will get her," said Enitan. When she got to the top of the stairs, she checked her phone and saw that she had a missed text from Charles.

How are you all settling in?

She calculated the time difference and decided to reply.

were fine. lost luggage ☹

I'm sorry to hear that.

Bubbles appeared on the screen.

Though Remi was well on her way to becoming what Charles jokingly referred to as their "radical leftist daughter," she had not complained when they had decided to switch from Androids to iPhones a few years ago as part of a promotional family phone plan. It had been Remi in fact who had taught Enitan the finer points of texting etiquette, explaining that when the gray bubbles appeared that was how you knew somebody was typing. And so Enitan waited. She knew that Charles liked to take his time when he texted, taking care to use proper punctuation, ending each text with a period or a question mark, or—on rarer occasions—an exclamation point. On this latter point, he was very strict. He could go on for twenty minutes at a time about how the "internet generation"—as he called the students he taught at the high school—had ruined the joys of the exclamation mark, using it too promiscuously, cheapening its adrenaline shot effect on the sentence.

Enitan had no stake in this argument. Her texts, which Charles frequently mocked for their lack of punctuation—"You text like my fourteen-year-old freshmen!"—all lowercase, no apostrophes, were functional. They were like Pidgin: they got the job done. Charles was a snob, she would tease him; he always believed he was more sensitive, more attuned to the cultural whims and sensitivities of other parts of the world than he actually was.

And how's Remi?

shes fine

Bubbles appeared and then disappeared.

Remember when I tried kilishi for the first time?

He did this with growing frequency now, a sudden intrusion of memory into an unrelated conversation, a kind of preemptive mourning for the relationship they had once shared. Certainly, they argued much less now that they had finally stated what had felt forbidden for so long—that their marriage wasn't working and it hadn't been for a while and it was time for it to end. And some of the old rancors—the fact that they had moved to Park Slope so he could bike to the private school where he taught English to the spoiled children of doctors and lawyers while she had to take two trains and a bus to get to work in Jamaica, Queens; all the years she spent working as a CNA while he did research for his novels that were ultimately never published—those had faded now.

And in many ways he was still her closest friend. She talked to Funmi and Zainab of course, more regularly now thanks to WhatsApp; no longer did she have to rely on Rebtel or use phone cards, thank God. But they were so far away. And since Grace had moved to Atlanta and Maya back to Trinidad, she hadn't really had any confidantes near her. Charles at least understood her reality on the ground. For venting about the patient who would graze his fingers across her bottom as she changed his bedpan and pretend as if he hadn't done anything when she looked at him, or the haughty white woman with blue hair who refused to believe that Enitan was her nurse and not the CNA, and had raised such a fuss Enitan's supervisor had had to come to the room to calm her down and assure her that yes, Enitan was her nurse, and since they were short-staffed, Enitan was forced to attend to her anyway after that and the woman would always grimace when she saw Enitan and would never say hello or good morning and would yelp anytime Enitan moved her—Charles was her listening ear.

She debated telling him about the robbery but then decided against it. She didn't want to alarm him.

are you grading right now??

Guilty as charged.

hows it going?

Well, I keep texting my ex-wife 😏

Enitan smiled again. The emoji use was new.
soon to be, she corrected. **when are you leaving for ri?**

Christmas Eve.

thats cutting it close

I know. But you know how they are.

She did.

Back when they were both teaching in Edo State, Charles had told her he was from a wasp family, and Enitan had said that she thought of herself more as a lizard because she loved to sit in the sun all day doing nothing, hiding in plain sight on a wall or in a courtyard. Charles had laughed and explained that he meant that he was a White Anglo-Saxon Protestant; that his descendants could be traced back to the **Mayflower,** the ship that had brought white people to America. Charles informed her that the telltale characteristics of a typical WASP included the inability to express emotion in healthy ways and a lot of passive-aggressiveness. In fact, one of the most striking things he had noticed since he had started teaching in Nigeria was how blunt everyone was: "What do you want?" "The fat woman will sell you groundnut." Even the innocuous, ubiquitous exhortation—"Ehn?"—was aggressive.

"In my family, you could never be that direct," Charles said. (Enitan would experience that lack of directness herself when she met his sisters the first Christmas after their elopement. She had thought they loved her; they had been so effusive with their praise, raving about how enviously skinny she was, and how darling her accent, how charming her haircut. It was only later, when she heard them speaking through the air vent in the upstairs bedroom she and Charles were sharing, that she learned the truth.

"I give it six months," the older sister said.

"Don't be cruel, maybe more like a year." This was the younger sister. "That's how long she has to stay with him to get the green card!" And they had broken out into laughter. Enitan had climbed back into bed afterward, her heart beating so loudly she could hear it thudding in her ears.)

Enitan headed to the guest room, walking slowly, because her back was still giving her some trouble. A fresh towel had been folded and placed on the bed, which had been made. Na wa o. These maids worked wonders. She headed to the bathroom, which had also been cleaned. On the bathtub lid were two boxes of bar soap. Enitan picked one up and sniffed it. It smelled like lavender, probably a soap Funmi had bought on one of her trips to Europe. Enitan missed the smell of the marbled soap you would buy in the kiosks for a few hundred naira; it reminded her of her mother. Her mother had talked and talked of Remi coming to Nigeria to visit her, but Enitan and Charles had simply never been able to manage it. It was easiest to blame it on the money when Charles spent years trying to sell his manuscript and they were essentially subsisting on monthly checks from his mother and Enitan's CNA salary. Then, even when he had finally eaten crow and taken the job at the school and Enitan had finally gotten her nursing degree, they went elsewhere for summer vacations—Rome, Paris, one year a cruise to Alaska. She had not wanted to go back. She was afraid that returning would highlight how much she had changed; that being back in that house in Abeokuta would only aggravate the fragile peace she and her mother had brokered.

It did not matter now. She was finally home with her daughter and her mother was not here to see it. When she had died, Enitan had searched in vain in all the Caribbean and African food stores in the greater Brooklyn area to find that specific brand of marbled soap. She hadn't been able to find it.

CHAPTER 8

Zainab

Destiny spent a few months with Zainab and Ahmed in Kaduna during her gap year, two years before Ahmed's first stroke. Funmi had called Zainab and told her Destiny wanted to go up north for a bit, to see the city where her parents had met, and experience some time away from the bustle of Lagos.

Zainab and Ahmed went to pick Destiny up from the airport. She was so delicate looking, seeming clearly out of place, wearing a sweatshirt and jeans, her hair in tiny box braids. A camera hung around her neck.

"Aunty!" Destiny said, and she was about to kneel but then caught herself. They both laughed.

"You don't need to do that with me," Zainab said. Even when Destiny was a toddler, before she could speak in full sentences, she kneeled whenever Zainab came to Lagos to visit, in accordance with Yorùbá rules of respect. Hausa people did it too, but in general Zainab found the whole practice unnecessary.

"How was your flight?" Zainab asked Destiny, steering her toward their car as Ahmed wheeled her luggage—just one carry-on—behind them.

"It was fine, Aunty," Zainab said.

"And your parents are well?"

"Yes, my mum sends her love."

They got into the car.

Ahmed asked her about the camera she had.

"Daddy gave it to me as a present before I started school."

"Do you like photography?" Zainab asked her. She wanted to draw Destiny out from within herself, free her from that tendency to answer in polite sound bites the way girls of a certain class were brought up to do.

"Yes," said Destiny. She seemed like she would say more but stopped herself. Zainab turned around from the front passenger's seat and smiled at her.

"Go on. Who is your favorite photographer?"

Destiny smiled shyly.

"Well, Ojeikere, of course, but I feel like that's an obvious answer," she began.

Ahmed nodded solemnly from the driver's seat. "His influence on Nigerian photography cannot be overstated. He is a towering force, a bulwark of African portraiture—"

"Don't mind him," Zainab interrupted, placing

her hand around the back of his neck and squeezing it lightly. "Was I asking **you**?" she added to Ahmed, and he shrugged sheepishly and winked at Destiny in the rearview mirror.

Destiny laughed then, a proper, full-fledged laugh.

"What a lovely sound!" said Zainab. "This is what we want. More laughter from you."

"Okay, Aunty," said Destiny, smiling. "I will try."

Destiny spent three months with them. She helped with the cooking, accompanied Zainab on trips to the market, sat with Ahmed and Zainab on their bench in their courtyard.

One day, Zainab and Destiny took a day trip to Kano and went to a market where they watched wizened old men tie-dye indigo fabrics. Afterward, Destiny talked excitedly about doing a photo series on such workers, but focused on women. "There's the market woman, the hairstylist, the seamstress," she listed as they sat on a bench on the verandah, looking at old photo albums.

"You know my stepmothers worked," Zainab told Destiny.

"Really? What did they do?" Destiny asked.

"One of them owned a suya catering company, the other one had her own hair shop."

"Wow," said Destiny. She was quiet for a moment. "I want to go to school for photography but I know Mummy and Daddy would never allow it."

"Why do you say that?"

"I saw how happy they were when I told them I wanted do to medicine. And you know Daddy always said that is what he would have done if he had stayed in school. I don't know how I could tell them no." She was quiet again.

"You know there are other ways for you to pursue photography; you don't have to go to school for it."

"I know," said Destiny. She turned the page of the album. It was a photo of Zainab, Funmi, and Enitan in their graduation robes. They were eating something out of frame and laughing. Zainab remembered that day vividly—mere weeks before she would finally marry Ahmed, a year after Damola's death.

"I don't remember ever seeing my mother looking this happy," Destiny said.

Zainab wondered if Funmi had ever told Destiny about Damola.

"Do you ever feel sad for no reason?" Destiny asked abruptly.

Zainab looked at Destiny, who seemed to be avoiding Zainab's gaze. Her finger played with one of the pages. "Sometimes," Zainab replied. "Especially after Musa was born."

"Sometimes I feel so sad I can't move," said Destiny. "I want to lie in bed all day. And my parents don't understand it. I don't understand it."

She turned and looked at Zainab directly.

"I could never talk to my mother like this."

"Why not?"

"You know how she is," said Destiny. "She doesn't listen to me. She thinks I'm too sensitive."

"You know your mother is trying in her own way."

"It's not good enough."

"I wouldn't write her off so quickly," said Zainab. She had been the recipient of Funmi's graciousness many times over. "I would at least try to have a conversation with her. She might surprise you."

Destiny didn't reply.

"You know that she loves you very much, right?"

Destiny smiled a half smile. "Yes, I know that," she said. "That makes it worse."

A month or so after Destiny left, Zainab received some photos along with a thank-you note in the mail. Destiny had snapped a picture of Zainab and Ahmed outside. The photo made Zainab tear up now. It was a portal into some other dimension, some alternative life where sickness and insolvency did not loom, threatening to overshadow all they had accomplished together. She and Destiny had kept in touch after that.

ZAINAB OPENED HER EYES. She blinked twice to adjust to the whiteness of the ceiling above her. She had had an awful nightmare, one that she couldn't remember at all now, only the feeling of utter fear and then an overwhelming sensation, a command really, to open her eyes. Once she opened her eyes, her surroundings began to register. She was not in mortal danger. She was in Lagos. She was here for a wedding. Yesterday she had been in a robbery. But today she was alive, in a comfortable bed in a spacious house in Lekki. She groped around the nightstand for her phone, which she had turned off to save battery since her charger was now lost. She turned it on and saw she had a text from Hamza.

hope u arrived safe.

She called him. The dial tone that she couldn't stand—such an ugly, grating sound—blared once, twice, three times. She texted him back.

yes, sorry I meant to call yesterday. Was distracted

Yes, distracted. Better not to alarm.
Someone rapped on the door.
"Who is it?"
"It's me."
Enitan.
"Come in."
Enitan entered, closing the door quietly behind her. It was amazing how much she hadn't

changed. The same medium brown skin now no longer marred by acne. The same frail build; she looked like she was drowning in the dress she was wearing; it was much too big for her. There were more worry lines on her face than there used to be, though. Two parentheses permanently surrounded her mouth.

"Sannu," Enitan said. "Did I wake you?"

"No, no, I was already awake."

Enitan sat down on the edge of the bed. She barely left a dent. She smelled like fresh soap.

"How are you feeling?"

Zainab sighed. "We thank God," she said. "I'm fine."

"I am glad to hear that," said Enitan. She smiled weakly, tapped Zainab's leg twice.

"It is so good to see you," she said.

"Yes, it is."

It was uncanny how after all these years apart Zainab could still sense when Enitan was upset. It helped of course that Enitan was incapable of masking how she felt about anything—her face was a window into whatever was churning inside her.

"How are you doing?" Zainab asked.

"I came here to check in on **you**," said Enitan. "How is Ahmed?"

"He is fine. I was about to call home just now."

"Oh, sorry." Enitan rose.

"Sit down, it's fine!" Zainab chided.

Enitan sat back down and then leaned in closer, taking Zainab's hand.

"When Funmi told me you were taking the bus, I had to admit I was very surprised. You know that we both are happy to assist you in whatever way we can."

Zainab felt the anger begin to mount; her face grew hot. It was not a malicious statement, Zainab knew, it was in fact a gesture of care, but it was still difficult to escape the feeling that she would now always be the most pitiful one among the three of them.

"We are all right, thank you," Zainab said. She hoped Enitan registered the brusqueness in her tone.

She did. Enitan was quiet.

"How is Charles?" Zainab asked. She had been wondering why he had not come with them for the wedding. She had still never met him in person.

Enitan looked down at her hands and then laughed a little sadly.

"Charles is fine." Then she said quietly, "We are getting divorced."

"I am so sorry to hear this, Eni." And Zainab really was. "Why didn't you tell us?"

"I would have rather told you in person. And with Ahmed's condition . . . I didn't want to trouble you."

"There's no reason to think that way," Zainab said. Why divorce? What did he do? Or had she done something? But as if to ward off these questions, Enitan asked:

"And how are my sons?"

Zainab picked up her phone.

"You have probably seen these pictures before," Zainab said, and Enitan had; she had sent them all to the WhatsApp group. But she showed Enitan the photos anyway, of Muhammad outside some glitzy mall in Dubai, of Hamza and the little ones, Musa and Ibrahim. Enitan responded with the appropriate sighs and coos and "how tall they are" and "beautiful!"

"So what happened?" Zainab asked Enitan after she handed the phone back to Zainab. She lowered her voice. "Did he cheat?"

Enitan laughed, a quick, unexpected laugh. "You know I don't know. I don't think so." She was quiet, seeming to really be considering Zainab's question. Then she said: "I don't know how you do it, Zainab, honestly."

"Do what?"

"Care for Ahmed like you have. I don't mean this in a rude way at all. I just, when I think about Charles, when I think about all the things I did for him, it all began to add up. My anger toward him, I mean. I never complained. I just did what needed to be done, but the anger, it grew until one day I just couldn't take it anymore."

Zainab nodded her head slowly. She wasn't sure she entirely understood, though she was trying to. She had only seen Charles on video calls sometimes; a ghostly white figure with a shock of red hair waving in the background, butchering her name. He was a presence certainly; he liked to make jokes. But marriages were private and mysterious things—even to the people in the marriages themselves. One spouse's perception of how the relationship was faring could be drastically different from the other spouse's. In marriage, you were ultimately alone together.

She and Ahmed had had their difficult moments. There were times when he could be so distant, so involved in his work, and it had a horrible effect on Zainab. It made her feel terribly lonely even in a house full of children. The way Ahmed could look past her sometimes; it had been chilling.

But she loved him still and he her. She had been looking forward to those years of getting to know him again as a grandfather. And what was the alternative with Ahmed anyway? Abandon him in the street? That was what Americans did with their elderly and infirm, they put them away in homes, stripped them from their families. Enitan had told her the horror stories and had always sworn that she didn't want to grow old in America. It was a cruel, cruel place.

Zainab was about to say something, when someone knocked on the door.

Without bothering to wait for an answer, Funmi bounded inside, carrying a dress. "We are leaving for the nail salon in twenty-five minutes o!" She handed the dress to Zainab. "So you can have a fresh change of clothes." She then turned to Enitan: "Sunday is ready to take you to the airport to pick up your luggage. You'll both have to go straight from the salon, though, the ceremony is starting at four."

"As if the traditional will possibly start on time . . ." said Enitan.

Funmi shot Enitan a look.

"How I have missed your sense of humor, Eni."

Smiling, Enitan got up from the side of Zainab's bed. "Tó," she said to Zainab. "We will continue this conversation another time."

Funmi raised an eyebrow, but Zainab shooed her away with her hand.

"I'll be downstairs in a minute, please give me a moment," she added. She watched them both leave the room and waited for the door to close.

Zainab had just brushed her teeth and changed into the dress Funmi had given her when she heard a timid knock on the bedroom door.

"I'm coming," Zainab said irritably, wiping her face with a towel.

"Aunty, it's me."

"Oh, Destiny, come in, come in!"

Destiny opened the door. "Mummy summoned me to get you."

"Destiny, my darling, so good to see you," said Zainab, and she came around to hug her. As they embraced, Zainab noticed how prominent Destiny's shoulder blades felt under her arms. She pulled away from Destiny so she could examine her more closely. She looked tired, very tired.

"You are looking so skinny," Zainab told Destiny.

Destiny looked away for a moment and then met Zainab's eyes. "This is my normal weight," she said.

"Are you sure?"

"Yes. I wanted to say I'm so glad you are all right. Mummy told me about the robbery. Thank God you were not hurt."

Zainab rubbed Destiny's arms; they felt like raw chicken flesh, pinpricked from the air-conditioning. "Thank you, sweetheart. But don't think I didn't notice you changing the subject. How are you feeling? You know you called me a few weeks ago, right? From some club of some sort? Are you all right?"

Destiny nodded. "I'm sorry, Aunty, I think I might have butt dialed you."

"You're sure?" Zainab asked.

"Of course."

"How are you feeling before the wedding?"

But before Destiny could answer, Funmi strode into the room.

"If we're going to make this appointment, we need to leave now!" She herded them out before they could finish their conversation.

CHAPTER 9

Funmi

THERE WAS TRAFFIC ON THE WAY TO THE salon, as Funmi had expected. That was what happened when you tried to go anywhere on Friday morning sha. Funmi had originally planned for Tinu to make a house call; that was what she usually did, but then she decided that they should all go to the salon instead. She wanted them to see it and she figured that it would be nice for all of them to leave the house if only to get away from Yinka's brother's family, who had made their eventual descent into the dining room and turned it to pandemonium as expected. Those children! The other good thing about going to the nail salon was that Funmi had been able to drive the Escalade so that all of them—Enitan, Zainab, and the girls—could fit in the same vehicle. Sunday would come round with the Jeep in forty minutes to take Enitan and Remi to the airport to pick up their luggage.

Funmi opened the car door and got out slowly.

It was a scorching hot morning; the sun was relentless; the sky a bright blue. Enitan and Zainab followed suit, stretching and yawning as they exited the vehicle. The salon was at the tail end of a small shopping complex; there was a jewelry shop and a store selling electronics next door. A beggar sat by the side of the wall closest to the salon; he was missing one leg and his eyes had the pale, cloudy blue color of the blind. Remi reached into her backpack and took out several new 1,000-naira bills.

"Ahn-ahn!" Funmi exclaimed, as Remi went and handed them to the beggar. This girl. He looked startled. As he counted the number of bills with his hands, his face turned toward her general direction and his lips cracked into a smile.

"God bless you," he said.

"Please, sir, what's your name?" Remi asked. Funmi looked at Enitan. Enitan shook her head, then shrugged.

"She is a good girl. You have brought her up well," said Zainab to Enitan. Enitan nodded and smiled slightly. Funmi shook her head. The young were idealistic until reality forced them to harden themselves.

Destiny was quiet; she leaned against the Escalade, rubbing her arms. "What's wrong?" Funmi asked her.

"Nothing," Destiny said.

"Are you cold?" Zainab asked. She used the ends of her hijab to rub against one of Destiny's arms.

"If the air-conditioning was too much, why didn't you say something?" Funmi asked Destiny, irritated. Destiny's inability to clearly express what she wanted had been the fodder for many of their oldest arguments, except to call them arguments would imply that Destiny was an equal partner in those exchanges—when really she would shut down and Funmi would have to pry the truth out of her, like she was extracting teeth.

"It's all right, Mummy, I didn't want to bother anyone and I knew we would arrive here soon," Destiny explained.

"Tó," Funmi said. "Remi, dear, are you ready?"

The back of Remi's ears crimsoned and she stood to her full height. What an interesting girl this Remi had turned out to be. So unlike her mother. Funmi wondered what kind of man Remi would end up marrying, if she married at all. She might be one of those girls who frowned upon the whole practice.

"I'm ready, Aunty," Remi said. Funmi walked up the tiled steps that led into the shop. As she pushed open the glass door, the pungent smell of acrylic nail polish wafted into the air. Tinu, the shop owner, was sitting at her desk opposite a giant shelf lined with a rainbow array of nail polish bottles. She was young, only thirty-two, but three years ago when she and Funmi had randomly been seated next to each other at a charity fashion show in Ikoyi, Tinu had mentioned her interest in owning her own beauty salon, specializing in intricate nail design. The salon would have the same amenities as any place in Europe or America, with a generator to ensure twenty-four-hour electricity. The girls in the salon would be highly trained, so there would be no need to worry about getting staph infections from tools that hadn't been properly cleaned. When a customer arrived, they would be invited to have a seat, while a girl would bring them a tray of nail polish options and ask if they would like a soft drink or tea. Soothing music would play from speakers. She had asked Funmi if she thought that having a TV would be appropriate and Funmi had told her yes. She liked watching Africa Magic as much as the next person, while a girl worked to declaw the last nail on her right foot. It had always been the bane of Funmi's existence; at other salons, the girls who had worked on that toenail would invariably suck in their breath as they got to work, whispering about the "fair madam with nails like vulture," as if Funmi couldn't understand what they were saying.

Funmi admired Tinu's vision. So when Tinu intimated that she might need some capital, Funmi was able to successfully persuade Yinka to give her some seed money. The shop had finally had its grand opening a few months ago. As a result of that generosity, Funmi had her own special chair in the salon reserved just for her, and she could reliably expect Tinu to accommodate last-minute appointments and if she was able, to show up to greet her.

"Aunty," Tinu said, rising as Funmi and the rest of the women entered the shop.

"Darling," said Funmi, and she and Tinu embraced. "I have some very special guests with me this morning. These are my two closest friends. We met in university." She gestured at Zainab and Enitan to come close to her. Funmi put her arms around them. "This is Zainab. And this is Enitan."

"It's a pleasure to meet you both," said Tinu, kneeling. Her eyes alighted on Remi. "Aunty, is this your daughter? Such a fine girl. Congratulations again on your wedding!" Remi turned red.

Funmi laughed. She supposed it was not impossible. Destiny was so dark, just like Yinka. "No, no, that is Enitan's daughter, Remi. They live in the U.S., in New York."

"New York," said Tinu, openly impressed. "Wonderful, just wonderful." She turned to Destiny and said, "Please forgive my mistake."

Destiny nodded and smiled slightly. "It's all right," she said.

"The girls are just finishing up their breakfast," Tinu told Funmi. Come to think of it, Funmi could detect the distinct smell of akara. "I'll go check on them, but please all of you, sit wherever you like." Tinu waved her hand toward the row of identical black faux leather chaise lounges arranged near the far wall. "And pick whichever color you prefer," she added, smiling at all of them. "You are very welcome." As she turned away from them, her facial expression suddenly hardened into the imperious look of a madam. "Girls," she called as she headed toward the back room hidden from view with a curtain. "Girls, get ready o! We have customers!" The sounds of her heels hitting the tiled floor reverberated around them.

"We don't have much time," said Funmi, walking up to the shelf of nail polish. She would go with red; it was her go-to color and matched with everything.

"I haven't gotten my nails done in a long, long time," said Zainab, walking up next to her.

"Remember when we used to give each other manicures?" Enitan asked, sidling up to Funmi. The three of them laughed at the memory.

"Funmi was always so impatient," Zainab said.

"Ahn-ahn!" said Funmi in mock consternation.

"Zainab would take the longest time of course," said Enitan.

"Is it a crime that I wanted to look beautiful? Haba!" Zainab joked. She turned toward Destiny. "Destiny, what are you planning to do for your nails?"

"She will have the bridal special now," Funmi answered for her. "Tinu has a special design that she does for brides. It's very beautiful. Let me pull it up on my phone now—"

"Was I asking you?" Zainab chided. "Destiny, what do you want?"

Destiny shrugged. "The bridal special is fine," she said, and she sat down in her chair.

Zainab looked at Funmi and Funmi gave a slight shrug. What was Funmi supposed to do if Destiny didn't speak up? "If she wants something else, she'll let you know," Funmi said, picking a bottle of oxblood-red polish and walking toward the center chair. There was a TV tucked in one corner above the giant mirror that made the shop look bigger than it was. A fetish film was playing on mute.

Zainab settled in next to her. She held up a silver vial. "That will look very nice," said Funmi. "I think I have a gèlè that will work well for you in that shade."

Enitan chose a bottle of clear nail polish and sat in the chair beside Funmi.

"Clear nail polish?" Funmi asked Enitan, slightly stricken.

"Yes now! Is it not a neutral color?"

So be it. Enitan had never been the stylish one of the group, it was true. Destiny sat down in the chair next to Zainab. Remi was the only one who had not yet claimed her seat.

She was sitting in one of the chairs reserved for manicures, rifling through sun-bleached copies of old **Life & Times** magazines. "Remi, have you chosen a color?" Funmi asked her. Remi shook her head. "I don't really like makeup," she said in a matter-of-fact tone. "The chemicals are so harsh."

"Ahn-ahn!" exclaimed Funmi. "So why did you insist on coming with us?"

"I wanted to explore the city," Remi said. "It's fine. I'll just watch you get your mani-pedis done. I feel like everything is interesting in a new country, you know?" This Remi was something else.

"Remi is our anthropologist for the weekend," Enitan said from her chair. Zainab laughed.

The metal ringing of a curtain being drawn interrupted their conversation. A team of young women wearing green aprons and carrying nail kits filed out, the smell of hot cooking oil following them.

"Good morning," they chorused one after another as they got into their positions, sitting on cushions in front of the women. Tinu came back out, a Louis Vuitton handbag slung on one shoulder. She was doing very well herself. Or was dating someone who was.

"Aunty, I'm so sorry I have to leave you now, but I have a prior engagement," she told Funmi. "I will see you at the trad tonight. So lovely to meet you, ladies," she said, turning toward Zainab and Enitan. "And, Destiny, congratulations again!"

"Thank you, Tinu," Destiny said.

Funmi gestured Tinu over with a finger.

"Please o, the girl knows to do the bridal special?" Funmi whispered.

"Yes, yes of course," said Tinu. "Patience!" she called out. The girl kneeling in front of Destiny looked up.

"Ma?"

"That is the bride. So you know what to do."

The girl nodded. "Yes, ma," she said.

"Good," said Tinu, her facial expression shifting from boss to supplicant once again. "Okay, ma, see you tonight." She kneeled quickly and then left the shop.

"How is the water, ma?" asked the girl who was assigned to Funmi as she gently placed both of Funmi's feet into the bucket under her chair.

It felt sensational. She closed her eyes. "It's good, thank you," she said.

"So Remi had some questions about the sequence of events this weekend," Enitan said. "I thought maybe you could help me, Funmi and Destiny. You know I didn't go through all of this for my own wedding."

"We know," said Zainab.

"You know Mom has never told me what her elopement was like for you and Aunty Funmi," said Remi from where she was sitting. "Were you shocked?"

"Shocked?" Funmi said. It was hard to remember. It was so long ago now, and that particular period of time was one Funmi had gone to great lengths to forget, for reasons that had nothing to do with Enitan at all.

"I was angry for some time," said Zainab quietly. Funmi turned to look at her, surprised at her forthrightness.

"But we've done a good job staying in touch," Zainab continued, placing her arm on Enitan's shoulder.

"She had to do what she had to do," Funmi offered, now that they appeared to be on this trajectory.

Enitan looked embarrassed. "What do you want to know about Nigerian weddings, Remi?" Enitan asked in a noticeable attempt to change the subject. "We've got the bride right here." Enitan smiled at Destiny.

"Yes, Destiny," Zainab now said encouragingly. "We should be focusing our attention on you. How are you feeling?"

Now Funmi turned to look at Destiny.

"I feel fine, Aunty," she said. She made fleeting eye contact with her mother and then added: "I'm looking forward to it."

"What I don't understand is the difference between what's happening tonight and what's happening tomorrow," said Remi.

"Funmi?" Enitan said.

"Tonight is the traditional and tomorrow is the church wedding," Funmi said. She didn't understand the question. Weren't the differences obvious?

"But what is the traditional?" Remi continued.

"The traditional is the traditional," Funmi said, realizing as she said it that this would not be helpful. She decided on a new method of explanation. "In the old days, when two families agreed that their son and daughter will marry, there were certain customs that were done. You've heard of a bride price for instance?"

"Yes," Remi said, her face reddening slightly. "I have always found the concept kind of troubling."

"It's not as if anyone believes that their daughter is worth a monetary price for goodness' sake," said Funmi. "Anyways, the traditional wedding is a way to celebrate our culture. And the white wedding or church wedding is the official ceremony. Doing both is just how it is done now."

Back in university, if one of the students in the union had been asked that question, they likely would have mentioned something about the aftereffects of Christian imperialism and how it had managed to leach its way into many traditional customs, as if marriage had been an oasis of equality between the sexes before white men came along. But Funmi had never really been one for that kind of talk. And that was all a long time ago now.

CHAPTER 10

Enitan

Enitan stared at her daughter, who was sleeping, her head resting in the crook of her elbow, which was snug against the car door. She noted the light brown freckles that dotted the side of her cheek, the smooth profile of her nose.

Enitan's mother, Sharon, had given Remi her name. Oluremi, God has given me comfort. Charles had insisted their daughter have a Yorùbá first name—a deliberate act of defiance toward his own mother. Enitan had supplied the middle name, Ayooluwa, the joy of God, which was so fitting when Remi was a toddler. She had been such a chunky baby, with a bright orange Afro and gummy smiles. How adorable she had been.

This is mine, she belongs to me, Enitan would think, sitting in their armchair, breastfeeding Remi at night, still finding it all so hard to believe. Flesh of her flesh. She knew that description was for marriage, but it felt so much more accurate for what she had gone through, what she had endured. The doctor had had to do a C-section because he was concerned about the narrowness of Enitan's hips and the baby was already seven pounds in utero. Surgery absolutely terrified her, but then when the drugs had coursed through her, she had mainly just felt delirious; the green wall of the curtain blocking her lower half and the vague tugging happening below her, the feeling of: They are getting this baby out of me, and it is a struggle of some kind; they have cut open my belly and have moved my intestines around. And then the unmistakable cry and the baby, a slimy gray-purple thing with a squished face and dark hair that would later redden. They placed her on Enitan's chest just for a moment before they cleaned her, and Charles, who had been wearing surgical scrubs and a surgical mask, was crying. Their daughter.

They had had their disagreements of course; what mother and daughter hadn't? About, for instance, her hair. When Remi started wearing it out like a madman—literally that's what she would look like—Enitan wished she had photos of such men and women to show Remi. They roamed the streets, probably suffering from some form of undiagnosed schizophrenia, with wild, matted hair that was un-combed and unwashed and sometimes looked like it had been dyed light brown when in actuality this was just the effect of all the dust that collected on their hair as they walked outside in callused bare feet, rags barely covering their private parts. You breathed through your mouth when you saw them approaching. Enitan had tried to explain this phenomenon to Remi, but she hadn't understood; she had been fixated on the perceived cruelty of such treatment. "So they're left on the street to suffer? There's no place for them?" And Enitan had grown weary of arguing with her yet again. Everything in Nigeria seemed comparatively cruel to liberal Americans who loved to act as if America was also not capable of cruelty and disregard.

That Remi was so thoroughly American still occasionally surprised Enitan. Her surprise wasn't logical; she understood this. When you had children in America, the children became American, that was the trade-off. But this reality could still be jarring. Even the way Remi pronounced her own mother's name, flattening the vowels so they sounded drawn out, made Enitan feel a deep sense of sadness. She had no misconceptions about what raising a child—a daughter especially—in Nigeria would have been like, but still she found herself sometimes mourning what might have been. Those rare, wonderfully surreal opportunities when Enitan would hear a cabdriver or a hairdresser speaking in Yorùbá would take Enitan's breath away. She would feel an ache deep in her gut, of a very specific and fleeting kind of homesickness.

That Remi looked so much like her father and so little like Enitan did not help mitigate the disorientation of having a child who was so different from its mother. No one ever thought they were related and while Enitan had become accustomed to this, there were always random moments—the pinprick of seeing a mother and daughter on the subway, each a mirror of the other for instance—when she wondered what that would be like. And she was not alone in this. "You don't understand because you're skinny!" Remi would yell at her mother when Enitan would ask Remi why she wasn't eating the jollof rice Enitan had made for her because it was her favorite, or why she had thrown out the pints of Ben & Jerry's Enitan had bought on a whim a few days ago, or when Remi would have a breakdown because Enitan had bought 2 percent milk instead of no fat.

The years of Remi's eating disorder, from twelve to seventeen, were arguably the most difficult years of their relationship. Eating disorders were spreading at a prolific rate at the school Charles taught at, and that Remi had attended (courtesy of a faculty discount that still made the tuition bill the most expensive check they wrote every month).

Remi's adolescent dissatisfaction with her body had been so hard for Enitan to fully fathom because in Nigeria, Remi's body was ideal: the ample bosom and the small waist and the thick thighs, all wrapped up in light skin. If she were living in Nigeria, men would be lining up to propose. But in New York, in the elite world of private schools, Remi was chubby—fat, apparently—and this was why she would only eat oatmeal for breakfast and an unseasoned chicken breast with raw kale for dinner, though eventually the chicken breast would be replaced with tofu she grilled in a frying pan herself, and then replaced with only unsweetened Greek yogurt. She would go on long runs in the evenings when the sun was setting before coming home to do her schoolwork. It made Enitan so nervous—New York was not as safe a city then.

Then Remi started smoking, only casually, only with friends she said when Enitan had confronted her about the pack of Marlboro Lights she had found in Remi's schoolbag. They had gotten into a blowout fight about why Enitan was searching through Remi's schoolbag; she had not been, she had picked up the schoolbag, which Remi liked to recklessly dump in the living room anyhow, creating clutter, and the pack had slipped out, but that didn't matter to Remi. What Enitan had done was a breach of trust; what about her privacy, and Enitan had been enraged, privacy kẹ, privacy was irrelevant. Remi lived in a benevolent dictatorship, she did not pay the bills, her name wasn't on the lease, and she would not start smoking, not when Enitan spent all day in the nursing home caring for patients who had smoked their way into lung cancer or emphysema. She would not start smoking while Remi was in their house and under their rules, and Remi had said fine, she wouldn't live in their house anymore and she had gone to stay with Francesca, her best friend at the time who lived in a Tribeca loft with her artist parents and burgeoning movie star brother. Enitan had been so upset and Charles had said not to worry, she was acting out, it would be fine and he had smoked a few cigarettes now and then, and Enitan had hated him too in that moment, had felt completely and utterly alone, ganged up on by the two most important people in her life.

She called Grace, who was still living in Queens at the time. Grace had told her to come over. They had sat together at the table in her kitchen and Grace heated up some kimchi fried rice and talked about what a little shit her ex-husband was while Enitan listened, soothed by Grace's self-absorption.

They had met at church of all places, Korean church. After her mother had died, Enitan had found herself searching for . . . something. She and Charles were fighting more and more in those days. He didn't seem to understand why she was so completely undone by her mother's death, when their relationship had still been so strained toward the end. He expected sadness of course, as he had felt for his own father, but not complete incapacitation.

She had been written up twice now at the nursing home for missing shifts even after the time off she had taken for the burial. They would have fired her outright but they were so short-staffed. Enitan just couldn't get out of bed; it was the strangest thing. Her mind willed it, but her body refused to obey. She found herself listening to Don Moen CDs over and over and over again. "God will make a way when there seems to be no way," he would croon, and she would hate it, the sound of syrupy certitude in his voice. Where did it come from, his certainty? And yet she could not stop listening. She felt unmoored. Uprooted.

So she decided to go to church. She thought that maybe she would find something of her mother there, an understanding of her spirit, a sense of peace. The burial had been attended mainly by people Enitan hadn't known, members of the congregation who had known Mama, as they had called her, all wearing celestial white. It had been a church member who had gotten ahold of Enitan's number somehow and informed her of the news. "She has gone to the Lord," the woman had told her on the phone. She had died in her sleep. (What phrasing! A massive brain aneurysm. She had been seventy-one. Not young, but no, not old. Especially when there were octogenarians in the nursing home, shackled to oxygen tanks but still talking, still laughing, still living.)

When Enitan had heard the news of her mother's death, it was her body that reacted first. She could no longer hear properly. It felt as though someone had taken a loud industrial fan and placed it close to each ear. Sweat began to trickle down her sides, pooling at the small of her back; her heart was beating frantically. No tears came, though, not yet, but she knew that she had to remedy this ailment immediately.

So to church Enitan had gone. She just walked into one after her shift one Wednesday evening because she recognized the song they were singing: "How Great Thou Art." It was a basement room and the door had been open, casting a prism of orange light on the sidewalk. She had slipped into the last row of metallic folding chairs that had been set up in two columns of four chairs each. An elderly Asian woman with permed hair stood up front, leading the song. Then they shared testimonies. In the beginning they weren't in English, but then the same elderly woman got up and said something and then they started speaking in faltering English, and Enitan realized that they were doing this for her benefit and found that gesture moving. The woman took her aside afterward and asked Enitan how she had found the church. She said she had just walked past it.

Enitan began to make the trek from Brooklyn to Queens on Sunday mornings. She wasn't sure why exactly. She just found it all comforting, the ritual of the hymns they sang together, the stale coffee and Dunkin' Donuts Munchkins to eat after the service. She had thought the church was Chinese (Remi was always telling her to stop assuming that all Asian people were Chinese, it was rude and incorrect; and Enitan would tell her that in Nigeria, all Asian people **were** Chinese). Enitan would learn the truth later, after Grace noted how she had seen Enitan at two of their church services and had asked her how she liked the service and then invited her over for lunch, where she made kimchi fried rice in a cast-iron skillet and explained how Reverend Park had moved to America from Korea fifteen years ago and founded this church.

They got on, Enitan and Grace. Grace talked a lot and Enitan didn't, but she found being around Grace soothing as a result. Grace's droning served as a soundtrack; her litany of grievances was long and at the top of her list were her ex-husband and lesbian daughter.

Charles was always trying to pry information out of Enitan—he took her silence as some form of reproach or rebuke. "We're not leaving until we settle this," he would tell her if they got into an asinine argument about something and Enitan closed up. He thought that her silence was immature. But Enitan didn't speak because her anger was incapacitating. She had never been a naturally gregarious person, the loneliness and isolation of her school years had ensured that, but she also found that when she moved to America it was harder to speak. Especially in those early months, when she talked, people did not understand what she was saying. They would ask her to repeat herself as if she wasn't speaking English, a language she spoke fluently. And then she found that there was a kind of soft power that came with being quiet; people were disconcerted at first and then flattered. They always thought she was listening to them.

She and Grace talked about their daughters, trying to understand them. Grace didn't understand why her daughter was gay. She lived in San Francisco and had shaved her head and stabbed a needle through her eyebrow. Grace had shown Enitan pictures. She would have been a pretty girl, if not for the shaved head and stabbed eyebrow and the generally angry, surly expression she wore on her face. She was gay but not only that, Grace said; she was something called polyamorous. At first Enitan had thought she said polygamous and Enitan had said, "Well we have that in Nigeria too." And Grace had shook her head violently, no, no, no, **polyamorous,** which meant she would never settle down with one person, which meant it would be highly unlikely that Grace would ever have grandchildren. "At least, when it's just one, there could be potential for children," Grace had explained. But now the entire situation was really just something straight out of Sodom and Gomorrah, as far as Grace was concerned.

Sunday pulled the Jeep into the parking lot of the airport. "Madam, make I wait for you here?" he asked. Remi yawned and stretched, blinking rapidly as she woke up.

"Yes, we won't be long." Enitan got out of the SUV carefully. She had forgotten how high up such cars were from the road. Remi got down from her own side and they began to walk to the main building. It was just as busy as it was yesterday, if not busier, the same crush of bodies making their way; groundnut vendors and phone card sellers, luggage boys and drivers, passengers with unwieldy trolley carts. They entered and headed to the arrival hall. They had been told their luggage was supposed to come on carousel #3. "We might as well sit down," Enitan said. The flight was delayed, according to the announcement a woman had given over the intercom. Remi sighed and they sat down on a rusted bench. A giant industrial fan blew whirls of ticket stubs and strands of hair weave around them. A bathroom attendant, wearing a blue apron and carrying a broom and extended dustpan, attempted to catch the whirls with her pan.

"So what is your verdict on Lagos thus far?" Enitan asked Remi.

"Overwhelming," Remi said.

Enitan nodded. "Yes, that's generally how I've always felt about Lagos. New York too, when I first moved there."

"There's just so much to process on so many fronts. All the poverty and then the way Aunty Funmi is about it all. The way Aunty Funmi is in general. She's just such a strong personality."

Enitan chuckled.

"I talked to Destiny a bit this morning," said Remi.

"About whether or not she's a Communist?" Enitan asked, smiling.

"Ha ha," said Remi sarcastically. "No. She's actually really cool. Did you know she runs this Instagram account?" Remi took out her phone and showed Enitan. "I didn't realize it. Her photos are gorgeous." And Remi showed Enitan photographs, mainly portraits of market women with weary faces in front of trays full of their wares; a young girl in her Sunday best, sitting outside a church, her chin in her hands. "We talked for a while about photography. She's really good at it."

"Yes," Enitan said. She remembered the last time Funmi and Destiny had visited New York, about seven years ago now, when Destiny was doing her gap year. She took a lot of photos on a camera her father had given her. Nice photos too, of Enitan and Remi standing by the Washington Square arch, of all of them at the Bronx Zoo. Remi had been twelve then; the acne that disrupted both of their adolescent lives, that genetic marker of awkwardness had begun to erupt on Remi's face. She was irritable, dramatically so, loudly groaning as they went on their tour of the Lower East Side, walking through the tenements the poor whites had once lived in even though this was one of Remi's favorite New York activities and Enitan had suggested it in an attempt to defuse Remi's irritation. Funmi meanwhile found the whole enterprise amusing. "It's still better than Lagos," she told Enitan in loud Yorùbá, laughing. Destiny was the only person that day who seemed genuinely enraptured by the words of the guide and who took diligent photos. "Our little photographer," Funmi would joke, and Destiny would smile this tight little smile and Enitan wondered then if there was some private discord between the two of them that she was obviously not privy to.

A few months later, she received some photographs in the mail and a thank-you note from Destiny written in scrupulously neat handwriting.

"I wonder what she sees in Dele," Remi said. "He kept trying to convince me that the med school he went to is really prestigious and was shocked when I told him I turned down Columbia. It was actually kind of funny."

Well, Enitan had been shocked by Remi's decision too. She recognized Dele's type immediately.

Ambitious for ambition's sake. No real sense of calling toward his profession, but a desire to attain prestige by any means possible. He was the kind of person who accrued degrees, collected them like art to display in his office. The kind of person who would subscribe to magazines he would not read, who would buy season tickets to the opera—that he did not like opera would not matter.

"Then again, Destiny is hard to read too. And I always felt like you used to compare the two of us and I would come out the loser."

Enitan looked at Remi closely when she made this confession.

"That's not true."

Remi shrugged. "Okay," she muttered.

"You know I'm very glad you are here," Enitan said after a moment of silence. She reached for Remi's hand. Remi allowed her to squeeze it.

They were quiet for a while until Remi asked abruptly, "Why didn't you tell me Aunty Zainab got robbed last night?"

Enitan was taken aback by the question. It reminded her of Charles, always going back to old fights, waiting for moments when Enitan thought all was resolved and then pouncing with an intensity that overwhelmed her.

"It was not your immediate concern."

"Not my immediate concern? What does that even mean?"

Enitan closed her eyes. "Please, Remi, we're not going to have this conversation now."

"So when are we going to have it?" asked Remi.

"Another time."

Remi rolled her eyes theatrically, something Enitan detested and Remi knew it. She felt her anger mounting in spite of herself. The bathroom attendant was watching them now, pretending not to.

"Stop it!" Enitan hissed. "You're embarrassing me."

Remi pulled her hand away from her mother's angrily, her face red and her eyes already brimming with tears.

They would sit in a tense, unhappy silence until their bags came.

CHAPTER 11

Zainab

T HOUGH ZAINAB HAD BEEN IN FUNMI'S HOUSE
many times over the years, she had never been
inside the master bedroom. It was preposterously
large—with tall floor-length windows, a huge
canopied bed underneath mesh mosquito netting,
a plush carpet on the tiled floor, a giant television,
an armchair, and matching vanities. The master
bathroom had a Jacuzzi tub and gold-plated sink
fixtures. And then there were the closets, his and
hers, as large as their kitchen back home in Kaduna.
Funmi was dragging clothes by the armful and
throwing them on the bed for Zainab to peruse at
her leisure. Since both dresses Zainab had chosen for
the trad and the church wedding had been dumped
unceremoniously on the roadside somewhere en
route to Lagos, she was searching for replacements
in Funmi's closet.

And wow, what clothes! There was a slinky dark
green number with a cinched-in waist and black

chiffon sleeves, a pink off-the-shoulder jacquard dress with fringe that looked like a complicated dessert, a floor-length maroon gown with a heart-shaped bodice. White foam mannequin heads lined two rows of Funmi's closet, each sporting their own pre-tied gèlè—gold, green, red, orange, silver, bronze. On one shelf sat high-arched shoes that looked like archaic torture devices, all ending with points that seemed like they could draw blood when pressed against skin. Zainab knew that those items were likely designer names but she was unable to recognize them. Her days of caring so much about her physical appearance were long behind her. Over the years, her waist had thickened; her hair had begun to gray. She went to the same tailor every year, who stealthily let out the dresses she wore to weddings and naming ceremonies.

"See anything you like? We don't have much time," Funmi said. They had come from the salon a half hour ago. Zainab picked up the green dress. "Are we the same size?"

"Close enough," Funmi said. "I have the perfect gèlè for that dress. See." She went inside the closet and came back with an extravagantly tied gèlè, all oblique geometric angles. The fabric was beautiful, a dark moss green embedded with complex cutout patterns.

"You think the green will look all right?" Zainab

asked, holding the dress against her body and eyeing the full-length mirror that stood just outside the closet.

"Of course! You can wear any color. It's me that has to worry. Try the dress on," she instructed.

Zainab turned her back on Funmi and untied her wrapper. She hoisted her blouse over her head so she was wearing just a bra and her slip.

"You will have to take the slip off. The dress is supposed to be tight," Funmi said. It would be quite a change of pace, that dress for Zainab. She took off the slip. In the mirror she could see her stomach, soft and striated with stretch marks courtesy of Muhammad. She bore the markings of his entry into the world on her body, and he could still forget to call her from Dubai for weeks on end. Oh, the reckless, unthinking cruelty of children! How they broke their mothers' hearts so casually!

Zainab unzipped the dress and placed one foot in and then the other. She shimmied it up over her calves, her knees, her hips. Then a problem.

The fabric did not give. She pulled a little harder this time and the dress finally went over her hips, but now it wouldn't zip.

"Funmi," Zainab said.

Funmi emerged from the closet, carrying a sparkly beaded ball gown and black high heels.

"I'm going to change into this for the reception

tomorrow," Funmi was saying, but then she stopped and gasped. "Ah ahn! Look at this model in our midst," she said, beaming. "Is it fitting?"

"It won't zip."

"Let me see," Funmi said, and she got behind Zainab. "Hold the bottom of the dress well," she instructed. She maneuvered Zainab so she was standing directly in front of the mirror. The dress **did** look nice, if it could fit. It had a fluted bottom skirt that clung around the thighs and hips, the neckline was modest, the sleeves were black chiffon. Funmi tried the zipper. Nothing. "Suck in your belly well well," Funmi joked, and then she tried again.

Zainab held her stomach in. She felt like she was eleven again, standing stock-still in a new dress Mama Fatima had sewn for her as she tried to make finishing touches, hovering over Zainab with pins sticking out the side of her mouth, pinning and tucking and letting hems down. The dresses were almost always too short at first; Zainab had had a giant growth spurt between the ages of eleven and thirteen.

"This tailor. She never knows how to do the zipper right! It's always getting stuck. Such a waste of money," Funmi muttered. "You want to try something else?"

She would try something else. There were so many options after all.

"Thank you, Funmi, for doing all of this. I know you must be feeling stressed."

"Oh, I have just the dress," Funmi said. She went back to the closet and came out carrying a sequined midnight-blue gown, long sleeved, floor length. "I have a silver gèlè that this would be perfect for."

Zainab nodded. She would try it. "Ṣé you heard me, though? How are you feeling before the trad?" She thought of the conversation she had had with Destiny, or rather, Zainab's attempt at a conversation.

Funmi looked at the clock. "I hope Enitan makes it back in time. Traffic can be so bad at this time of day." She smiled at Zainab. "I am fine. A wedding is a blessing."

Zainab took the dress and stepped into it. It slipped over her hips easily. Yes, this would be the one. She reached for the zipper and up it went, sliding smoothly.

Funmi smiled. "Perfect." Funmi moved some of the dresses from the bed and sat down. "One crisis averted."

"You know, Funmi, you really are too hard on that girl," Zainab said.

Funmi looked taken aback. "Ahn-ahn! What do you mean?"

"You spend so much of your time being angry that she doesn't do everything you say with a big smile, but then you expect her to stand up for herself without giving her any encouragement." Perhaps now was not the best time to have a conversation like this, but Zainab knew that there was truth to her words. She saw the way that Destiny had looked at Funmi in the nail salon. A cauldron of resentment was bubbling inside of Destiny and it would spill over at a moment's notice.

"Have you talked to Destiny?" Zainab continued. "Are you sure this is what she wants?"

"What do you mean? Of course, I've talked to Destiny. Of course, this is what she wants. Did she not choose him? Did I hold a gun to her head and say it's by force?"

Zainab sighed. "She's lost weight," Zainab said quietly, sitting down beside Funmi.

"Stress from the wedding now."

"Are you sure?"

"Of course! I don't even understand why you are talking about this now."

"It's important, abi no be so?"

"Marriage will be good for her," Funmi said firmly.

"Why?"

"What do you mean why?" Funmi asked Zainab, as if her question was so unreasonable.

But Zainab did want to know. "Why is it so important that Destiny marry Dele right now? What will happen if she doesn't? It just seems so fast."

"Has she said anything to you?" Funmi asked Zainab suddenly, suspiciously it felt like.

"Not in so many words."

Funmi sighed. "You know this life I have? I couldn't have gotten it if I hadn't married Yinka."

"Oh, but, Funmi, my dear, Destiny is a smart girl. She's going to be a doctor for goodness' sake. She doesn't need a man for that."

Funmi was quiet for a long moment, it seemed like to Zainab.

"I just want her to have a better life than I have had," Funmi said. "No complications."

"I understand that but—"

"I don't want to talk about this anymore," Funmi said.

Zainab nodded. They sat in silence.

"Why do you think Charles is not here?" Funmi asked after a few more awkward minutes had passed.

Zainab turned to look at Funmi. "Enitan did not tell you?"

"Tell me what?"

Zainab hesitated for a brief moment. Surely if Enitan had not told Funmi, she had her reasons. But she would find out sooner or later anyway.

"They are getting divorced."

Funmi turned to look at Zainab now, processing it. "Hey ya. That is sad."

"Yes, very," said Zainab.

They were quiet for another moment.

"I wonder why she has not told me . . ."

"She probably doesn't want to distract you with bad news now. This weekend is supposed to be a joyous occasion."

Funmi nodded. "Yes o," she added.

They were quiet again.

"Remember the day we found out they had eloped?" Zainab said after a moment's silence.

Funmi laughed. "How can I forget?"

"I was so angry. I still don't think I've ever been so angry in my life."

Funmi shrugged. "She had to do what was right for her."

"Was it right?"

Funmi smiled, a bit wryly, Zainab thought. "Only she can know whether it was right."

"And what about Destiny and Dele?"

"What about them?" Funmi asked sharply.

"Do you think they are doing what is right?"

"It is good for Destiny to marry," Funmi said, the expression on her face hardening ever so slightly. "Marriage will provide some security for her. He comes from a good family."

Zainab didn't say anything. She thought about the voicemail she had received from Destiny.

"And you are positive she is all right?" Zainab ventured to ask yet again. Funmi shot her a look. Zainab recognized it well; it was a more subdued derivative of a look Funmi had given when Zainab had asked her to read for the part of Juliet back in their uni days.

"How many times must you ask this question? Would we have gone through all this trouble if this was not what she wanted? Haba!" Funmi sucked her teeth.

Zainab raised a hand in surrender. "I am just confirming. I know how quiet she can be."

"Of course now," said Funmi, again with a bit of edge to her tone. Zainab was silent. She knew Funmi well enough to know that now was not the time to press.

They heard the gate clank open. Enitan was back. They both got up to meet her.

CHAPTER 12

Funmi

"SUNDAY IS HERE. ARE YOU READY TO LEAVE?"
Yinka stood at the doorway of their bedroom,
where Funmi sat in front of her vanity, dabbing
powder on her T-zone rather viciously, irritated by
the conversation she had just had with Zainab. She
was annoyed that she was annoyed—that as Zainab
had spoken she had begun to feel a slight panic.

But Destiny was prone to fits of moodiness; they
had even been told to see a professional about it
once, some years ago now, just after Destiny had
begun her second year of university. A teacher of
hers had taken the trouble of emailing Funmi and
Yinka, telling them that Destiny appeared to be far
less animated than she used to be in her photography class; she was one of their most promising
students, had something happened at home and
perhaps Destiny should see a therapist? Both Funmi
and Yinka had agreed that the idea was absurd.
Therapist for what? Destiny had had a charmed

childhood, the likes of which Funmi could only dream of. Two parents who loved and pampered her, admission to one of the best boarding schools in Nigeria, now a slot at a university in England. Had Destiny become increasingly reticent of late? Yes, but that was how Destiny could be sometimes, especially when she was stressed. When the wedding was over, she would relax, Funmi was sure of this.

She stood up, put the compact into her purse, and picked up the ostrich feather fan Yinka had given her for Valentine's Day a few years ago. Then she moved over so she could see herself in the full-length mirror.

This outfit was in Funmi's standard silhouette, an off-the-shoulder lace peplum blouse that framed her breasts magnificently and then a long skirt, which sat just beneath her bust, holding in her stomach. She wore a 24-karat gold chain around her neck (it was an early Christmas gift from Yinka) and had chosen her wine-red gèlè and ìborùn. She readjusted her ìborùn so it did not block the view of her cleavage.

"How do I look?" she asked Yinka, who was tapping on his BlackBerry.

"Are you ready to go?"

She nodded and slipped into her heels.

She tried not to take it personally—Yinka's steadfast refusal to be romantic. Though there had been some of that in the beginning when he was still trying to woo her, she had learned the hard way that romance left you too vulnerable, too exposed to the wanton cruelties of the world. And she liked Yinka's practicality, his brutality even, the way he ate his swallow (amala was his favorite, bafflingly to Funmi) with his thick, meaty fingers, cracking chicken bones with his teeth to suck out the marrow. To be clear, he could be charming; this charm was something he accessed as needed, when he was courting government officials for lucrative contracts for instance, and he gave her plenty of gifts, jewelry and shoes and clothing, but he could also be intimidating. He had hit her once during an argument early in their marriage and it had stunned her, literally stunned her. The world had flashed to white for a moment and, though he later apologized (with a Coach bag and single long-stem red rose the following night), it had confirmed something for her that she had suspected, namely that he was capable of a kind of cruelty she found both intoxicating and terrifying.

All the guests had been herded into the chartered bus that would take them to the hotel and so the house felt eerily quiet, the first time it had been this tranquil in months. Doors were still ajar, showing flashes of unmade beds, clothes strewn onto floors. There were children's toys from Yinka's nieces and nephews in the foyer. The maids had not yet begun tidying up.

She and Yinka reached the courtyard. The coach they had ordered was still sitting there, emitting a low hum. The driver was waiting for Sunday to lead them to the hotel. She could see Enitan and Remi sitting in the back of the bus with Zainab behind them. Remi was even wearing her own gèlè—how charming. Funmi would have wanted them to drive with her and Yinka, but she knew Yinka would not allow it, preferring to be alone.

Funmi had called the wedding planner first thing in the morning, as soon as she had gotten out of bed, to triple-check the itinerary of the proceedings. She made the planner text her photos from the venue that morning too. It looked beautiful. Truly they had both outdone themselves. She couldn't wait for the guests to see what would be in store for them.

Funmi thought back to her own wedding. The total tally had been something like five hundred guests. They had married in Yinka's village, so essentially all the villagers had crashed the wedding. They had had armed motorcades to escort the VIP guests coming in from Lagos—Yinka's closest military friends, the governor of the state. Funmi had known very few of the guests, Aunty Buki and Zainab had been the only people she insisted on inviting; her father was dead, she didn't speak to her stepmother, Dorcas, or her half siblings, and Enitan was an ocean away. But it hadn't mattered, how few people Funmi actually knew or recognized. She was the bride. She felt like a celebrity, because for all intents and purposes she was one, in her white dress and veil; the shoulder pads that were then in fashion flanked either side of her head; her hair curled about her face, her bouquet of plastic flowers thrown into the crowd during the reception just like the Americans did. All eyes fixated on her when she walked down the aisle in the church amid gasps and fawning looks. The same looks had been magnified when she danced with Yinka during the reception. She had felt like a star.

Funmi had given her own wedding dress to Destiny to wear for the church ceremony. (Destiny was also wearing a custom-made Duro Olowu dress for her second outfit change during the English reception.) The tailor had done some rearrangements for Funmi's dress, taking in the waist quite a bit and removing the shoulder pads. The dress was long sleeved and lacy, with a square-shaped bodice, classy and elegant, like the dress that thin-lipped woman in England had worn when she married Princess Diana's oldest son. Funmi couldn't wait to see Destiny wear it tomorrow, which she would in Jesus' name!

Sunday opened the door for her and helped her climb into the SUV. Yinka had already entered from the other side. She could not expect him to see that her mobility was severely limited in this dress. Sunday practically had to boost her up onto the car ledge and then she collapsed onto her side and shuffled in so all of her was in the car. What could you do? Fashion was not always practical.

Sunday started the car. The radio turned on automatically to the Pidgin news station. Funmi snuck a glance at Yinka, who, as usual, was looking at his BlackBerry. "Mind your neck," she said.

Yinka looked up. "What is it?"

"Doesn't your neck hurt after looking down at your phone for so long?"

Yinka looked irritated. He sucked his teeth. "Please don't bother me again." Funmi was quiet then and slightly embarrassed. She wondered, not for the first time, if he was cheating on her. It would be utterly unsurprising if he was, of course. Most men of his age and status had some young illiterate harlot they were harboring in some apartment in Ikoyi, giving them monthly allowances so they could stick their wrinkly penises into something young and waxed twice a month. She took solace in the fact that at least Yinka was discreet. He was not like Mercy Ladipo's husband, who had paraded his young girlfriend all up and down Lagos Island, even bringing her to the tennis club. Poor Mercy had only found out his mistress was pregnant when one of the waiters at the club's restaurant (subsequently fired) had asked her if she was excited for her daughter's pregnancy. "We don't have any daughters," Mercy had said, but she barely needed to get the words out before she knew exactly what the waiter had meant. What a disgrace! She did not divorce him of course. The child was supposed to be the spitting image of his father.

Yinka would never do that. He did not like to make scenes. Even his anger was controlled. When he hit Funmi, it was calculated, and after he hit her that one time, he decided he would not do it again. It was not in his best interests. Showing off a young girl, getting her pregnant—these were messy decisions, signs of excess. Everything Yinka did was disciplined. And he doted upon Destiny, really doted on her. "Girls are more reasonable than boys. You can train them," he told Funmi early in the pregnancy, when they had found out the sex of the baby and Funmi had wondered if he was disappointed. "I would rather have one Destiny than a million Babatundes," he would tell Destiny all the time. His love for Destiny was partly why Funmi knew even if he was cheating, and he probably was, he would never leave Funmi. He would not hurt the mother of his only child. He would not embarrass Destiny like that.

Sunday eased up in front of the security checkpoint for the hotel. The security guard began to run his weapon detector stick over the SUV when Yinka rolled down the window.

"Ah, boss," said the security guard, hurriedly genuflecting. He went back into the little security checkpoint hut and lifted the rope attached to the cylindrical iron barrier that blocked their entrance into the hotel courtyard. The barrier rose and Sunday drove in, the coach pulling in right behind them.

Other guests had already started arriving. They stepped down from an assortment of tinted SUVs blinking in the bright sunlight, stretching, preening, their iPads at the ready for photographs. So many colors, bright pinks and magentas, yellows, reds, purples, lavenders, blues, and greens began to fill the courtyard.

Funmi loved this—the unabashed clash of colors, the opulence. There was no question that Nigerian weddings were the most beautiful weddings in the world. Well, maybe Indian weddings were a close second. She liked to watch their movies, even though she usually didn't have the stamina to finish them as they were often quite long. She liked the extravagant dance numbers, the fancy jewelry, the henna and the music, percussive and loud and vibrant. And their weddings were even longer than Nigerian ones—they could last for a week in fact! The grooms would ride in on horses. A small part of her had hoped that Destiny would meet an Indian man in her same program in London, and then they would have a joint Indian and Nigerian wedding. Imagine how splendid the wedding would be: the colors, the dancing, the music! She felt a general affinity toward the country—it had been very hard for her when acquaintances started circulating videos of Nigerian students being beaten in India on WhatsApp. Almost like a betrayal.

A small cabal of street photographers had begun to circulate in the courtyard, preying on the foreigners, looking for the just-come-backs and swarming them with photographs, printing them while the guests were inside, only to later pester them to buy the prints once the ceremony was over. Funmi could already see Remi in passionate conversation with one such photographer. She had forgotten to warn Enitan.

"Mother of the bride!" Funmi turned to see Nike George, the wife of one of Yinka's business associates and a woman she absolutely detested, standing in front of her.

"Nike! Thank you so much for coming. I am so glad to see you." Funmi summoned the nicest smile she could muster from deep within her spirit. "You are looking beautiful this afternoon," she added. This was a blatant lie. Nike looked, frankly, ridiculous, eschewing traditional attire for some long, slinky red dress, with a fur around her shoulders as if they weren't in Lagos in December.

"Haba, you, my dear, are **radiant.** Must be the glow from all the wedding preparations." Funmi knew that was a thinly veiled dig at her shining forehead—she couldn't help it, she had started sweating as soon as she had stepped down from the SUV. Even after her explicit instructions that Sunday blast the air-conditioning, she still over-heated easily.

Funmi smiled. "Yes, we thank God. And how are the children?"

She had heard that Nike's oldest son had just gotten a divorce.

"They are well, we thank God. My youngest, Joseph, just got into Stanford's medical school. We are grateful for His mercies."

"Yes," said Funmi. "You know I actually have to go and find my daughter, but I hope I will see you later." She couldn't be bothered to play this game with Nike now. There would be so much of this later today and tomorrow. They gave each other air kisses and she headed into the hotel lobby, welcoming the arctic air that greeted her when she walked in. What sweet relief. The bridal suite was on the eighth floor so Funmi made her way to the elevators. When she got into the lift, the light flickered off and on for a moment, and Funmi became briefly stricken, contemplating the possibility of being trapped in an elevator when NEPA took light. She had heard some true horror stories. Yinka still generally refused to use lifts for this reason, preferring to huff and puff his way up the stairs. It was good for his heart at least. The elevator managed to make its rickety ascent however, and when the door slid open, Funmi said a silent prayer of thanksgiving. The smell of burnt hair was overwhelming when she got off the elevator. She could hear the muted bass of an Afrobeats song and a girl's grating hyena laugh. There was no question that she was on the right floor. The burnt smell became stronger as she drew closer to the suite.

When she got there, she could barely see Destiny amid the general commotion. Bridesmaids were primping themselves in the mirror. Half of them were already dressed in the rose-gold aso-ebi chosen for the ceremony while the other half were still wearing the light pink silk robes Funmi had had monogrammed personally for each of Destiny's ten bridesmaids. Someone was blasting Afrobeats from a speaker and there were empty glasses of champagne on the floor, on the sink, on the long countertop laden with makeup brushes, lipsticks, and other paraphernalia.

One of the bridesmaids was dancing lustily in one corner, thrusting her buttocks in and out to a song while the others cheered for her, but when they saw Funmi by the door, they stopped abruptly.

"Good afternoon, ma," the maid of honor said, kneeling, and then the other bridesmaids joined, and there was a chorus of "mas" and a discreet lowering of dress hems and clutching of bridesmaid robes.

"Hello, ladies, I trust you are well," Funmi said.

"Hi, Mummy," said Destiny, who was sitting in the center of the room, her eyes closed as a makeup artist carefully attached an eyelash extension with a pair of tweezers. A photographer crouched down to take a photo. Why would he photograph that moment? Funmi wondered. But increasingly, as she had learned browsing wedding photography sites on her iPad at night when she couldn't sleep, wedding albums included these banal moments— the bridesmaids getting ready, the makeup being applied, the wedding dress hanging on a curtain rod in the window, a close-up of the rings in their jewelry boxes. It was supposed to be artistic. And they did this even for the traditional. In fact, Funmi had coordinated with the photographer to make sure that some of the choice photographs of Dele and Destiny would be displayed during the English reception tomorrow.

"My darling girl," Funmi said, heading to the center of the room. She lightly squeezed Destiny's shoulder. "How are you feeling?"

Destiny turned to the makeup artist. "I'm so sorry, would you mind if I get up for a moment?" The makeup artist nodded and stepped aside. "Mummy, could you come with me?" Destiny asked. Funmi nodded and helped Destiny make her way past the clutter and into the bathroom. The makeup artist hadn't yet wiped away the setting powder under Destiny's eyes and on her cheekbones. Only one eyelash had been attached so her face looked sunken, unsymmetrical, not unlike a clown.

Funmi shut the door. "What is it?"

"Mummy, how did you know Daddy was the one you were meant to marry?"

Funmi stared at her daughter. What a question to ask at a time like this. How did she know Yinka was the one she was meant to marry? What could she say?

The day she and Yinka met he had told her he was going to marry her. Not **I want to marry you**. But **I am going to**. Funmi had found that sort of clarity—that certainty—strangely attractive. After Damola's death, she had felt so unmoored. She had committed to him; she had let herself fall in love with another person, had given in to the fear and uncertainty such love required and he had ended up dead, murdered by police.

The following months were a blur for Funmi. To this day she could not really remember what she did, whom she saw, whom she talked to. Everywhere she went carried memories of Damola. She could no longer walk pass the junction that led to the dam where they had first made love. She would walk out of the hospital half expecting to see Damola's Peugeot idling across the street, one hand dangling out the window to feel the breeze.

So when Yinka had come into the emergency room a year later with a cut hand in those frenzied days of the '87 riots, when she was working all those back-to-back shifts doing her clinical training, tending to patients with gruesome wounds—when he had told her that he was going to marry her one day and that he had been sent by the army to sort out "this nonsense"—when he said his name was Yinka and he lived in Lagos and she should come and visit sometime—Funmi had remembered him. It was then still too early for her to take his proposal seriously but there was something about his arrogance, his certainty. And also his determination. He wooed her doggedly for more than a year, calling her aunty Buki's house every Sunday without fail, then the hostel where she stayed with her fellow corpers when she served in Bauchi. He sent her lavish gifts—designer handbags, soaps, and expensive perfumes. She had to admire that level of persistence, which gradually, then suddenly, diminished over the course of their twenty-six-year marriage. Now that he had won his prize, there was no need to exert himself. But before she had known any better, he had promised escape. And she liked that. She knew she would never love him the way she had loved Damola, and that was part of the appeal. She was in control. And he would spirit her away to Lagos, to a new life of leisure and luxury and stability most of all. In a marriage, that was the best you could hope for.

"Why are you asking this question now? What is it?"

Destiny sighed and sat down on the toilet seat. "I'm just feeling a little overwhelmed."

"What do you mean?"

Destiny looked down at her hands. The bridal special looked beautiful on her, as Funmi had expected. There were swirls of silver and white on each nail and they were each studded with tiny ersatz pearls.

"I feel like everything is happening so quickly."

"You are just tired. It's natural to be nervous. Take a deep breath. Dele is a good man."

Funmi remembered the first time she had met him, at an upscale Indian restaurant in London. He had prostrated for both Yinka and Funmi amid stares from other diners. Yinka had been thrilled that he spoke fluent Yorùbá and wanted to get his MBA after getting his MD and that he had bought them all tickets to see **Les Misérables,** which was Yinka's favorite musical (the only musical he had ever seen in fact, but he loved it so much he made a point of watching it every time they were in London). Dele was a predictable man, slick in his own way, but Funmi sensed that he would never hurt Destiny, that he valued what she offered him: beauty, intelligence, a certain degree of docility. They were a good, stable match.

"I know he is," said Destiny. "It's just that—"

"You're just stressed from the wedding now," Funmi interrupted, squeezing Destiny's shoulder.

This line of talk was a dangerous one from Destiny and Funmi was not interested in pursuing it further. "It will all be over soon, don't worry. I know you don't like being the center of attention." Funmi dropped her hand from Destiny's shoulder and adjusted her iborun. They really did not have much time. "Destiny, my dear, they need to finish your makeup. Let us go back."

Destiny looked at her mother for a moment and it was startling, because the face she made was one Funmi recognized in herself and had given to her stepmother on many occasions. It was a look of deep fury and exasperation. But then in an instant, it disappeared and it happened so quickly that Funmi wondered if her eyes had been playing tricks on her.

Part II

Zaria, Kaduna, 1983–1988

CHAPTER 13

Funmi

October 1983

FUNMI WAS NOT ACCUSTOMED TO BEING ignored the way that Damola ignored her. Since she had started menstruating at eleven, she was used to the fixed stares of men. They watched her when she walked to the market to buy plantain and yam for the house. They watched her walking home from school and walking to church. Her stepmother, Dorcas, had certainly noticed Funmi's budding breasts and the new curve of her thighs, and had become alarmed. It was why she was such a horrible person. Well, part of the reason. She was mostly just anxious about Funmi's father, Emmanuel, and his continued lack of fidelity—and rightly so. Dorcas and Emmanuel had started sleeping together when Funmi's mother, Leila, was still alive. It was only Dorcas's pregnancy that had persuaded Emmanuel to marry her soon after Leila's death (a car accident).

Dorcas was quick to bear him a son—and then three more children after that, twin girls and another boy. She thought that the sons would be enough, but Emmanuel was a wealthy businessman. He traveled a lot and so did his eye. Constantly worried that he was looking for someone younger, for someone fairer, Dorcas bleached her skin and had the twins pluck her chin hairs with tweezers. And she took out her anger on Funmi.

When she was younger, Dorcas beat Funmi for stupid infractions—for not kneeling when greeting her in the morning, for not answering Dorcas immediately when she asked a question, for letting one of the twins smear lipstick all over the master bedroom wall while Funmi had been reading her Mills & Boon romance novels. Funmi would report these unjust beatings to her father when he was home, which was once every week, and then over time, once every two weeks. She would exaggerate for effect, calling upon her powers of embellishment, adding bits from the fairy-tale books her father would give to the children; how Dorcas hit her so hard she bled, how Dorcas poisoned her food and she had to go to the toilet for twelve hours straight. Her father would listen silently, sitting in his favorite armchair with his hands pressed together as if in prayer, his eyes closed. It would take him so long to answer that Funmi would occasionally wonder if he was even listening. Then his eyes would flutter open and he'd say, "Funmi, where do you get these stories from?" There was always a hint of admiration to the inquiry—just enough so that those weekly confessions would serve as one of the fonder memories she had of her father. As Funmi grew older, both Dorcas and Funmi wanted Funmi to go to boarding school but her father refused. He didn't see the point of continuing women's education and thought having Funmi home would reduce the need to hire help. Though he was rich, he was very cheap.

When Funmi was fourteen, she and Dorcas got into a screaming match, the likes of which the other children had never witnessed. Dorcas backhanded her and Funmi, who already towered over the barely 5'3" Dorcas, picked her up and dropped her into the unfinished borehole hired men had been building on their property. It wasn't very deep and there was no water in it yet, but it didn't matter. One of the older children ran screaming for the neighbors. Dorcas cursed her that day in florid, sensational Yorùbá. She refused to have Funmi sleep in the house. She insisted Funmi stay off the property. When her father returned from Lagos later that evening, he told her that she could not disrespect his wife and she would have to find some other place to live.

"But I'm your daughter," Funmi had told him, sobbing. Emmanuel didn't say anything in response. He had a younger sister, Buki, who lived in Kaduna, all the way up north, so far from Port Harcourt. Funmi would go and live there with her. Funmi's protestations did not move her father; he would not change his mind.

She would never forget the smug look on Dorcas's face as Funmi got into the taxi that would take her to the train station, where she would begin her two-day journey from the southernmost part of the country up north to Kaduna. With one baby balanced on a hip, a scar still scabbing above an eye (a souvenir from their last encounter), Dorcas grinned ferociously. She had won, and both she and Funmi knew it.

Aunty Buki worked brutally long hours as a nurse at the teaching hospital and so Funmi had the two-bedroom bungalow mostly to herself. This was how Funmi discovered her powers of attraction and how much she loved that power. She began to develop a system. She would let a boy walk her home and then ask if he wanted to come inside. "I have malt and chin chin," she would say to entice him. She would fish a cold bottle of malt from the fridge and serve chin chin in a tiny china bowl. They would sit at opposite ends of the rickety circular table that served as both study and dining room table. She would take out her exercise books to show that she intended to work. She would ask him to help with her mathematics equation.

"Bring your chair here," she would tell him.

"I'm still not sure I understand." He would move his chair closer to hers bashfully. She would rub her ankle against his school trousers, and he would stiffen in the middle of explaining a concept she already understood. She would look him in the eyes and unbutton her blouse slowly. The bras she had picked out with Aunty Buki weren't designed for looking. They were absurdly practical. But her breasts were large and yellow. She would watch the boy stare. It was that look that aroused her.

"Go on. What are you waiting for?"

And then the boy would do a variety of things, fondle them ineptly, attempt to stuff her nipples in his mouth. Once word got out, the more brazen of the boys would unzip their pants and let their penises hang there stiffly, waiting for her to put them in her mouth. She was happy to appease them; she liked being wanted. She never had actual intercourse with any of them; she always made sure of that. They could play with her breasts and she could put their penises in her mouth, and sometimes if she was feeling especially aroused, she would touch herself with her free hand. Later at night, when she scrubbed her tongue with her toothbrush to erase the taste of semen and had finished her homework and had left rice and stew on low heat on the stove for Aunty Buki to eat, she would run through the images, the involuntary shudders the boys would make, the way they grasped her neatly plaited hair and moaned. Thinking about their moaning could bring her to orgasm without her having to even touch herself.

As her reputation grew, more boys began sending her notes in class, asking if she needed an escort home. But their desperation bored her. She discovered that she liked challenges—quiet boys who were hard to read, who seemed almost surprised that she had picked them. There was nothing more satisfying than the moment their hot, bitter semen hit her tongue and she knew that she had made them come, a power that they couldn't dare hope to reciprocate.

This pastime did not make her popular with the girls at school. It was already hard enough for her to make inroads as a day student, that she was "loose" only made the other girls whisper "ashewo" and stay away.

By the time she managed to score high enough on her JAMB to get into the region's best university (she was a naturally bright student, just unmotivated), she hadn't had any female friends since she was in primary school. She would go to university because she had won a full scholarship (there's no way in hell her father would have paid), and she would read nursing sciences because she was actually quite good at maths and science and she figured that nursing jobs would be easy to find.

She first saw Damola in the sculpture garden—one

of the university's crown jewels. It was filled with statues built by graduating students in the fine arts program. They ranged from abstract, geometric shapes to life-size renderings of recognizable humans. The figures gave Funmi a sense of calm. Other students preferred to work in the botanic garden, which had long swaths of green grass that looked like it could be in England or the U.S. But Funmi liked to work in the sculpture garden, which didn't have much in the way of seating and no green to speak of, just brown dust that got on her textbook and on the seat of her skirt. No matter. Funmi carried a plastic lawn chair around when she wanted to work, placing it in front of whatever sculpture she felt would give her inspiration that day.

She wasn't used to living with three other girls. In Aunty Buki's house Funmi had had a whole room to herself. Here, she only had a bunk. They had to line up to use the toilet and to have their baths. Sometimes she would walk to Aunty Buki's house, which was halfway between campus and the teaching hospital, to bathe in the mornings as a result.

She needed space, and she found it in the garden. The evening she first saw Damola she had selected an abstract sculpture to sit in front of. It was made of thin corrugated metal. She was working on her problem set when she heard the distinctive sound of something—bones—it sounded like, cracking. She turned her head to find the source, and when looking didn't give her any results, she got up and walked around. She saw his back first; it was shining with sweat, little beads of perspiration forming in the middle of the deep groove between his shoulder blades that curved downward to his buttocks, which were firm and round and covered in paint-stained trousers. A dirty singlet hung from one shoulder. His hair rose in tightly coiled corkscrews above his face.

"You're being very loud," she told him. He turned to see who was talking to him. He had a nice face. A flat, broad nose and full, wide lips. But it was his eyes that made her heartbeat race. They were light brown, like the color of honey in the sun, an aberration, albeit a beautiful one, for a man with his deep brown complexion. He raised his shoulders and continued hitting the cinder.

"You're deaf, abi?" Funmi felt emboldened. Emboldened and a bit reckless. She waited for him to say something. When he didn't, she walked in front of him.

"Did you hear what I said?"

Silence. She moved closer to see what he was doing. On the block was a small skull from an animal of some sort, probably a goat. The skull looked old; it was yellowing. Holding a stone with his right hand, Damola brought it down and the skull fractured, making a satisfying cracking sound.

She wondered if he was some kind of fetishist.

"What are you doing?"

"I'm making art," he said without turning to look back at her.

"Which kind art is this?"

He pulled a tiny nylon bag out of his pocket and used his hand to sweep the bones into the bag. Then he cradled the block and stone in the nook of his free arm.

"You shall see soon enough," he told her, and he walked away.

She watched the sinews of his back muscles moving in tandem for as long as she could. She knew she wanted to see him again. Maybe he would come back.

The next evening, she hustled over to the sculpture garden, carrying her plastic lawn chair in one hand and her chemistry textbook in the other. She waited to hear the cinder block. Nothing. She went the next evening and the evening after that and the evening after that. There was a 9 p.m. curfew on weeknights that she couldn't miss, so she would make it to her dormitory room just under the wire. Her roommates would groan, especially since Funmi had a top bunk and there was no easy way for her to climb up without waking the roommate below her.

"Can't you come in at a reasonable hour?" one of them, Mariam, asked, irritated. Funmi just shrugged. She didn't care what they thought.

Mariam only became useful two weeks later, when she and Funmi were walking back to their hostel. Funmi had spent three hours in the garden, hoping to see Damola, when he walked past them, holding a canvas in one hand. Funmi was so surprised, she turned back to watch him walk away. Mariam laughed. "You think he's fine, abi?" She laughed again, a particularly unattractive laugh.

Funmi's cheeks burned with irritation and humiliation.

"You better wait in line, o!" said Mariam. "He has a girlfriend. In the English department. Her name is Zainab."

CHAPTER 14

Enitan

E NITAN DIDN'T REALLY WANT TO HELP. SHE didn't know the first thing about plays, what they entailed; she certainly wasn't going to act, given her shyness. Her acne was bad enough that she was reluctant to look people in the eye when she talked to them, so naturally the thought of hundreds of eyes watching her at the same time made her want to hyperventilate. Though Zainab, at fifteen, was a year younger than Enitan, which was still quite young even for the other first-years at the university, she had quickly established herself as the more dominant of the two. And she was insistent that Enitan help her since they were roommates and new best friends.

They had glommed onto each other instantly, each fascinated by how different they were from the other. Zainab, tall, dark-skinned, slim, exasperatingly beautiful, with her brilliant engineering scholar of a father and her large polygamous family, the two women she called Mama Fatima and Mama Gimbya. The whole family had fussed over her as they had helped her move into the hostel. Armed with brooms they had brought from home, Mama Fatima and Mama Gimbya swept the bedroom floor on their hands and knees, eyeing Enitan with suspicion.

It was so different from how Enitan had grown up, her mother's only daughter, living in Abeokuta, where her mother worked as a bank teller, her father completely out of the picture since before she was born. She went to school enduring nasty rumors about her father's origins, how her mother had been impregnated by a Lagos oga who promptly abandoned her; how her parents were too ashamed of their daughter's sexual proclivities to take her in; how they had left her virtually penniless.

Sharon had sobbed the day Enitan got her test results that would ensure admission into the university. "But Kaduna is so far away!" her mother had cried. She didn't understand that distance had been part of the appeal for Enitan. She needed to flee the desperate, incipient need of her mother. Enitan was suffocated by her love, by the way she would sometimes slip into Enitan's bed late at night and put her arms around her waist and hug her so tightly, she couldn't breathe. How when Enitan was younger and money was tighter, she would use the last grounds of garri to make eba for Enitan and would watch Enitan eat all of it and would wait until Enitan had gone to the other room to suck the chicken bones in the remnants of the okro soup Enitan had greedily consumed. Enitan knew, **knew,** that if ever her life was on the line in any way, her mother wouldn't hesitate to kill herself in Enitan's stead. And that kind of love frightened her.

It was the promise of putting a solid five hundred miles between them that made Enitan decide to attend the premier university in Kaduna State, located in the city of Zaria. When she stepped down from the danfo she had taken from the train station, and walked toward the main campus, passing the university's signature white and green gates, she took a deep breath and inhaled. This was the start of her new life. This was freedom.

In addition to their drastically different familial upbringings, their religious differences were also a source of fascination. Though Zainab's father was a professor of engineering at the polytechnic, he was enthralled with the art and intellectual rigor of the Islamic empire and was not a strict doctrinaire. As a result, Zainab was a dutiful but somewhat lackluster Muslim. She prayed once a day in the morning, waking up early to go to the bathroom to do her ablutions and then returning to her bedroom and unrolling the prayer mat her father had given her that he claimed was from Saudi Arabia. She covered because her mothers covered and her female siblings covered and so she knew no other way. But even from an early age, she covered with flair, wearing sequined, lacy scarves, ones with sophisticated beading. She started lining her eyes with kohl when she was twelve. She took pride in her appearance, especially as her intelligence became more readily apparent at the day school she attended. She did not like the connotation that smart girls were ugly girls.

Enitan, meanwhile, had grown up attending church every Sunday and reciting Bible verses with her mother before bed every night. She was accustomed to praying before she ate and could recite the names of all the books of the Bible in the order in which they appeared. But she too had no strong religious inclination outside of force of habit and in later years, as her mother became more and more devout, Enitan became less interested in adhering to any sort of religious dogma.

Enitan had fled the room when Zainab and her family had arrived, instead going to the main office to find out her schedule and to familiarize herself with the buildings where her classes would be held. When she returned to the room, Zainab was sprawled on her bed, reading a book called **Wuthering Heights.**

Zainab put down her book when she saw Enitan enter.

"I hope my family did not scare you off," she said matter-of-factly. "They mean well."

Enitan nodded because she was too intimidated to speak and sat down on her own bed. "What book are you reading?" she asked. Zainab handed her the copy. It was well-worn; the pages were yellowing. The cover was partially torn. Enitan could see that certain lines had been highlighted in black biro.

"It's one of my favorite books," said Zainab. Enitan looked at the back cover.

"Why? What is it about?"

"It's about love. Passionate love. I'm telling you it's better than those Mills & Boon books. If I ever meet somebody like that Heathcliff, I'll die! I'll die!"

Enitan quickly learned that Zainab was fond of dramatic declarations. It made sense in a way. She was reading English literature and was an aspiring playwright. She told Enitan this later that night when they were both in bed, unable to sleep, thinking of the classes they would start the next day. Zainab's father was a literary man even though he taught at the polytechnic. He gave her books by the major African novelists—Chinua Achebe, Wole Soyinka, Ngugi wa Thiong'o—and would have her write reports on them. He bemoaned the fact that a Hausa man had yet to achieve the same widespread literary acclaim of Soyinka and Achebe in particular. But Zainab didn't like their books. She found their writing about sad men boring. She wanted romance. She wanted epic declarations and quaint English or American or Canadian novels about incorrigible little girls who later have torrid love affairs. **Pride and Prejudice** and **Emma** and **Anne of Green Gables** and **Wuthering Heights** and **Little Women**—and when she was really desperate, **What Katy Did**. She loved Shakespeare too. All of the lecturers in the English department were British foreign nationals who were all too happy to encourage Zainab's interest in the Bard. Just a month and a few weeks into their first semester, Zainab announced that she wanted to mount a student production of **Romeo and Juliet**. And she wanted Enitan to help her.

"We can do it in the drama village," Zainab said. "We can have auditions!" Enitan was reading nursing sciences and was struggling to keep up with the mathematics in her chemistry class. She would leave the lecture and head straight to the library, trying to finish yesterday's assignment as well as that day's—wondering how on earth she had ever thought she was a good student in secondary school. Here, she was simply outmatched. She honestly didn't feel like she would have the time to help Zainab and believed that anything other than schoolwork would be a distraction. But Zainab told her she had to do something. Otherwise, what was the point of their being bosom friends—a phrase she said came from one of her favorite books, **Anne of Green Gables**.

Enitan didn't really understand what Zainab meant, but she was touched nevertheless. Hers had been a very lonely childhood. The cystic acne hadn't made her very popular. Coupled with her absent father and the persistent ashewo rumors about her mother, she hadn't had many friends in primary or secondary school.

And so reluctantly, Enitan agreed to help Zainab with auditions. Enitan had better penmanship than Zainab, who wrote in furious scribbles, so it was Enitan who designed the flyers. Zainab used the photocopier in the English department building to make copies and together they distributed them around campus. They went door to door in the female hostel, slipping flyers under the door of each room and pinning them to the notice board in the common rooms.

The morning of auditions, Enitan and Zainab dragged their bedroom table down three flights of stairs and carried it to the drama village. The distance wasn't very far, but the table slowed them down significantly. They stopped every five minutes to catch their breath. Enitan privately thought that this was something Damola, Zainab's new boyfriend, could have helped them with. The boyfriend had been a surprise for Enitan, though it shouldn't have been, as she witnessed firsthand the steady parade of men who wooed Zainab. Zainab would show Enitan the letters boys bribed female friends to slip under their bedroom door, letters declaring their marital intentions. They left her packs of Nice biscuits, which everyone knew Zainab loved. She was constantly buying them at the tiny market close to the edge of campus, where people could purchase candles, kerosene, and soft drinks. (Zainab had shown Enitan how to mix the biscuits in condensed milk to form an even sweeter, sticky mush that you could eat out of a mug with a spoon.)

Men were never lewd with Zainab; they treated her gingerly like a fragile thing. Zainab said it was because she covered. It communicated a kind of chasteness men liked. They wanted to parade her on their arms, this beautiful woman with uncanny angular cheekbones. Christian or Muslim—it didn't matter. Her hijab only made her beguiling to them, as a signifier of virtue and piety. That and the fact that Zainab steadfastly refused to sleep with any of them. She was waiting for marriage. "Sex is a sacred act," Zainab had told Enitan during one of their first conversations about boys. Enitan had just handed her a five-page letter that a boy in her biology class had asked her to give to Zainab. Enitan was happy to play the courier and to live vicariously through Zainab's marriage proposals. Her own love life was nonexistent and had always been. How Damola, who always smelled of turpentine and had paint stains on his trousers, had managed to win Zainab over, Enitan didn't understand. But he had.

Boys weren't allowed in the female hostel, only in the common room, and only during daylight hours, so Zainab and Damola would sit quietly together at one of the tables in the recreation area, playing Scrabble or sometimes watching a movie if one was screening on the VHS. Often Enitan would join them. Other times, Zainab read one of her novels while Damola sketched on a notepad with his pencil or would read books too—rarely novels, only books about Marxism—which made Enitan vaguely nervous for reasons that she couldn't quite articulate. Also, Damola barely acknowledged Enitan's presence if she was there. It was as if her lack of beauty made her invisible to him.

The drama village, or the University Theater as it was technically called, had been designed by an American who had taught at the university's architecture department in the '70s before going back to the U.S. It was inspired by traditional Hausa architecture. Four adobe huts in a circle surrounded a central stage. They were buttressed by two white entranceways carved with intricate bas-relief sculptural designs. A student group had performed **The Trials of Brother Jero** there just the other week.

By the time Zainab and Enitan had finally sat down and had taped **Romeo & Juliet Auditions** on the front edge of the table, they were both sweating. Zainab took a sip of water from the sachet she had purchased and began fanning herself with her copy of **Romeo and Juliet**. She had circled the passage she wanted prospective actors to perform.

"I hope people show up," she said. Enitan opened her chemistry textbook. She was not holding her breath.

They had been sitting at the table for half an hour when Enitan noticed a pair of thighs moving toward them. She noticed the thighs immediately in part because girls did not generally wear shorts on campus. And these shorts were short—revealing yellow thighs that jiggled slightly as their owner walked. They sprouted from hips that were round and full. Enitan felt newly embarrassed by her own legs, "chicken legs" the neighborhood boys called them; they were skinny and bruised easily so they were covered in faded dark spots. How she wished she had thighs like this girl. Enitan looked up beyond the thighs and the hips to her blouse then to her face—and realized that she recognized the girl. She was in her biology class. She always sat in the last row of the lecture hall. The girl was staring at Zainab intensely. Zainab was flipping through the play. The girl started walking toward them, her eyes still fixed on Zainab. She stopped just a few inches away from the table.

"Ahem," the girl said.

Zainab looked up, noted her shorts, but quickly recovered and smiled. "Yes?"

"Are the auditions still happening?"

"Yes, they are! You are our first!"

Zainab tore out a piece of paper from Enitan's composition book.

"I'm sorry, I forgot my notebook upstairs," Zainab said quickly before Enitan could say anything. "Please, what's your name?"

"Funmi," the girl said. She had an unnerving gaze that she fixed on Zainab.

"Funmi. So you are Yorùbá. Enitan is Yorùbá too."

Funmi turned to look at Enitan for the first time. Enitan felt her face grow warm at the intensity of Funmi's stare.

"I think we are in the same biology class," Enitan said, but Funmi had turned away, her eyes back on Zainab.

"Okay, so what do I have to do?" Funmi asked.

"Well, if you have a monologue prepared—"

"I don't."

"Okay, well which part are you auditioning for?"

"Juliet of course."

"Okay, great. I have underlined the monologue for that part. You can just read it out loud."

Funmi picked up the book. She narrowed her eyes and began reciting in a flat monotone. "O-Romeo-Romeo-wherefore-art-thou-Romeo-deny-thy-father-and-refuse-thy-name—"

She went on like this for quite some time. Zainab and Enitan exchanged looks. When Funmi was finished, she didn't say anything but looked at Zainab expectantly.

"Actually, perhaps it would be helpful if I provided some context. Have you read the play before?" Zainab asked.

Funmi shook her head.

"In this section, Juliet is really anguishing over her love for Romeo. She's just discovered that—" Zainab stopped talking abruptly because Funmi had begun laughing. It was a low rumble that slowly grew into something more raucous.

Zainab and Enitan stared.

"How many people have stopped by that you are giving me notes? Na wa o! Who else is here?" She started laughing again, so hard that tears were forming in her eyes.

"Just let me know when the rehearsals start. If enough people show up."

She bent down and scribbled something on Zainab's piece of paper.

"That's my room number so you know where to find me. I will see you at rehearsals," she said, and turned on her heels and walked away. Zainab and Enitan watched her go.

"I don't like that girl," Zainab said.

"I know," Enitan replied automatically, but she continued staring as the thighs receded into the distance.

CHAPTER 15

Funmi

AT FIRST, FUNMI GENUINELY HAD NO recollection of the girl who was standing in front of her, claiming they had met before. The biology lecture had just ended and other students were filing out, but Funmi was taking her time packing up her things. She didn't like being around so many other students, forced to hear their asinine commentary on the lecturer, whom many girls found attractive (he was not).

"We met a few weeks ago," the girl was saying. "At the auditions."

Ah. That joke of an audition for that joke of a play. Funmi remembered the girl's friend, the infamous Zainab, with her high cheekbones and her purple-black skin. Funmi seldom felt threatened by other girls, but as soon as she had seen her, she could see why Damola would be besotted. She was strikingly beautiful. This girl in front of Funmi now, though, she was quite plain. It was unfortunate. She was very skinny and short and she had that paunch that skinny girls sometimes have. It made her look slightly pregnant.

"Okay, yes, I remember you. What do you want?"

"Well, I wanted to tell you that the play is canceled. Nobody else came to the auditions."

At that Funmi had to laugh, low and loud and long.

The girl stood watching her.

"Thank you for informing me," Funmi said. She gathered her things and started walking toward the door. The girl followed her.

"So how are you liking your classes?" the girl asked as they headed outside.

"They are fine." Funmi hoped she was communicating her lack of interest in furthering the conversation.

"You never seem to pay much attention in class and yet you always do so well on exams," the girl said.

Funmi stopped walking and turned to look at her more closely. She had a smattering of acne on both cheeks. It really was quite unfortunate. "That is true," Funmi said. "I have always been good at maths and science."

The girl looked down at her feet. She was murmuring under her breath, almost as if she was counting. Then she looked up at Funmi. "Would you be able to help me?" she asked her. "If I don't pass this next exam, I'm in danger of losing my scholarship."

Funmi took another look at the girl. If her skin cleared up and her fat magically realigned itself to the right places—breasts and yansh—she would look all right.

"Okay," Funmi said. "I'll help you."

They agreed to meet that weekend in Enitan's room.

The female dormitory was a squat cement building painted bright fuchsia, with an outdoor balcony on each of its three floors that connected to stairwells on both ends of the building. If you had to go to another room on another floor, you had to go outside. During the dry season, girls opened their windows to let in fresh air and hung their laundry from the balcony railings to let them dry. But after there were some reports of bras and pants being stolen by male students, the practice had died down somewhat.

Enitan lived on the third floor, in one of the corner rooms. Funmi lived on the ground floor. She got up early that morning to jog around the track field, a decision that always drew commentary from her roommates, who thought it was odd and dangerous for a young woman to go out by herself like that. But Funmi welcomed the stares. She liked the risk and she loved this time of day, just as the sun had risen. It had rained very lightly the night before, which was unusual for this time of year, and the smell of wet earth hung in the air. She breathed it in deeply as she ran. The smell reminded Funmi of her father's village, on the outskirts of Ibadan, where they would stay every Christmas. Funmi's grandmother Mama, a tall, imposing woman, would walk Funmi through the rows of cocoyam plants. "This is your land," she would tell her. "This is your inheritance." It was as if she was forcing Funmi to remember something about herself, as if she didn't trust Funmi to fully comprehend this truth without explicitly showing her the land her grandparents had tilled. She had approved of her son's marriage to Funmi's mother only grudgingly, it appeared, even though her mother's family had lived in Port Harcourt for three generations. They made their money selling imports from Britain—cans of baked beans, tinned sardines, Darjeeling tea, and English biscuits. They had convenience stores all over Port Harcourt.

The story, as her mother told it when Funmi was very small, is that her father had walked into the convenience store one day on a lunch break from the oil refinery and had seen the most beautiful woman in the world. She had long curly hair that fell around her shoulders, full lips, and such fair olive skin that her father had thought she was a white woman from England. But she wasn't. Her name was Leila and she descended from a line of

Lebanese Christians who had lived in the area since the '30s. Funmi's father had seen Leila and asked her for a can of baked beans and a loaf of agege bread for lunch.

"You don't know how to cook?" she teased him. Her father replied that he was a man, of course he did not know how to cook. Leila said that this was a shame, that every man should know how to cook or have a good woman to cook for him. That she could make really good baklava. Funmi's father had never heard of this famous dessert. He struggled to say the word and Leila had laughed at him. She had the most beautiful laugh, low at first and then steadily rising in volume. Emmanuel began to visit the store every day. He would always buy a can of baked beans and a loaf of agege bread.

One day, Leila made him a plate of baklava; she wrapped it in cling film for him, and Emmanuel had never tasted anything like it. It tasted like biblical food, the kind of dessert the Israelites dreamed of in the promised land, the land of milk and honey. Emmanuel went back to his parents' village and told his parents he had found the woman he was going to marry. His parents were not pleased. They didn't trust oyinbo people and Leila's parents had no land. Emmanuel said that it did not matter, that Leila was the most beautiful woman he had ever seen, that her beauty would make him rich, that the children they would bear would bring him wealth. They married; they had a small church wedding in Port Harcourt. There was one photograph of her parents together, happy and beaming, and it was Funmi's prized possession; she kept it folded in half in her tin of most cherished items. The tin also contained her mother's jewelry—her wedding ring, a pair of ruby earrings, a gold necklace. Shortly after her parents married, they had a daughter. Emmanuel chose her name himself, Olufunmilola, God has given me wealth. Funmi's earliest memories were of being in the convenience store, strapped to her mother's back as she made change with customers. Funmi first learned how to count in that store, with the British sterling that was the nation's currency until the naira was introduced in 1973. She was convinced that she got her maths skills from her mother's side of the family.

That first Christmas with Aunty Buki she had expected to go back to Port Harcourt, where they would then all drive to the village for Christmas, but her father had called and told her in so many words that he thought it mutually beneficial for her to spend the Christmas break with her aunt in Kaduna. "What about Mama? What about my brothers and sisters?" Funmi had asked, her voice breaking in spite of herself. She found that she missed them, which she had honestly not expected. When she had lived in Port Harcourt, she was their child minder, forever making sure they didn't accidentally kill one another or themselves. She washed their dirty nappies and hung them up to dry in the courtyard. She wiped their runny noses. The youngest child, the boy, had just started walking when she left. He should be talking now, a few words here and there. And she loved spending those Christmases with Mama, who still regarded her as someone worth loving, someone worth caring about.

Her protests didn't work. She spent Christmas with Aunty Buki, who said that they would travel to the village to see Mama themselves by train when she was able to take off more time at work. Eventually they did, but Funmi never got over the betrayal. A few days after the New Year, her father appeared at their front door with a bulky TV set in his arms. He was in town for business, he said. He could only stay for an hour or so. The TV was a belated Christmas gift, but it was really a way to assuage whatever guilt he was feeling, Funmi knew. She served him beans and plantain and a bottle of malt, which she knew he always liked. She sat across from him at the table and watched him attempt to make awkward conversation. "I hope you are doing well in school," he said, looking at her forehead instead of her eyes. Funmi didn't say anything. She didn't say anything because that was the moment when she realized that there was something deeply cowardly about her father. The way his eyes darted as he began to talk in a transparent attempt to fill the silence between them. How was her aunty? How did she like the school? In his day, he had been sent away to boarding school when he was just eleven years old. You became accustomed to being separated from your parents at a young age; it was a noble thing in fact that taught people self-sufficiency. That he had forbidden Funmi from attending boarding school when she lived in Port Harcourt seemed to escape his memory. She looked at the deep forehead wrinkles that were exposing themselves now as her father talked, the furrow of skin that pinched and narrowed between his two eyebrows. She was suddenly filled with pity, pity and contempt. How easily distractible he was. How simple it was for him to go from woman to woman, and to leave behind those he claimed to love.

At the end of his meal, after she had put the dishes in the sink and set the glass bottle aside to give to the boy who collected them, she stood in front of her father as he gave her a stiff one-armed hug.

"Daddy," she said, "there's no reason for you to come here." He opened his mouth in surprise, then shut it, then opened it again. His face shifted slightly; his eyes looked bewildered. "Close your mouth, do you want flies to enter?" Mama would tell Funmi when she was small. (Mama would die two years later, and whatever connection Funmi had to the village and to her father would sever completely.) But then he nodded and pressed some naira into her palm and left. It was that feeling, that small nod, the money in her hand, the realization that he would never fight for her—had never fought for her, really—that made her cry hot, angry tears. He would call occasionally, once a month, then once every other month, until it became once a year, and even then Funmi always found ways to avoid talking to him.

AFTER HER RUN, SHE went back to her room to grab her bucket and bowl to bathe. She was walking to the latrines when she saw a familiar figure headed toward her. It was Damola. He was reading and walking at the same time. She could just make out the title of his book: **Violence** by Festus Iyayi.

He froze when he saw her. Boys, even if they were students, were absolutely forbidden from entering the female hostel. Maybe he hadn't been inside the building, but he was close enough that it was suspicious. And it was 8:30 a.m., early. She wondered how he had come in without being seen. Then she wondered with a pang of jealousy whether he had spent the night with Zainab. Sometimes boys snuck into their girlfriends' rooms dressed in niqab. The girl would bribe her roommates with money or with food so they wouldn't tell the hall advisor and they could have the room to themselves that night. But those were usually the especially reckless girls, and typically, the couples were very serious and essentially engaged to be married.

He looked at her and she suddenly felt hyper-aware of her running clothes and the patches of sweat under her arms and across her stomach. He stared at her steadily, not cutting his gaze when most people would have turned and looked somewhere else.

"What?" Funmi finally asked him, unsettled.

He walked toward her then stopped again, now close enough that she could see herself reflected in his eyes.

"This is our secret," he said. He continued walking.

God. What was this feeling? Funmi had to steady herself. Why hadn't she asked him which dormitory he lived in or what he was studying, or why he had chosen Zainab as his girlfriend? He looked like the kind of man who had had sex and Zainab did not look like the kind of girl who had had sex. Had she put his penis in her mouth? Had he taken her from behind? Had she ridden on top of him, her body moving in an undulating rhythm, arching forward so her breasts hovered over his face, so she could breathe closely in his ear and tell him how good he was making her feel? Had he come inside her? Had she swallowed his semen and told him she loved him? Funmi couldn't see Zainab doing any of those things.

After she had bathed, she dropped off her bucket

in her room and then climbed up the stairs that led to Enitan's room. When she reached their floor, the door was shut. She was about to knock when she heard the sounds of footsteps behind her.

"Funmi! I hope you weren't waiting long!" It was Enitan. Zainab was standing beside her. Enitan was holding a paper bag that smelled like freshly fried akara. The smell made Funmi feel nauseous. She hated akara. Enitan looked so pleased Funmi had actually shown up.

"No, I just arrived," Funmi said.

Enitan smiled widely and opened the room door with her key. "Please come in. We brought breakfast." So they were roommates.

Their room was neat and nicely decorated. There was a large window that looked out onto the city; they had a close-up view of the central mosque's minaret. A bookshelf stood in the far corner. A prayer rug leaned against one wall. There was a table too—Funmi recognized it from the auditions—and two chairs. But the central feature of the room, the chief perk, was a large circular Persian rug that covered most of the ugly cement floor. It looked plush and luxurious, and Funmi wanted to sink her fingers into it. She took off her shoes and sat on the rug. Enitan grabbed three plates from the shelf and set them on the table.

"You don't have any additional roommates?" Funmi asked, noting that the top bunks of both beds were missing a mattress. Each room was supposed to house four girls.

"No," Enitan said. Funmi wondered how they had made that happen. It had to be Zainab. She had the air of a rich girl.

"So you are reading nursing sciences?" Zainab asked in a tone of voice that sounded like she was just barely tolerating Funmi's presence. Funmi resented it.

"Yes, I am."

"Enitan tells me that you are really good at maths," Zainab continued.

Enitan had put two pieces of akara on a plate. She handed it to Funmi.

"That's all right, I'm not hungry, thank you, though," she said.

Enitan looked crestfallen. "Are you sure? They are warm, freshly made."

Funmi didn't have the heart to tell her she hated akara. Her face was all quivering approval. Funmi took the plate and bit into the akara. It was hot. "Yum," she said between bites, forcing it down her throat.

Zainab picked daintily at her own plate.

"I take it you are reading literature," Funmi said to Zainab.

Zainab nodded proudly.

"What are you going to do with a literature degree?" Funmi asked.

"She's going to write plays," Enitan said.

"A play? I heard **Romeo and Juliet** is no longer happening," Funmi said.

"Yes," Zainab said slowly, her eyes narrowing. "There was a misunderstanding."

"A misunderstanding," Funmi said, and she laughed. "Maybe Nigerians don't want to do all those oyinbo plays. Shakespeare in the drama village." She sucked her teeth. "Na wa o."

"Maybe we should get started on our schoolwork," Enitan said uneasily.

"What is that supposed to mean?" asked Zainab, ignoring Enitan. She was practically vibrating with anger. Funmi loved it.

"You don't know any African writers? African plays you can put on? You want us to pretend we are oyinbo?" She pinched her nose and mimicked an English accent. "Romeo, Romeo, wherefore art thou, Romeo—"

"I don't only do foreign plays! I'm writing my own play. It's a historical romance set here in Kaduna. It's about Queen Amina. She's in love with one of her soldiers, but they can't be together because she has to lead the army during an uprising, so they meet at night in secret—" Zainab stopped abruptly, catching her breath as she had been speaking very quickly.

"Go on," Funmi said, her curiosity piqued. She loved romance. She had read her Mills & Boon books so many times the covers were all falling off.

"They can't be together in public, so they meet in secret late at night," Zainab continued. "And then one day he is called into battle. He is kidnapped by a rival army and Queen Amina has to devise a way to free him. She decides to dress up as a rival soldier. She cuts off her hair and dresses in men's clothing and then sneaks over in the cover of night into enemy territory to rescue him—"

"Here's the chemistry equation that I am having trouble with," Enitan announced, thrusting her notebook in front of Funmi.

"Right," Funmi said. "Don't worry, I will help you." She got up from the carpet and wiped her hands on her dress. She turned to Zainab.

"When are you finished with your play? I want to play Queen Amina."

CHAPTER 16

Zainab

November 1983

UNDER INSTRUCTIONS FROM HER HUSBAND, Mama Gimbya took Zainab to the market to buy fresh goat meat. Zainab watched the goat-killing process with rapt fascination; the blade across the throat, the dark blood that had bubbled forth from the incision, the way the goat's legs had feebly kicked the air in protest, its eyes glazing over in death. The butchers prepared the goat for cooking the traditional way; one of the men blew into the mouth of the goat to bloat it up for skinning. He took a razor blade and ran it over the hide. And then he hacked the goat into pieces with a cutlass, wrapping them in newspaper and putting them in two black nylon bags that bulged unnaturally as she and Mama Gimbya walked home.

The meat had been bought to celebrate the success of Zainab's play. **Queen Amina and Her**

Secret Love premiered that November at the drama village to immediate broad acclaim, particularly among the swarm of first- and second-year female students who attended. The newly formed women's empowerment group on campus gave Zainab an award for the play's "positive representations of strong female characters." The vice chancellor of the university had even attended a performance; how incongruous seeing him sitting on one of the plastic lawn chairs she and Enitan had had to hastily grab from the common room because they had run out of wooden ones.

The women's group even reached out to a small independent publishing press, which agreed to print thirty copies of the play for Zainab to keep for posterity. That had been surreal. She and Enitan had carried the box containing the copies up three flights of stairs to open in their room. She gave herself a paper cut ripping the box open. But seeing the row of copies of **her** play—thin little blue pamphlets with her name, **Zainab Hassan,** printed at the bottom—had been worth it. She gave a copy of the play to her father when he came to pick up Zainab, Enitan, and Funmi to stay at the family compound for the weekend. He held it in his hands, sitting in the front seat of the car, flipping through the pages quietly. Then he turned to her and said, "I am so proud of you." For the rest of her life, Zainab would remember that moment, and the feeling of deep warmth that suffused throughout her whole body. She had never loved her father more.

Now that she was in university and had met the few other Hausa girls her own age, she was more appreciative of her own extraordinarily good fortune, that she was in school, that she hadn't been forced to marry when her breasts developed at fourteen or fifteen, that she was her father's unabashed favorite. Mama Gimbya, the senior wife, and Mama Fatima, her co-wife, treated Zainab with grudging affection, also a rarity. Her mother, the about-to-be third wife, the youngest wife, the wife that her father had fallen so deeply, madly in love with—that wife, Nafisah, had died giving birth to Zainab, thereby solving all of Mama Gimbya and Mama Fatima's problems.

Feeling somewhat guilty over their happiness about a young woman's death, a death that had set the patriarch into a depression so prolonged and profound it scared them, they treated Zainab like one of their own. After all, there was no one else to look after her, and Mama Fatima was still weaning Zainab's youngest half brother, so there was breast milk available. And Zainab had been an easy child to love, such pretty, delicate features, like a baby doll.

The wives were smart, industrious women. Zainab's father didn't believe in women's seclusion. He wanted his wives to work and to excel. Mama Gimbya ran a suya catering company in Kaduna's busiest marketplace. A team of muscular men, their arms slick and shiny with sweat, worked for Mama Gimbya, who would sit in the front room, barking commands as they cut the meat, roasted, and seasoned it. Her suya mix was legendary. Nobody could determine what it was exactly that made her suya so fragrant, the perfect piquant combination of spicy and sweet. It was highly requested at weddings, naming ceremonies, and burials.

Mama Fatima braided hair and sewed clothes by the market close to the Christian side of town. She rented out a stall and hired the best and fastest girls. Sure, you had to sit amid the smells of fish and raw meat, and the flies were relentless, constantly buzzing by an ear, sitting on a toe. But the end result was always something breathtaking, intricate cornrow designs, or later, box braids, and she was by far the cheapest place to get a really convincing weave-on. She was also a tailor who made beautiful bridal gowns. Women were perpetually stopping by the compound with a magazine cutout of the style they wanted, and Mama Fatima would replicate it and somehow even make it better, adding beading or gently nudging customers toward the more expensive fabrics.

The success of Mama Gimbya and Mama Fatima's businesses, coupled with Zainab's father's senior teaching position at the polytechnic, meant that the family was quite well off, able to provide for the ten children total, five for Mama Gimbya and four for Mama Fatima, plus Zainab. Nafisah's death had also appeared to deaden any instinct her father might have for romantic love. The wives could rest assured that he would not one day walk into the compound, a young nubile woman on his arm, and announce that she was his new wife.

Because Zainab had grown up in Kaduna and their house was only about a twenty-minute drive away from campus, she often went home on weekends, at least twice a month. Her father would pick her up on Saturday mornings. Once it was clear that she and Enitan were going to be best friends, Enitan would come too. The weekend after the play's performance, Zainab invited Funmi to come home with her as well. It turned out that all Funmi had needed to become an actor of some distinction was the right muse, in her case Queen Amina. And once Funmi had signed on to play Queen Amina, it had been fairly easy to convince a group of fellow first-year boys to play members of Amina's army. They each got to wear sixteenth-century Hausa costumes, billowing shirts and trousers that tightened around the ankles, and they got to pretend-fight with scimitars made out of cardboard. Zainab was still not sure she trusted Funmi. She was a peculiar girl, loud and rude and blunt in a way that Zainab thought was very unladylike, but the play would obviously not have succeeded without her performance and early encouragement. Zainab figured an invitation to her family's compound was the least that she could do.

Zainab's father picked them up in his lime-green Mercedes-Benz on Saturday morning. When they pulled up into the compound, Mama Gimbya was waiting for them, in the courtyard, hands on her hips. "We are going to buy a goat," she told Zainab when they had gotten out of the car. "Come along." And so she and Zainab had trekked to the market and Zainab had watched the butchers kill the goat and had carried bulging bags of goat meat back into the compound. Mama Fatima and Zainab's older sisters, Fatima and Adama, had already started a fire for roasting and preparing the beans for dan wake, the bean dumplings that were a delicacy here and something neither Enitan nor Funmi—Yorùbá girls through and through—had ever heard of. Enitan had asked if the mothers needed any help, and they had taken the girls up on their offer and put them to work.

"Nice house," Funmi told Zainab, as the three of them sat outside in the courtyard with trays of beans balanced upon their knees. They were fishing out the weevils.

It **was** a nice house, her father's pride and joy. He had designed it with one of his colleagues at the polytechnic, though over time, he had kept adding rooms, so the house on the northern end of the compound had a narrow, unfinished look. The house had five bedrooms and a borehole and small garden where Mama Gimbya grew vegetables. Ten children meant siblings inevitably had to share, but Zainab had had her own room since Fatima and Adama had gotten married and moved in with their husbands' families.

"Thank you," Zainab said, fishing out what looked like a tiny wood chip from her tray. Her eight-year-old brother, Bakary, darted past them, pushing a tire with a stick.

"Bakary!" Zainab yelled. "Go get us some bitter lemon from the fridge!" He pretended not to hear her so she repeated herself, increasing her volume.

"Bakary, do as your sister says!" Mama Fatima shouted from somewhere in the bowels of the house.

They soaked the beans in water and then Mama Gimbya dismissed them. They went to the living room, where her father, after much insistence from the rest of the household, had allowed a small television to be installed. For years he had been opposed, arguing that television dulled the mind. "Can't you children think of something more edifying?" he would ask them. But with political tensions rising, he had changed his mind. He needed the TV and the newspaper and the radio to keep close watch on what was happening in the country.

When there was light, everyone gathered around the television. When there was no light, the family gathered around it anyway. It had a centrifugal force, as the sole portal for life outside of Kaduna. There was light that afternoon, so Zainab switched the television on. "How amazing for you all," Funmi said. "A television."

"Thanks," Zainab said. She couldn't tell if Funmi was being sarcastic or not. She could never tell. Only one channel had a clear signal, so they were forced to watch **Scooby-Doo.**

"You know Velma wouldn't be so ugly if she took off her glasses," said Funmi after a few minutes.

Enitan laughed.

"She's playing a type. She's the plain best friend, that's the point," said Zainab.

Funmi rolled her eyes. "This cartoon is stupid. I can't believe this is the only thing we can watch. So boring."

Zainab resisted the urge to ask her why she was here, then. Did she have a television in her aunty's house when she went home to visit her on weekends?

"It's not so bad," said Enitan. "Though I think I prefer **Tom and Jerry.**"

"**Tom and Jerry** is racist," said Zainab.

Funmi eyed Zainab curiously. "Who told you that?"

"Damola said. He has a cousin in the U.S. He says that the woman on the show, the woman whose feet you never see, is mocking black Americans. That she is a mammy figure."

"That sounds like rubbish to me," said Funmi. "So he has a cousin in the U.S. So what?"

Zainab couldn't help herself. "Why did you even come here if all you are going to do is complain?"

Enitan looked distressed. Funmi was quiet for a moment, staring steadily at Zainab. She picked up the copy of Zainab's play that her father had left on the coffee table.

"Sorry," Funmi said after a moment, flipping the pages and not looking at her.

"Did you hear her, Zainab? She apologized," Enitan said.

"Yes, I heard," muttered Zainab. Really, she could not stand this girl. And she didn't understand why she had to attack Damola's credibility like that. Damola was sweet and kind. She had learned so much from him. He was quiet at first, but he could talk a lot when he was comfortable. She had seen him drawing in the botanic garden and she had asked him what he was drawing. He had stared at her for a moment, his eyes resting on the book she was holding, and then he told her that he was designing flyers for a student union meeting. He asked her what book she was reading. She held it up. Her father had given her a copy of the play **I Will Marry When I Want**. He told her that Ngugi had been jailed for this play. "The power of words alone can send a man to jail!" her father had exclaimed. Zainab told Damola this. Damola had responded in kind by saying that he had read the play too and liked it. He asked Zainab if she had read any Festus Iyayi. She had never heard of him but she pretended that she had, because she sensed that Damola might be the kind of man who would judge her for reading books by oyinbo people. And she had discovered on closer inspection that he had beautiful, warm, light brown eyes, incongruous with his milk-chocolate skin. He was a romantic, an artist like Zainab was an artist, and he was respectful. He walked her to and from her classes. He encouraged her artistic production. He was quiet. He had kissed her once, when they were sitting in the botanic garden. Zainab had been reading **The Forsyte Saga,** and Damola was amused at how thick the book was. He picked it up. "It's as big as the Bible," he had said, and Zainab's face grew warm, in part because it was a reminder of why their burgeoning relationship would never work. Her father would never allow her to marry a Christian. Never. Then he leaned over and kissed her quickly on the lips, and she had been surprised at how anticlimactic it had felt, just warm, soft lips on her own for a millisecond. So many of the novels she read hinged on illicit kisses on red lips, from **Tess of the D'Urbervilles** to **The Scarlet Letter.** **This** had been what broke up marriages and ruined lives with death often to follow?

She quickly hit Damola's hand anyway to show him she was not a prostitute; she was not like those girls who would sneak off to the dam to do God knows what with their boyfriends. She was a good, virtuous woman. She would wait until marriage. But she had been kissed, so now she knew she was desirable. She had a boyfriend. He gave her thoughtful gifts, sketches mostly of flowers and some designs made out of animal bones. She felt comfortable in his presence. She liked the fact that he was a year ahead of her at the university. In her mind, it made him seem more worldly.

Mama Fatima yelled for them to come to the dining room for lunch. Zainab noticed there was an extra place set at the table; the smaller children typically ate in the courtyard.

"Who else is eating with us?" Zainab asked Mama Fatima, who had just put down the last fork.

"One of your father's friends from the polytechnic, Mr. Ahmed."

Zainab resisted the urge to groan. She wasn't thrilled at the prospect of sharing her celebratory meal with one of her dad's polytechnic friends, because she knew that all they would talk about was President Shagari and rising inflation rates and the precarious nature of Nigerian democracy.

"Please, our guests, you must sit," said Mama Gimbya to Enitan and Funmi, who had been eyeing the table nervously, their hands grazing over the backs of the chairs.

A sumptuous feast lay before them; they usually

only ate like this for Eid. Mama Gimbya had used the goat for pepper soup (Zainab's favorite), which was still bubbling in a tall steel pot with a ladle. There were individually cling-film-wrapped spheres of tuwo masara with miyan kukar and trays of still-simmering suya, accompanied by freshly fried masa. Dan wake with hard-boiled eggs sat next to a plate of fried plantain, and there was a small pot of plain white rice and beef stew for Zainab's father, who was a picky eater. "Na gode," Zainab said to Mama Gimbya and she hugged her. Mama Gimbya tolerated the hug for a few seconds and then peeled her arms off. "Go and get your father and Mr. Ahmed. They are in the study."

The study was on the opposite end of the house. It had been the latest addition to the compound and had been built two years ago. Zainab had rarely been inside. It was lined wall-to-wall with books that smelled like dust. The door was open and her father was in the middle of what sounded like a long speech.

"Absolute foolishness," her father was saying. "Blaming Ghanaians for the corruption and malfeasance of the Nigerian government. Shagari really is just astounding in his incompetence—"

Zainab knocked on the door.

"Daddy, we are ready to eat," she said.

A shadow moved across the room and then a tall

man was standing before her, smiling. "You must be the playwright," he said, and he extended a hand.

Zainab's cheeks grew warm at that.

"Yes," she said, and she shook his hand. He was much younger than Zainab expected. He couldn't have been more than twenty-three or twenty-four. He had exquisite cheekbones and the whitest teeth, all the more dazzling in skin so dark.

Her father clapped his hand around Ahmed's shoulder. "My protégé," he said, and he took Ahmed's arm in his. "You know this is a very brilliant man right here. A tenure-track position at such a young age. I am glad you are eating with us today." He led Ahmed out of the room. Zainab followed behind, unsettled by the rapid beating of her heart.

CHAPTER 17

Funmi

December 1983

Funmi's thighs were burning, quivering with each step she took up the rock. She had never felt so sore. And even though the sun was setting, and the sky was a muted blaze of orange and pink obscured by Harmattan dust, she was too tired and hot and irritable to enjoy the view.

"Come on, we are almost there," shouted Enitan from up above her somewhere.

"Jesus," Funmi muttered, and she took a swig from one of the two sachets of water she had bought for the journey. The water was warm now; it made her want to gag.

"Behold the land of my ancestors!" Zainab's voice boomed from atop the summit. She had been ahead of them for most of the climb.

It gave Funmi no satisfaction to realize that all those mornings she would jog around the track on campus and around the perimeter of the hospital when she was home with Aunty Buki did not mean she was fit enough for this form of rigorous exercise. Though the jogging cleared her mind and tamed the widening of her body, this climb had been unexpectedly grueling.

The most maddening thing of all—this had all been Funmi's idea.

They had been studying feverishly, cooped up in the library or in Enitan and Zainab's room prepping for end-of-term exams. Enitan, in particular, was a nervous wreck, perpetually convinced that she was going to fail out of school for good this time, even though Funmi was an excellent tutor if she did say so herself. Zainab was fretting over her new play, or rather its lack of existence. She suffered through her writer's block by being generally very irritable. She and Funmi were constantly bickering. The weekend before their final exams, Funmi suggested they go to Kufena Hill the weekend they were done. You were supposed to be able to see all of Zaria from the very top—the vast stretches of farmland, fertile thanks in part to the dam. The rock formations were older than Queen Amina herself, existing way before there had been any Hausaland to speak of. Trekking to the top would be a fun diversion. Enitan had needed no convincing; she was always eager to do Funmi's bidding. Zainab had been more skeptical.

"The hills are almost ten kilometers away from

campus. How are we supposed to get there? Ṣé we are supposed to walk?" Zainab asked.

"Why not? It's part of the experience," said Funmi.

"You must be joking."

"We can take a danfo, then."

"Danfo kẹ? You must be mad."

"Oh, right, I forgot Queen Zainab must ride in a chariot."

"Damola has a car. I don't know how to drive it, but, Funmi, you can, right? What if we borrow his car? He'll let us use it. He's going back to Jos for the holidays."

Funmi felt her face grow hot at the mention of Damola's name. He still hadn't spoken more than a few obligatory words of greeting whenever she happened to run into him sitting with Zainab in the common room or outside in the sculpture garden. But there was evidence of his presence everywhere. Funmi could finally now see what he did with the skulls he smashed. Zainab's side of the room she shared with Enitan displayed his handiwork—he arranged the splintered bones into various domestic tableaus that he glued onto stock paper. Funmi's favorite was of a woman huddled over a big mortar and pestle, a baby tied on her back. Composed entirely out of bone fragments that varied in size and shape, the woman's form seemed to change depending on the light. Each piece of bone was like part of a jigsaw puzzle; Funmi marveled at how he had been able to make them fit. He also drew sketches; there was one of the madman who was always shouting unintelligible things by the side of the main gate. Damola had captured his lean, haggard face, and his wild, matted hair. Underneath Damola had written in all caps: **WHO IS MAD?** Funmi wanted to ask him a million questions about his art. But she kept quiet; they acknowledged each other with head nods, but that was all.

She and Damola agreed to meet early that Saturday morning, a few hours before she, Zainab, and Enitan planned to leave. He said he would park the Peugeot across the street from the female dormitory and would wait for her to hand off the keys. She dressed that morning feeling hyperconscious of what she was wearing. She had opted for a loose adire dress she could sweat in and tennis shoes. She had gotten her hair relaxed the weekend before, so she tied her hair back and had worn a cap to block the sun.

Damola was sitting in the front of the car. He had cranked the seat back so he was virtually horizontal and had his arm flung over his eyes. He smelled strange, like a kind of dead animal. Marijuana, Funmi realized. She rapped politely on the roof of the car. Damola jerked awake.

"What happened to you?"

Damola blinked a couple of times as if he was still taking in his surroundings.

"Late night." He cleared his throat. "Late night," he said again, more authoritatively this time. Then he looked at her more closely.

"Why are you always looking at me like that?" Funmi snapped. "Don't you know it's rude to stare!"

Damola's expression changed to one of mild amusement.

"Sorry," he said. He opened the car door and got out. "You know how to get to the dam?" he asked.

"Yes." What kind of question was that? Everybody knew how to get to the dam.

"We have meetings there sometimes . . . every other Saturday night. You should come. Starts at eleven. Bring a flashlight."

Funmi was slightly stunned, as these were the most words he had ever spoken to her.

"What about the curfew?"

Damola smiled. "You do not seem like someone who always obeys curfew."

Funmi secretly glowed under this assessment. Then she asked, "What about Zainab?"

"What about Zainab?" he asked her evenly as if there was absolutely no reason why it shouldn't be at least remotely suspect that Funmi would be spending time late at night with her sometimes-friend's boyfriend. He added, unprompted, "This doesn't concern Zainab. Don't worry about it." He took the keys out of the ignition. "Take care of my pikin," he told her gravely, and at first Funmi thought he was talking about Zainab but then she realized he was talking about the car.

That had been hours ago now. They were supposed to have left earlier, but Zainab had had some kind of sudden divine inspiration for her play and had spent the morning sitting at her desk, writing chicken scratch. Funmi and Enitan had been forced to amuse themselves; she braided Enitan's hair and then they took advantage of the empty common room to play three rounds of Scrabble. They had finally left around 2 p.m. It was going on 5 p.m. now and they were close to the top of the rock formation, but the ground beneath them was getting rougher and steeper. Funmi was forced to go on her hands and knees up, up, slowly, even as the rocks cut into her hands.

"Watch your step here," Enitan shouted.

With one final heave, Funmi was at the summit. She lay there on all fours, catching her breath.

Zainab was standing in the center, her arms outstretched. A slight wind whipped up the ends of her hijab so it looked like she was wearing a cape.

"Are you all right?" Enitan asked Funmi. Funmi nodded. She just needed a second to catch her breath.

When Funmi felt sufficiently rested, she slowly stood up and took in the view. There was no question that it was beautiful. She hadn't fully realized how high up they were; they must have been at least eight hundred meters above the ground. There was so much to take in—the small brown blips that were humans walking between rows of greenery and mud huts that resembled dollhouses from this distance. The trees looked like tiny green lollipops.

Funmi felt giddy, excited at what they had actually accomplished. She had felt a similar sort of achievement when she had run five miles for the first time and had reveled with a strangely disassociating feeling of pride at what her body had done. She was able to move across many distances, to climb up the side of a rock, to make real progress with nothing but her hulk of fat and bone and muscle.

Zainab was lying flat on her back. "It's beautiful!" she said. "I wish we had a camera."

Enitan began spinning in circles, her arms out. "Yippee, we did it!"

"Haba! You two are behaving like children!" Funmi said.

"Don't those look like a man and a woman?" Funmi asked, pointing to artfully shaped rock formations in the far distance, positioned next to each other, and arranged in such a way that they did appear to look like two giant people, sitting on their haunches, gazing out over the land.

"Yes, it does," said Enitan. "It's beautiful."

"You saw how we passed by some of the city walls

that used to protect this area when this was Zazzau," said Zainab, who was still lying on her back.

"Ṣé you are talking to me?" asked Funmi. "Abeg, am I not the one who chose this place?" She sucked her teeth.

"Must everything be a competition with you?" asked Zainab.

"Ladies, please stop fighting. Let's enjoy the view," Enitan said. She took a deep breath. "The air even seems cleaner here, sef," she said dreamily. She stopped spinning. She put one foot out in front of the other. "I wonder if I could . . ." She didn't finish her sentence but instead placed her hands in front of her and kicked her legs up so she was doing a shaky handstand.

"Eni, I think you should be careful," Funmi said. "We're too high up . . ." She was beginning to feel a bit dizzy, actually. How far from the ground they were and how hard and bumpy the landing would be should they fall resonated now to a degree she hadn't expected. She lowered to a crouch.

"Relax," said Enitan. "There is no need to be afraid. See!" She did a slow cartwheel and almost tumbled into Zainab.

"Watch it!" Zainab sat up.

"Sorry. I can do another one," said Enitan and then—Funmi would never forget this moment— Enitan's feet were in the air and then they were not and then she was gone over the edge of the rock and there was a dull thud and then Funmi and Zainab were scrambling to see if she was still alive.

"Enitan! Enitan!" Zainab and Funmi peered over the edge of the rock. Enitan was moaning softly, lying in a completely unnatural position, her right arm bent crookedly near her head, which was slowly oozing blood.

"Don't move!" Funmi shouted. That much she knew from her nursing classes thus far.

"Oh my God, oh my God," Zainab was saying over and over again.

"Zainab!" Funmi snapped. She put her hands on Zainab's shoulders. "You've got to calm down. Stay with her; I'll go and ask for help."

"No, **you** should stay with her!" Zainab said. Funmi frowned; now was not the time to be territorial.

"I just mean, I am faster than you. I speak Hausa. It will be easier for me to get help."

Funmi nodded. Zainab was right. "Make sure you hurry; the sun is already setting."

Zainab nodded and then she was scurrying down the rocks.

Funmi dropped her water sachet down to where Enitan was lying; it landed softly near her left leg. She crouched down and then slowly, carefully, delicately on her hands and knees like a lizard, crawled down the rock so she was at the same elevation as Enitan.

Enitan was looking at her, her eyes wide open in abject terror. "Don't worry, Eni, I'm here," Funmi said in the most soothing tone she could muster. She didn't want to alarm her and she knew it was important to keep her awake. She also knew she had to stop the bleeding. She didn't have anything to wrap the wound so she took off her dress.

"I need to stop the bleeding," she told Enitan, who was trying and failing to form words with her lips. Funmi bunched up the dress and then carefully slipped one hand under Enitan's head. Funmi had plaited Enitan's hair that morning, simple cornrows that filed backward, while they waited for Zainab to finish releasing whatever droplets of writerly inspiration she had magically conjured up. It had been a surprisingly soothing ritual for both of them as Enitan sat between Funmi's legs and Funmi oiled each part with Sulfur 8 before working her fingers through each row. Zainab plaited hair much better than Funmi; she had had more practice courtesy of Mama Fatima and all her half siblings, but Enitan had been gracious and grateful for the effort Funmi had made.

The memory of that moment now made Funmi's eyes burn with tears. Enitan could be annoying; she was so guileless, so eager to please and keep the peace between Funmi and Zainab. But Funmi recognized the deep loneliness within her; she possessed it too. And though Funmi preferred to mask her own loneliness under layers of bravado, sometimes even outright cruelty, at the end of the day Enitan's loyalty to her was endearing, as easy as it was for Funmi to exploit it. Now Funmi regretted every callous remark she had ever uttered.

She placed the dress underneath Enitan's head; she could feel the cut with her fingers; it was right in the hollow where the base of the skull connected to the neck.

"This will hurt," she whispered, because she didn't have the heart to speak any louder. Then she bunched as much of the fabric as she could into the wound; Enitan screamed.

"Sorry, sorry," Funmi said, and she realized that she was crying and her tears were sliding down her nose and falling onto Enitan's blouse.

The sun was a waning orb. Funmi reached for Enitan's hand and Enitan squeezed it tightly. Funmi hoped that Zainab was already on her way back. "Pèlé," Funmi whispered. "Sorry," she said over and over again like an incantation.

CHAPTER 18

Zainab

January 1984

ABOUT A MONTH AFTER ENITAN HAD RECEIVED four stitches at the back of her head and an accompanying gnarly scar as a result, Zainab, Enitan, and Funmi were all over at Zainab's compound watching the new president deliver his New Year's speech. He reminded Zainab of a bird with his thick, black frame glasses and his fingers, long and slender like a woman's. He rolled his r's like her father did when he was giving lectures at the university; this president was Fulani, though, not Hausa. In clipped English, he justified his bloodless coup, pledging to rid the nation of corruption once and for all.

"Well, there goes democracy . . ." said Ahmed, who had come over for lunch.

Her father sighed. "This country . . ." Filling in the pauses appeared to be a futile endeavor.

Over time Zainab had come to learn a little more about her father's protégé. From Kano originally, Ahmed had graduated college at sixteen and was now the youngest assistant professor at the polytechnic. He taught in the environmental studies department, but he, like Zainab's father, had a fondness for the humanities, in languages specifically. He could read and write in Ajami script and he had a way of carrying himself that suggested he was older than he was. He liked to talk in long, slowly unspooling paragraphs.

After the speech had concluded, Ahmed offered to give the three of them a ride back to campus. He was headed toward that area anyway.

He had parked his Mercedes-Benz outside the gate, by the garbage-filled ditch that ran alongside the house. "You all come in on this side, I don't want you to fall into the ditch," Ahmed said, gesturing toward the side of the car closest to the road.

The three of them climbed into the backseat.

"I'll be your chauffeur this afternoon," Ahmed said as he started the car. The radio was on and was replaying the new president's remarks. Ahmed turned the radio off. As they slowed at the junction to let a truck pass, Ahmed turned around and smiled at them. "What are your thoughts on the new president?"

Enitan, Funmi, and Zainab all looked at each other.

"Come now, you must have some opinions,"

he suggested after they were silent. He looked at Zainab. "The play you wrote about Queen Amina implied you have quite a few strong ones in fact."

"You read my play?" Zainab asked, surprised and slightly awed. Ahmed intimidated her. Though he was only a few years older than her, she knew how much her father doted on him.

"Of course! How could I not look to see if the intelligence has been passed down from father to daughter?" Zainab felt her face grow warm. Funmi rolled her eyes, but Zainab ignored her.

"And what did you think?" she asked tentatively. A lot of the discussions he got into with her father had to do with literature. They were always arguing about the health of writing on the continent; sometimes talking about new books, but other times rehashing the value of old classics. They had had a long argument about the writer Amos Tutuola and his book **The Palm-Wine Drinkard** in particular. Her father thought it was embarrassing—the poorly written English, the plot holes. Ahmed thought it was representative of a certain homespun style. He said her father was too concerned with what the West thought. That had been one of the few arguments that had threatened to dip over into something much more cutting, more personal. Her father had hated the intimation that he might be anything other than a proudly African man.

"A valiant first effort," said Ahmed.

"What does that mean?" asked Zainab cautiously.

"You wrote something interesting about Queen Amina, even though sometimes it seemed as though you were more invested in the love story at the expense of everything else."

"And what is wrong with the love story? Isn't love the stuff of great fiction, of great novels too? Shakespeare and Anna Karenina and Jane Austen . . ."

"Mills and Boon!" Funmi added. Enitan laughed.

Ahmed looked in the rearview mirror and smiled. "You are right."

"I know," Zainab said, and she felt her face grow warm in spite of herself, thrilling at the way he looked at her in the rearview mirror.

"So you want to be a playwright when you graduate?" he asked as a follow-up. "Not a nurse like these two?"

"Yes," said Zainab. "I want to write plays and novels and poetry. All sorts."

"That's very good. Very noble. I hope it comes to pass for you."

They were silent again for a few more moments, and partly as a way to break the silence and also because she was curious and feeling uncharacteristically bold, she asked: "And what about you? Did you grow up wanting to be a professor?"

Ahmed was quiet for a moment. "I don't think I had a good conception of what it meant to teach.

I know I liked to read. I liked to write. In university, it became clear that writing creatively was not my strong suit, so I suppose teaching happened by a process of elimination."

He eased the car into a roundabout.

"Do you like teaching?" Enitan asked him.

"I do. I do. It's not easy. I'm forever at the mercy of whatever dysfunctional head of state is in charge, cutting back our salaries. But I enjoy the rigor of the work. It is important that northern Nigeria have as much access to education as the rest of the country."

They were quiet again. Zainab wanted to keep the conversation going. "My daddy says you know how to write in Ajami script."

Ahmed looked at her in the rearview mirror, seemingly surprised and perhaps flattered that he had come up in conversation.

"I do," he said.

"I still don't know how to write properly in Hausa. I think my father regrets not teaching me when I was small, and now it seems too late."

"It's never too late to learn!" Ahmed said, hitting his hand on the steering wheel for extra emphasis. "In fact, I'd be happy to teach you. Should that interest you," he added. "Or anyone else here."

Zainab looked at him in the rearview mirror. She nodded. What did she have to lose, she wagered.

CHAPTER 19

Funmi

February 1984

UILT IN 1973, THE DAM WAS A SOURCE OF
pride in the region and had become a go-to spot
for students hoping to socialize away from campus.
It was not a large dam, objectively speaking, but it
was a scenic one, surrounded by lush green grass
and trees that provided ample shade on all sides.
If you stood on the narrow concrete bridge that
jutted out onto the main expanse, you could watch
sheets of water pour into the reservoir like a giant
drain, spitting mist into the air. During the rainy
season, villagers could catch fish with their bare
hands. Couples would stand on the bridge and
gaze out onto the water. And there were all sorts of
nooks and crannies for discreet conversations. Tall
grass grew wildly on either side of the bank, grass
that was conducive for hosting small clandestine
gatherings. Nothing too extreme, usually somebody

had a cooler of some Star beers, and someone else a portable cassette player. They would listen to Fela or Michael Jackson while some of the more brazen, drunker students would attempt to dance like him. Sometimes there was reefer. Funmi learned all this after she took Damola at his word and headed to the dam around 11 p.m. two months after she had used his car to drive to Kufena Hill.

Carrying a flashlight that she only turned on once she was sufficiently far from campus, Funmi walked tentatively in the direction of the dam, wondering how on earth she would find Damola. She needn't have worried. She could hear laughter soon enough and see orange light from cigarettes floating in the night air like fireflies. She recognized Damola's Peugeot parked nearby. A group of students were sitting in a semicircle in metal chairs they must have carried in the car. Three kerosene lanterns had been placed around the circle, casting the students' faces in eerie shadows. Damola was sitting in a chair rolling some reefer on a small tray in his lap; one joint was already sitting snugly behind his ear. Funmi didn't know any of the people by name, but she recognized some of them—they were students who were very active in student organizing and were always getting dragged into the Senate Building for reprimands from the vice chancellor. The university was still on edge from 1978, when students had protested the rise in tuition costs courtesy of Obasanjo's austerity measures and had been shot by state police for their trouble. The local chapter of the National Union of Nigerian Students, or NUNS, had been banned from campus and key members expelled.

Feeling very self-conscious about being there, Funmi decided to wait outside the circle of light, hoping for an opportunity when she could approach Damola, when they seemed less engaged in serious, heated conversation.

"This guy," said one of the students. He was tall and lanky with protruding front teeth. He pointed his open bottle of beer at Damola. "Cannot be serious. Communism will never work in Nigeria. Our people are too self-interested for that," he added.

"But only because they have had no choice," Damola replied, fitting lingering stray buds onto the paper he was rolling. "Our government has no incentive to look after its own people—they cannot even provide decent services sef. It was not so long ago when we used to have light for twenty-four hours. What of NEPA now?"

"Never expect power always," they all chanted in a chorus. They each took swigs from their beer.

"Kai!" said the tall guy. "But don't you see how you're proving my point? How can you expect communism to work here when the government is so inept? The Buhari administration is padding its coffers with oil money as ordinary people cannot find a kobo to buy bread. How can you expect the government to be able to provide housing and food and jobs nationwide? It will not work!"

"And what about what is happening in Afghanistan? The Soviet Union there invading a Muslim country. You think the Communists are so pure in their motives but they're just as imperialist as the U.S. They are just as greedy." This was from the only woman in the circle. She was wearing a headscarf and drinking a bottle of malt.

"Enough of international politics, let's focus on what is happening here," said another student. "Teaching faculty have not been paid for two months now. I say we should conduct a protest in solidarity in front of the Senate Building—"

"I'm going to graduate this May, and I can't afford to get expelled before then."

"No, let's do it." This was Damola speaking now, with a calm assertiveness Funmi had not heard before. He twisted the ends of the joint with his fingers. "We just need to get everyone involved. If there are many of us, the administration will be less likely to cause trouble."

Funmi felt something scurry over her foot and jumped. Her flashlight landed on the ground with a thud and went out. The students all froze, looking around suspiciously.

Cursing, Funmi picked up her flashlight.

"Who is there?" the tall man asked.

Funmi emerged from the tree she had been hiding behind.

Damola looked up. He didn't seem surprised to see her.

"You made it," he said. "Come join us."

The tall guy handed her a bottle of beer. "Welcome," he said. Funmi nodded as a gesture of thanks. She hated the taste of beer, but she took a sip anyway.

"So how much of this meeting did you hear?" the tall man asked her.

"Easy, bros," said Damola.

"Ahn-ahn? There's no problem here. Friendly fire." He flashed a smile at her.

"Your name is Zainab, right?"

"Ousmane." Damola put his tray down and stood up.

Ousmane laughed, waving Damola off. "Take it easy, take it easy."

"Wawa," one of the other students muttered, and they laughed. Whatever tension had been in the air dissipated.

"How did you hear about our group?" the hijabi woman asked Funmi.

Funmi looked at Damola for help. He nodded as if encouraging her.

"Damola invited me," Funmi confessed, suddenly

feeling sheepish. "I don't know much about your beliefs," she added.

"Our beliefs are fairly straightforward," said the hijabi woman. "We believe that the money we are spending on this education should ensure a quality education for every student. We believe that faculty should be paid a living wage. We believe in democracy and the premiership of the working class. And we believe that Ousmane is an idiot." The other students laughed at that.

"Your father!" Ousmane muttered.

"Some of us identify as Marxist. Others of us are not so sure," the woman continued. "Our university is supposed to be the premier university of the North. But students are barely getting by. Overcrowding is becoming rampant as they cut our services but still expect us to pay. My father and his father both attended this university and the stories they tell of how it has fallen into disrepair are tough to hear. But I believe if we fight for the right of our brothers and sisters—"

"Aisha, it's enough now," said Ousmane, springing to his feet. "We don tire. Bros," he said, gesturing toward the guy who had a portable cassette player in his lap, "play some music now."

Aisha looked annoyed but didn't bother coming up with a clever retort.

Some of the students stood up then, moving

the chairs around. Damola took a matchbox from inside his pocket and lit the joint. They began to pass it around while Fela's wives sang "Zombie oh zombie" over and over again. Some students began to shuffle to the music, sipping from their beer. Aisha sat in her chair, her lips pursed. Ousmane went over to her. "Come and dance, Doctor," he said with a drunken smile. Aisha kissed her teeth and turned away from him. "Ahn-ahn, why must you be so rude?" Ousmane said. He grabbed her hands and tried to pull her out of the chair.

"Ousmane, leave me alone!" she shouted and pushed him away firmly so Ousmane stumbled, tripping over a lantern. The other students laughed. Aisha cursed and angrily whipped the dangling end of her headscarf to the other side of her neck.

Damola looked up from the new joint he had been rolling. "Ousmane, if you don't cut it out right now, you're expelled from this group." He said it quietly but with that same calmly assertive power Funmi had heard for the first time only minutes ago. The laughter quickly died down. Only Fela's saxophone played now.

"If you think I am joking, try me," Damola added. Ousmane was lying on the ground, his right hand still holding his beer. They eyed each other for a while, a long while, it felt like to Funmi. Then Ousmane sucked his teeth and spat on the ground. "Forget this shit, mahn." He struggled to get up for an excruciatingly long moment, as no one helped him but just watched him, on edge. When he was finally able to stand, he grabbed two more bottles of beer and stalked off into the night, raising his left palm at them as one last curse.

There was some stunned silence as Fela's voice warbled on the cassette player. Then Damola patted the empty chair beside him.

"Won't you sit down?" he asked Funmi. With that request, the tension broke. Students began to laugh and dance again. Funmi sat down slowly beside him. Damola went back to rolling his joint, his fingers moving nimbly. He wet his fingers and twisted each tip. "Do you want to try it?" he asked her. Funmi nodded. Damola lit the joint with a match, his face awash in orange light.

"You know how to do it?"

She nodded. She did not. But she would never admit this.

He took a hit, sucking in his cheeks, and then exhaled. Two puffs. It smelled awful.

He handed it to her. She inhaled.

"Hold it, hold it, hold it until you feel it in your lungs," he said to her. She held the smoke until her eyes teared up and the inside of her chest felt like it was on fire. She exhaled finally, two puffs and then coughed for good measure. Damola laughed and patted her back a few times. She sat upright. It was the first time he had ever touched her. She accepted the joint and took another puff. She felt momentarily dizzy, and then a shift. She looked at Damola's face as he took another hit, and she thought he looked very funny, with his cheeks sucked in like that.

"Why are you always staring at me?" she asked him.

"Staring at you?"

"You are always looking at me like this." And she pursed her lips and stared at him the way she felt Damola stared at her.

Damola laughed.

One of the students almost bumped into them. He had been trying to execute a complicated dance move. He seemed properly drunk or high or maybe both.

"Sorry, sorry," the student said, holding out his hands in apology. Damola handed the student his tray and stood up.

"Here, you can have the rest," Damola told him. He turned to Funmi. "Come on, let's go somewhere more private." He held out his hand. She took it and he pulled her firmly out of her chair.

He picked up the lantern at his feet.

"What about your car?"

"I'll get it later."

He led her through some bush; the grass was higher now and kept cutting into her legs. He held her hand tightly as he led her, moving with purpose until they arrived at their destination: near a small aqueduct. Below them, the water shimmered.

"Are you afraid to sit there?" Damola asked her.

"No!" Funmi said defiantly. "Why would you ask me something like that?"

Damola laughed. "Okay. Sorry. Let's sit."

He led the way, holding her hand with his left and the lantern with his right. With the light in front of them, Funmi could see that the aqueduct was made of cement and that the water below them looked shallow, more like a stream than a river. When he reached the middle of the aqueduct, he sat down, placing the lantern beside him. He helped Funmi sit as well. Their legs dangled out in front of the water.

They were both quiet for a moment, listening to the nocturnal sounds around them—the chirp of the grasshoppers, the slight rustling of the water.

After a moment, feeling emboldened, Funmi turned to look at Damola. He was staring out at the water, his face in profile. She had never been this close to him before, she realized, had never felt comfortable enough to look at him with abandon as she was doing now. It felt almost greedy.

Then he turned suddenly to look at her. They stared at each other for a long time, gazing unabashedly into each other's eyes. Funmi knew in that moment that whatever he asked her to do that night, she would do. Without hesitation.

"How are you feeling?" he asked her finally.

"I feel fine," she said. Great, even, like her body wasn't part of this world anymore. The water looked like a piece of glass God had gently set down on top of the earth. She told Damola this and he looked out at the water too.

"Yes, you're right. You have a good artistic eye for a nurse."

"Is that supposed to be an insult?"

"No."

"Good. You'll get in trouble if you insult me."

"What sort of trouble?"

"Why did you bring me here?"

Damola was quiet. "I like this place. I can think here."

"Why did you invite me to this meeting tonight?"

"You ask a lot of questions."

"Is that a bad thing?"

"No. It's one of the things I like about you."

At that, Funmi felt her body grow warm. **One** of the things. Things. Plural.

"What else do you like about me?" It was the alcohol and the marijuana that were making her feel reckless.

"When you want something, you won't stop until you get it. We need that energy in the group."

"So is that why you asked me to come?"

"It's not the only reason."

They were both quiet. Funmi's heart was beating so loudly, she could hear it pounding in her ears.

She was about to say something to break the silence when he stopped her, putting a finger on her lips and caressing them softly. Then he leaned in and kissed her. He tasted like beer and marijuana, surprisingly not unpleasant. He paused to gauge her reaction. She pulled him close to her and they kissed each other more passionately. His right hand reached for her breasts.

"Get up," he instructed in a low voice. He stood and held out his hand to guide her. She took it. He led them off the top of the aqueduct, up the bank, until they were standing under a tree. He set the lantern down. He pulled her toward him, and they kissed again; when he bit her lower lip gently with his teeth, she felt her body turn liquid. He pushed her toward the tree so she was facing it.

"Put your hands up."

She obeyed, placing her hands against the jacaranda tree, spreading her legs apart.

He began kissing the back of her neck slowly.

She moaned. He nibbled on her lower ear, as his right hand went up and under her shirt, squeezing her nipples gently, and his left hand crawled under her skirt.

"Do you want me?" he asked her.

"Yes." She heard the clink of his belt unbuckling.

"Say it," he said, hiking up her skirt and pushing down her underwear.

"I want you." She could barely get the words out before he thrust deeply into her and she gasped both in pleasure and pain.

"I want you, I want you, I want you," she cried with each thrust, until he put his hand over her mouth, and she screamed the words against his callused fingers. He came with a violent shudder, whipping it out just in time to finish all over the back of her legs. She wanted to tell him to wait, to touch her with his fingers; she had not yet come. But she said nothing, just watched him move away from her, shaking his penis as he walked toward another tree. The stream of his piss hitting the earth was the only sound besides the insects for a long moment. She knew she should pee too, but she couldn't, not now. The semen on the back of her legs was already drying. She hitched up her underwear and tried to assess her own feelings. He had been the first man to enter her, despite all her secondary-school forays. She heard him zip up. Now that he was standing outside the radius of the lantern light, he was just shadow. She had never noticed how skinny his legs were. They were incongruous with his toned arms and broad chest.

"Are you all right?" he asked her.

She nodded. She did not know what else to say. She was too overwhelmed to speak.

CHAPTER 20

Zainab

May 1984

AFTER THE CAR RIDE, AHMED HAD GONE OUT of his way to avoid Zainab whenever she was home, or so it seemed. Her father still invited him for weekly dinners and arguments about the direction of the country, and he came but avoided her gaze, only inclining his head slightly in greeting. He never offered to drive her back to campus and Zainab found herself wondering with a disproportionate amount of intensity what she had done to upset him—the first sign that perhaps she liked this man more than a little bit. Things with Damola had come to an end. It wasn't so much a set ending as a sustained lack of energy from either of them. He had stopped trying to see her. She didn't care to know why.

When Zainab was home and she knew that Ahmed was coming over, she went out of her way to make sure she looked presentable, wearing her shiniest hijabs and silver bangles that clattered chaotically when she moved. But his face was always inscrutable, kind and warm yes, but without the slightest hint of sexual interest. Finally, she took matters into her own hands.

"Daddy, I want to learn how to write in Hausa," she announced to her father one afternoon, an hour before Ahmed was scheduled to come over for lunch. "Ahmed said he could teach me."

"Did he now?" said her father.

"I know you are busy with your book. We could have lessons here in the study."

She broached the subject again at lunch.

"You said you were going to teach me how to write in Hausa," Zainab told Ahmed when he arrived, holding his weekly gift—a crate of soft drinks. He looked her in the eye finally for the first time since their car ride.

From then on, every Saturday afternoon, after lunch, for an hour in the study—the door wide open so there was not even the suggestion of scandal—he would give her lessons. Modern Hausa used the Roman alphabet, but the Ajami style was indebted to Arabic languages—it had the same curlicue script and only Islamic scholars tended to be able to read it. They argued about the arrival of Islam to the region, and Zainab quickly learned that he liked to play devil's advocate. When she would parrot the words of her father, make mention of how much Hausaland had thrived before the murderous, marauding white men with their Christianity and slavery came to ruin their land, Ahmed would push back. Slavery was an integral part of Zaria's economy even before white people began plundering what would become northern Nigeria. And Islam was not native to the area either. He did not condescend when he talked to her. He considered her arguments and her opinions, taking them seriously. It made her delirious to receive his attention in this way. Enitan noticed too. She still came over on weekends and watched Zainab go into the study. Zainab's father had encouraged Enitan to take lessons as well: "You are in the North so do as the northerners do!" he had insisted, but Enitan, thankfully, had declined. "I'm too busy with my own schoolwork," she said demurely.

Ahmed dropped them both off at campus on Sunday afternoons. Nothing untoward ever happened. Nothing **could** happen—there was no way in that house in the study with the door open or in the car, where Zainab sat in the backseat with Enitan, Ahmed looking for all intents and purposes like their brother. But Zainab grew to love him; she recognized it in herself. It did not feel like the fairy-tale books; it did not make her lose control.

"You like him, don't you?" Enitan said one afternoon, after he had dropped them outside their dormitory and they were making their way up the stairs to their room.

"I don't know what you are talking about," Zainab said hastily, too hastily she knew. Enitan simply turned around to look her in the face.

"Okay o," she said. "Denial is not just a river in Egypt."

Zainab sucked her teeth.

When Ahmed came down with an acute case of malaria that sent him to the hospital and then left him bedridden for days, Zainab made pepper soup and asked her father if she could come with him to deliver the food. She wrote a note, just a quick thing hoping that he would feel better soon and that she missed their lessons, and slipped it into an envelope inside the nylon bag where the soup sat in a thermos. She waited in the car when her father went to deliver it—her father did not think it appropriate for her to see Ahmed convalescing. For an agonizing month there were no more lessons.

Then Ahmed appeared at their house for lunch one Saturday afternoon, looking noticeably thinner. His eyes were feverishly bright. He came with his customary crate of soft drinks. When Zainab reached to take it from him, he took an envelope from his jacket pocket and slipped it on top of the crate. Barely able to wait to open it, she ran to the kitchen, slammed the drinks down—the glass bottles rattling in the crate—and raced to her room.

She lay on her back and looked more closely at the envelope, with its red, white, and blue lining on the edges and her name written in his cursive on the front.

My dearest Zainab, the letter began. **These past few weeks have given me time for ample reflection.** It continued. It was a love letter. There was no other way to describe it. How as he tossed and turned in a malaria-fueled delirium, he dreamed of her. How those moments of forced reflection made him realize how desperately lonely he was, how it was time for a wife. He praised her fierce intelligence, her great beauty. He ended with a question: **Will you do me the great honor of considering my hand in marriage?** adding in parentheses (**you do not have to answer now**).

She came down for lunch and avoided his gaze. When her father idly asked if he would be resuming lessons today, Ahmed said he was not quite up to it. Zainab stared down at her plate. When Ahmed got up to leave, she felt her stomach heave. He said his goodbyes, avoiding her eyes as he bid farewell to her siblings. He was out of the compound and walking to his car parked across the other side of the street when Zainab grabbed a newspaper and dashed out of the house. "Wait, wait!" Zainab shouted, and she ran toward him, her slippers kicking up clouds of dust. She held out the newspaper like it was his most valuable possession.

"You forgot this," she said, struggling to catch her breath.

"Oh, na gode," he said, not making eye contact, as if to look her fully in the face would be too much to bear.

"I also wanted to respond," she said, feeling nervous, her hands suddenly clammy. "I wanted to respond to your question." She ventured a look at his face now; he was fully at attention, his eyes wide and fixed on her.

"My answer is yes."

The look on his face at that moment was one Zainab would never forget. His smile spread rapidly, working its way through until his face was just dimpled cheekbone and glistening white teeth. He laughed and clapped his hands together. "This is wonderful," he told her. "This is wonderful news!"

He turned his car keys in his hand and ran his hand over his hair. "I will talk to your father right now!" he said, and he began walking back to the compound.

"Wait, I think, maybe we should wait," Zainab said, but he was already gone, running now toward the house, and in hindsight, of course her father acted the way he did.

CHAPTER 21

Enitan

I'M MISERABLE," ZAINAB ANNOUNCED BEFORE collapsing onto her bed, her arms splayed out in melodramatic fashion, like one of the protagonists in the novels she was always prattling on about.

"Daddy refuses to talk to me!" she added. Enitan nodded charitably. Zainab had come dashing into their room, announcing that she was engaged to Ahmed. Zainab's infatuation had been obvious, her sudden interest in wanting to learn how to write Hausa, the long deliberations over what color hijab would go best with the dress she would wear for such lessons—it was all very strange to see Zainab, never frazzled by the myriad marriage proposals she received, suddenly besotted with someone. And it had never been clear to Enitan that Ahmed had reciprocated those feelings.

Zainab's father was furious. Even though Zainab had told her father Ahmed was willing to have a long engagement and would certainly not encourage

Zainab to drop out of school, there was no trying to persuade him. He was incensed.

"We ambushed him; we took him by surprise," Zainab moaned. "Why did we do it like that?" Apparently, Zainab's father had gotten so upset, he had had Mama Gimbya fetch a switch and had methodically beaten Zainab's legs for fifteen minutes, demanding to know as he did it whether Ahmed had ever touched her. Zainab had never been beaten by her father before, she told Funmi and Enitan, limping into their room. Both Enitan and Funmi had found that implausible. Enitan did not know her father of course, but she imagined that if she did, eventually she too would do something so upsetting he would feel the need to have her hunt for a stick.

Funmi told them that what Zainab had experienced was minuscule compared to the punishments she had received as a teenager. She regaled them with stories of her stepmother, Dorcas, of the slaps and the kicks and the thrown pots and pans and sometimes even the bricks, the punishing rituals that were rites of passage: fly to Mecca, where you stood with your arms outstretched and your knees slightly bent; the monkey dance, where you held your left ear with your right hand and your right ear with your left hand and squatted up and down and up and down for hours.

Funmi relayed these stories with clear sadistic

pleasure; it was obvious that she considered those sufferings to be badges of honor, indication of her superior mettle, her inner strength.

Enitan's mother had smacked her bottom when she was very young and had wielded the occasional ear pull with great embarrassing effect (the ear pull was always most humiliating when done in public), but by the time Enitan was ten, the physical punishment had mostly abated. What was left in its wake was equally as manipulative, the emotional strings her mother could pull, the heavy and implicit cloud that lingered over Enitan's actions as she was always made aware of her mother's sacrifices, of her mother's suffocating love.

"What would you like us to do?" Enitan asked.

Zainab sat upright suddenly, as if she had just realized that Enitan was in the room.

"Can you come with me for dinner this weekend?" she asked. "I think if we're all there, if we all try to convince my dad——"

"Why would he listen to us?" Enitan interrupted. "And convince him of what? If you really wanted to marry Ahmed, you could always just elope."

"You must be joking."

"Why would I be joking?" Enitan was suddenly very irritated. She had had enough of Zainab and Funmi's phallic problems. There were more important things in this world than men. She had clinical training to prepare for.

"I think maybe if all three of us are there, then you can tell my dad how nothing has happened, how I have not slept with Ahmed, how there is nothing haram about our relationship . . ."

Funmi stiffened. "Is that what you really think?" she asked Zainab.

"What do you mean?"

"If you had slept with Ahmed, would that have been so wrong?"

"What are you saying?" Zainab asked. "First of all, Ahmed would never have allowed such a thing to happen, second of all, it's just not what I would ever think to do—"

"You know Damola and I are sleeping together," Funmi announced. Enitan felt her body fold in on itself, bracing for whatever cavalcade of angry words Funmi had now sparked.

But Zainab shrugged. "Good for you," she said. "I don't care."

"Really?" Funmi asked, and her tone had shifted, had become more earnest and beseeching in the process, as if she actually had really needed to hear Zainab's approval. Zainab noticed it too; Enitan could tell.

"Yes," Zainab said again, more confidently this time. "I really don't care. I love Ahmed." She smiled at them widely. "I love Ahmed!" she said again with more conviction. She got down on her knees and clasped her hands together. "Please, girls, you have to help me."

Funmi and Enitan looked at each other. "Okay," they said.

ENITAN HAD ALWAYS FOUND Professor Hassan intimidating but never more so than at the dinner Zainab had invited them to, though Mama Gimbya and Mama Fatima had happily set places for them at the table, eager for the family to be at peace. Zainab had told Funmi and Enitan that they were excited for her to marry. "Then I'm out of the house," she had quipped.

The professor was taciturn, his usual wry smile nowhere to be found. Ahmed had not been invited, according to Zainab; her father had banned him from their residence. Enitan was extremely doubtful about the impact she and Funmi could have on the man who sat at the head of the table; this man who ate his tuwo masara with a fork and knife and didn't need to sip water in between bites as Enitan was doing now, wishing she had accepted the invitation to help herself to a soft drink even if the crate of drinks had been left in the courtyard and would thus to be too warm. The combination of something cold and carbonated paired with something warm and spicy was always ideal.

"So you and Funmi will be doing your clinical training soon?" Mama Fatima gamely asked after they had sat through fifteen minutes of utter silence, save for the sounds their mouths made as they ate.

Enitan nodded. "Yes, ma."

"Very good," Mama Gimbya said. "It is good that you girls will soon have a practical degree."

Professor Hassan made a noise, a grunt of displeasure as he speared his morsel of tuwo masara in the soup Mama Gimbya had prepared.

Enitan looked at Zainab, who was staring at her own barely touched food.

"Do you have any idea where you might want to be stationed when you do your youth service?" Mama Fatima asked Enitan. Because Enitan had come to their house more often than Funmi, she was the recipient of all their questions. It was very much a reaching question considering the fact that graduation was three years away for the three of them.

"Yes," Enitan said, though to be honest she wasn't sure if she was excited. She knew it would be highly unlikely that she, Funmi, and Zainab would end up working in the same state.

"I'm not planning on going," Zainab announced. Her father looked up at her.

"I'm not planning on entering the workforce. When I marry Ahmed, I'll write in my spare time," she added. Funmi let out a stifled gasp; as bold as she tended to be, even she had been cowed to silence by Professor Hassan. For good reason. Professor Hassan sent his fist down hard on the table, clattering the plates. Both Mama Gimbya and Mama Fatima jumped.

He spoke to her in Hausa, in a shockingly quiet voice as if he was mustering all his power not to explode.

"I have done nothing wrong!" Zainab exclaimed in English. "I love him! Why won't you let me marry him? Other fathers would be proud of me, happy that I've chosen such an honorable man—"

"Honorable man!" Professor Hassan yelled. "Honorable man! I forbid it! You hear me? That's enough! It's enough that I forbid it!"

"But, Daddy—"

"Don't Daddy me. This is the last time you will show your face here if you continue to carry on this way."

"Professor Hassan—" Funmi now began, and the prof looked momentarily surprised that Funmi had even dared to speak. So was Enitan.

"With all due respect, Professor Hassan," Funmi continued. "I don't mean to intrude. But I think you should listen to what Zainab has to say. I've always respected you as a father, so unlike my own," she mused, then she stopped. "We live with Zainab. If she were sleeping with Ahmed, we would know. She is telling you the truth. Please, at least take the time to talk with her privately. If she marries him, is it really the end of the world?" she added. Everyone was silent as her question hung in the air. Enitan looked down at her soup. Zainab was looking at her father with hungry, pleading eyes.

The silence dragged on for agonizing minutes, until her father sighed—one long, heavy sigh.

"My study. Now," he said, and Zainab grinned at Funmi as she leaped from her chair and her stepmothers smiled tight little smiles at themselves and Enitan and Funmi looked at each other, Funmi with just the slightest hint of triumph in her eyes. Perhaps there would be a wedding after all.

CHAPTER 22

Enitan

September 1984

Enitan had never been so glad to be back in Zaria. The two months she had spent at home for the summer holiday in Abeokuta had been tense; her mother's newfound religious devotion perplexed Enitan. The cultural religiosity she had grown up with, the memory verses recited at bedtime, the prayers they had said before eating, had now given way to something more ardent, more desperate. They had gone to Shekinah Glory off and on for most of Enitan's life, but Sharon had never been heavily involved. They always sat in the back and Enitan was never permitted to go off to Sunday school with the other children; maybe her mother was afraid that they would mock her for having no father. But they teased her about this in school already. Enitan wasn't sure what protection her mother thought she was offering by keeping her separated from them.

But now Sharon had become a member of the Celestial Church—she wore their signature white robes for service on Sundays and covered her hair with a headtie. She attended prayer meetings on Wednesday evenings and all-night prayer vigils on Friday nights. She was newly concerned with the state of Enitan's soul and with Enitan's chastity.

"I trust you are not spreading your legs for anybody anyhow?" her mother had asked her that first night Enitan had been home. Apparently, the church had been an essential emotional support for Sharon when there were talks of redundancies at the bank. Sharon had been spared, and she was convinced the prayers of the church members had saved her. She wanted Enitan to attend service with her, but Enitan hated it, wearing the white clothes, which Enitan inevitably got stained with dust or once with menstrual blood. Sharon had rushed her out of the hall when she had noticed the blood on the seat of Enitan's skirt. Bleeding women were impure; they weren't supposed to be able to attend services. They were required to abstain from entering the church until seven days had passed, like the Israelites in the Hebrew Bible. Enitan didn't like the fact that men and women were separated during the service, that only men could teach. It just seemed fundamentally unfair. And why should a woman be blamed for her own bleeding body? Wasn't it natural? But at least her period had meant that Enitan hadn't had to attend church on her last day at home with her mother.

Being home had highlighted the suffocating narrowness of her childhood, the claustrophobia, the limited mobility. At least when she was bored at university, she could play Scrabble with Zainab or Funmi or they could give each other manicures or go see a play at the drama village. At home, with her mother at the bank all day with the car, there was nothing to do but read the same three books she had kept in Abeokuta over and over again. Her mother had sold their television, newly convinced of its contagious sinfulness.

And so yes, when she had stepped down from the danfo in front of the school's gates to begin the new school year, noting how much drier and cooler it was up in this part of the country—the muez-zin blaring prayers from the loudspeaker attached to the mosque minaret, the men doing ablutions with their plastic water kettles in preparation of jumat—she had felt relief and realized that she had developed an attachment to Zaria, and that this place felt like home.

ENITAN WAS UNPACKING HER suitcase in her room when Funmi came in and shut the door behind her.

They shared a room with Zainab and Mariam now because whatever favoritism Zainab's father had managed to get from the administration was moot in the face of budget cuts and aggressive overcrowding in the dormitories.

"Where's Zainab?" she asked.

"Bawo ni to you too," said Enitan. "She's not coming back to campus until tomorrow."

"Good." Funmi sat down at the table.

"What is it?"

"I need your help."

"With what?" Already Enitan felt a current of excitement, of intrigue. Whatever it was, judging from Funmi's wan expression it was serious, and Enitan was flattered by the attention, that she had been entrusted with the weight of this request.

Funmi was quiet for a moment. She looked out the window. The sunlight hit the side of her face, highlighting a sprinkling of acne on her jawline that Enitan had never noticed before.

"I'm pregnant," Funmi said.

Enitan had to ask her to repeat herself.

"I'm pregnant," Funmi said again.

Enitan didn't know what to say. She was overwhelmed by the twinning, paradoxical emotions she was feeling at the moment—utter disbelief that Funmi could be pregnant, because that meant that Funmi was having sex and it was strange to imagine any of them having sex—and also complete acceptance, because of course Funmi had had sex; of the three of them, she was by far the most likely to have had it. Enitan had seen the way the men watched Funmi on campus. She had a magnetism that drew men to her; there was nothing remotely surprising about this news. Enitan now had a sordid curiosity about the whole thing: What had it been like and how and **where**? But also, was Funmi positive? Sometimes stress could delay periods.

"Are you sure?"

Funmi began to drum her fingers on the table, as if she were playing an imaginary piano.

"Yes, I'm sure. It's Damola's." She turned now to face Enitan, seeking Enitan's eyes and looking into them defiantly, as if daring her to say something.

Enitan was quiet. She was still trying to process what Funmi had just said. Still slowly absorbing its implications.

"I need your help."

Another pause.

"I'm not having this baby."

For the second time in less than five minutes, Enitan was stunned into silence.

Of course, Enitan had grown up hearing of certain methods, procedures that existed even though they were illegal and dangerous. In secondary school, there had been stories about a girl a few years above Enitan who had accidentally killed herself trying to get rid of her pregnancy over the

Christmas term. Apparently, she drank bleach. The father was rumored to have been the mathematics teacher who had mysteriously been placed on leave with no explanation. And then there were the witch doctors women consulted who would claim to have secret concoctions, certain herbs, plant leaves, tinctures that could make your belly go away as long as you were willing to offer something to them first; more often than not it was money; sometimes it was sex.

In darker, more brooding moments, Enitan had occasionally wondered if this option was something her own mother had ever considered. Even though her mother loved her and this love was often stifling, how drastically different would Sharon's life have been had she not been so immediately cut off from the rest of her family and turned into the living embodiment of sin.

Enitan knew Funmi didn't have a good relationship with her father. And that she and her aunt were not close. Enitan would not fight the decision. She would help as much as she could in any way she could.

"There's a medical student who's willing to help me," Funmi said. "She told me I need to bring someone with me, though, for . . . afterward. Will you come with me?"

Enitan nodded. Of course she would.

She had so many questions but she wasn't sure

how receptive Funmi would be to answering any of them.

The procedure had been scheduled for that same night. Apparently, if Enitan hadn't agreed to go with her, Funmi would have gone by herself, and in fact had been planning to go alone. But Aisha, the medical student, had insisted she bring someone with her. That it was the immediate aftermath that carried the most risk of infection, of bleeding. And that if anyone were to find out what Aisha did, not only would she be unable to practice medicine, she would likely go to prison. Or depending on which fundamentalist cleric was in the mood, she would be made an example of—publicly. When it came to this particular issue, Christians and Muslims shared a united, proudly opposed front. How Funmi met Aisha, Enitan did not know.

Aisha told them to meet her at the teaching hospital and to register at the front desk. They took a taxi there. It was late, around eleven at night, and there was only one woman at the reception desk, who had been dozing quietly when they entered. Funmi told the woman whom she had an appointment with while Enitan sat down in one of the three plastic chairs that lined the room. It was a small, sparsely furnished space. There was a tiny TV in one corner that had been switched off and a coffee table with a broken leg. Some cement blocks had been placed underneath the table to prop it up.

Faded newspapers and one magazine were scattered on top of the table. A single flickering fluorescent light strip attached to one wall illuminated the room feebly, so most of the room was still in shadow. Enitan was holding the bag she had been instructed to bring—it contained heavy-duty maxi pads, some paracetamol, and a change of underwear. Funmi sat down next to Enitan. She leaned back in the chair and closed her eyes. Enitan took her hand and squeezed it.

"Ms. Ojo?" A woman appeared in the hallway, wearing a purple hijab and a white doctor's coat. "Please follow me," she said. Funmi stood up and so did Enitan.

She led them down the hallway and into the first door on the right. Inside there was a standard hospital bed, a sink and a table with blue gloves, a flashlight, some towels, and several silver instruments that looked vaguely like kitchenware. Aisha shut the door behind her. "You'll need to change," she told Funmi, and she handed her a gown. "You don't need to take off your brassiere," she added. "I'll be right outside." She left.

Enitan and Funmi looked at each other. Enitan set down the bag she had been holding. "Do you need help?" she asked, but Funmi muttered, "I can do it." Funmi took off her jeans. Enitan tried not to stare. Her belly seemed so flat; it was hard to believe that there was supposed to be a baby in there. Her calves needed lotion. Funmi took off her blouse next and then put on the gown, slipping off her underwear afterward. Then she folded each item of clothing meticulously, placing them on the chair next to the bed. She nodded at Enitan. The doctor could come back in now. Enitan opened the door and Aisha entered, holding a sheathed syringe. She told Funmi to lie down on the bed.

"Unfortunately, I have not been able to procure an ultrasound machine for this procedure," she said. "So we'll have to trust that there has not been much change since I last saw you. I was able to get some local anesthesia, but it may not be enough."

"So I will be awake for the procedure?" Funmi asked her.

Aisha nodded. "Yes. But you shouldn't be able to feel too much." She turned to Enitan. "It is good that you are here. I'll need you to hold this flashlight as I work."

"What exactly are you going to do?"

"A dilation and curettage. I have the tools here. I'll be using this to extract the tissue from her uterus. But first I'll use the anesthetic to numb the area. And then she may spend the night in this room. We'll need to monitor her for bleeding. You're in the nursing school, correct?"

Enitan nodded.

"Good. So you'll be able to monitor her."

"You've done this before?"

Aisha didn't respond.

"What are the risks involved?"

"We're not going to have this discussion now," Funmi said from the bed. "Just start."

Enitan remembered that Aisha wasn't a doctor, not yet, not really, but only a medical student.

"In that cupboard, there's a blanket," Aisha told Enitan. "You can place it over her lap for decency's sake."

Enitan opened the cupboard and took out the blanket. Together they draped it over Funmi's legs. Aisha asked Funmi to spread her legs wide. Then she put on the gloves. The light fixture flickered ominously. They all looked at each other.

"I am going to use this to examine your cervix. And then I will inject the anesthetic," Aisha told them. "If you can please hold the flashlight," she instructed Enitan. Enitan took the flashlight and shone it between Funmi's legs as Aisha picked up the speculum.

"Take a deep breath," she told Funmi, and she did, but she winced regardless. Funmi closed her eyes and Enitan could see that she was crying silently, twin tears sliding down her cheeks. She wanted to reach out, to hold her hand, but she had to keep the flashlight steady.

"Okay," said Aisha. "You're going to feel a sting." She unsheathed the injection and in the bad light, the needle looked frightening, long and thick, painful. Funmi gasped when the needle went in. Enitan's hands shook.

Aisha turned to her. "I need you to hold the flashlight steadily." Enitan nodded. She would concentrate. She would pray too, she decided. On an occasion such as this, it seemed necessary even though she knew God likely didn't approve of such procedures. Aisha worked quickly, methodically, even as the bleeding began almost immediately and she was quietly cursing to herself as she used the one silver instrument Enitan didn't recognize to fish the tissue out of Funmi's uterus, dropping the remains in a silver bowl. Funmi was sweating and grimacing. Enitan moved the flashlight where Aisha directed and tried not to look too closely. It felt like they were locked in that small room forever. At one point, the light did go out, but Aisha kept working anyway, and the torchlight was the only source of illumination, while they waited for the generator to judder on. Enitan held on to the flashlight with all her might. A hum from the generator finally sounded and then a few moments later, the light came back on too. Aisha put down her tools, now dark with blood.

"We have to monitor her now," she said to Enitan. She had placed towels underneath Funmi and around her.

"I think it's best if she spends the night here, and I will come and check up on her early in the morning."

"I'll stay with her," Enitan said. There was no question of that. She didn't see how Funmi could possibly stand, let alone walk back to the dormitory without attracting suspicion. If there was a surprise dormitory inspection, they would both be in trouble, but they seemed far past the point of no return now. Aisha took off her gloves, putting them in a black nylon, and rinsed the instruments in the sink.

"I can see if I can get you a pillow and some blankets," she whispered to Enitan. It looked like Funmi had fallen asleep.

"She's going to wake up in quite some pain," she said. "It's good that she is getting some sleep now."

She left the room and Enitan sat down on the plastic chair. She suddenly felt so tired; all the adrenaline had left her body. The room smelled of something animal, flesh and sweat and blood. She looked over at Funmi, whose eyes were now open. Enitan got up and placed her hand on Funmi's forehead; it was damp with sweat.

"How are you feeling?"

Funmi groaned. Then she let out a feeble laugh. "How the tables have turned."

"We do seem to have a penchant for calamity."

"Penchant for calamity, you sound like Zainab. That is one way to put it." Then, softer, "Thank you."

Enitan nodded. "Of course."

"Are you going to stay with me the whole night?"

"Of course."

She moved the chair closer to Funmi's bed.

"I'm going to stay right here," Enitan said. And she did.

CHAPTER 23

Funmi

October 1984

FUNMI AVOIDED DAMOLA IN THE IMMEDIATE aftermath of her recovery. Aisha had told her that Damola would understand, that Funmi should have told him from the very beginning, but Funmi refused. She had seen the way Ousmane and some of the other more obnoxious activists reacted when they found out a classmate their year had become pregnant. They had told dirty jokes, mocked her inability to keep her legs closed. Their radical politics didn't extend to the women they indiscriminately slept with apparently. Damola had told them to stop, but it didn't make a difference if they decided to reserve the worst of their commentary for when Funmi and Damola weren't there. She only had to imagine the conversations. It was bad enough that the others didn't seem to understand why she attended their meetings half the time. She had done a crash course of study in Marxist theory with Aisha, had volunteered to participate in various protests they had mounted, but she could not shake the feeling that everyone thought she was there because Damola had decided he wanted to sleep with her. And wasn't that the truth ultimately?

She looked forward to meeting Damola. It was the highlight of her week. It wasn't just the excitement of finally being with him, this person she had hungered for, who had given himself to her. It was the clandestine nature of the meetings in and of themselves. Being outside at night, the only illumination coming from the moon—the nocturnal sounds her ears were now attuned to hear, the insects and the crickets, the occasional lone dog barking.

They fucked in his car after the other activists had dispersed for the night. They would play music as they fucked, Fela of course—Damola loved him, though Funmi was finally comfortable enough with Damola to admit that she found Fela's songs too long and repetitive. She liked the music by the South African pop group Brenda and the Big Dudes; she liked to sing "I'm your weekend, weekend special" to Damola as she rode him, and he tried not to laugh and come at the same time. They listened to King Sunny Ade too and highlife and Miriam Makeba's folk songs. They would fuck plaintively to her ballads, Funmi's hips arching backward on top of Damola's skinny knees, which she teased him for. Afterward, she would rest her head against his chest, listening to the vibrations of his voice as he talked to her about his aspirations, how he wanted to merge his art and activism, about the uselessness of the current administration, the curse that oil had brought to the country, the greed. She listened to him and admired his speech, the strength of his convictions, his certainty. She felt so narrowly focused in comparison. He dreamed of revolution, of wholesale change; she just wanted to get her degree so she could have a modicum of independence from her father and her aunt. When they saw each other on campus, they looked past each other, pretending they had no idea who the other person was; it only made their eventual weekly consummation that much sweeter. "You looked so sexy in this top today," he would tell her as he slowly peeled it off her.

Afterward, when she would sneak back to the hostel at dawn, pushing open the door Enitan had left slightly ajar for her, Funmi would lie in bed and think about the world she and Damola had created for themselves. Being with him felt outside all time and space and memory. She had never felt this way about anyone before. It frightened her.

Now when she saw Damola, she would turn and walk in the opposite direction. She knew that he would seek out her gaze. He slipped notes under her door that she took and threw away without opening. Aisha had reached out indirectly on his behalf, but Funmi rebuffed all exchanges.

It had become easier to avoid meetings at the dam anyway because the clinical portion of her nursing training had begun. Funmi spent weekdays at the teaching hospital now, learning how to draw blood, how to read blood pressure, how to intubate a patient should it be necessary. The training was long and tiring—good for Funmi to keep her mind preoccupied. She and Enitan spent more time together going to the hospital to do their shifts.

In the aftermath of that miserable night, Funmi was consumed not with shame exactly but a kind of deep embarrassment, a humiliation really, that she had become pregnant, though she knew rationally that it could happen even though he pulled out before he came. She never asked him to wear a condom and he never volunteered to.

She was walking out of the hospital entrance about a month after the procedure when somebody horned at her, so loudly Funmi jumped. It was Damola. He was parked across the street. When he saw her continue walking, he got out of the car and hurried toward her. "I have to talk to you," he said. She kept walking. She had nothing to say to him. "Why are you avoiding me?" he asked her as she quickly picked up the pace, kicking up clouds of dust that clung to her standard-issue hospital pumps. She'd have to clean them thoroughly before her next shift.

The mosque was blaring its call to worship. A man leaning by the side of the wall took his plastic water kettle and began to perform ablutions.

Damola grabbed her arm. Funmi twisted it away. "Leave me alone!" she shouted.

"I know what you did!" Damola shouted back and because this was the first time she had ever heard him raise his voice, she stopped walking. "I wish you had let me help you," he said quietly. She was surprised at the relief she felt suddenly and powerfully coursing through her. It made her weak. Damola caught her as she slowly crumpled. He led her across the street, weaving between traffic, to his car. He sat her in the front seat.

"Aisha swore to me she would never tell you," she said after she finally felt strong enough to speak.

"Well, I am glad she did."

She turned to look at him. His light brown eyes looked like honey in the fading sun.

"You should have told me you were pregnant."

"For what? So you can call me an ashewo and make dirty jokes behind my back?"

"You know I would never do that."

Funmi said nothing. She leaned back against the seat. The muezzin had ceased his call. People were beginning to gather, headed toward the mosque. She closed her eyes and remembered with a sudden pang the last time she had lain in Damola's arms. He had asked her if she believed in God. She had been surprised by the question; they had not been talking about religion, they had been listening to "Malaika," a song that always made Funmi feel sad in a perfectly contented way.

She was going to say yes reflexively, and she did, but stopped herself to really think about her answer. She believed in God because it made more sense to her than the alternative—randomness, no meaning or purpose to the universe. But then she thought about how God had taken away her mother, the first person she had any conscious memory of, who had smelled of good things, of soap and hair oil and sweat, and had left Funmi with her father, so selfish, only obsessed with his latest conquest. Where was the justice in that?

For so much of Funmi's life, she had attempted to understand this early tragedy, to find the narrative in the events that had taken her from Port Harcourt to Kaduna, from her father's chosen pet to abandoned outcast, and she was realizing now with an immediacy that felt stifling, an awareness that made her face suddenly hot and trickles of sweat begin to accumulate underneath her arms—that there was no order, that she was truly alone, that the world, as it was, was a capricious place.

"I'm not sure," she told him then. "If there is a God, I'm not sure I understand Him."

"Can anyone?" asked Damola. He ran his fingers up and down her arm.

"Do you believe in God?"

"It shifts," he said. "Sometimes I do, sometimes I don't. When I am with you, though"—he kissed her temple—"I believe."

The heat that suffused her in that moment—and the terror—made her uneasy. She pulled herself off his chest, put on her pants, and pulled down her skirt.

"Why are you leaving so soon?"

"I have a test I have to study for," she lied. She had to get out of the car immediately; it felt so small, so confining.

Two weeks later, she found out she was pregnant.

THEY SAT IN HIS car, watching people enter the mosque in silence for a while. Then Damola turned to her. "Funmi," he said. "Funmi, I love you."

She felt something bubbling deep in the bottom of her stomach, her gut, which had been excavated, or at least that was what it had felt like, only a month prior. It was the urge to laugh and it came over her powerfully. She opened her mouth and she laughed; she could not stop. Damola's face morphed from confusion to concern as the force of the laughter overtook her. She was no longer emitting any noise, just hunched over in the corner of the front seat, head down, body convulsing. She felt his hand on her shoulder as the laughter turned to wracking sobs.

She sensed the doom in this proposition, the absurdity of what he had just said. Her parents had been in love, and what did that give them besides grief and heartache ultimately? Love had its limits. And what did Damola know of it anyway? Love existed in the romance novels she read and in the plays of the dead white men and the poetry she had grown up reciting in secondary school, but the sentiments they described were as alien to her as the language they used to describe it. She couldn't imagine herself having that much spare emotion for anyone else, driven to suicide over the death of a lover. And did he even really love her or was it the idea of her? The fact that she listened to him when he talked, that she let him enter her and that when he came his whole body shuddered, that sometimes she put his penis in her mouth and swallowed whatever came out of it, but did he know her? Did he care about her as a person outside of himself? She did not know the answers to these questions yet. She was only dimly aware that they were present and swirling around her. One day she would have to account for them somehow, but when that day would come she didn't know. For now, she could only give in, to the arms that were now hugging her, to the sentiments that had been uttered, to the hope and the optimism that had been presented to her. "I love you too," she told him. She would take it. She would try.

CHAPTER 24

Funmi

May 1986

DAMOLA HAD BEEN TALKING ABOUT THE march for months, one last hurrah before his graduation. It was supposed to be a denunciation of the rumored round of new austerity measures as well as a public commemoration of the brave students who had lost their lives protesting the austerity measures of 1978.

"It will be simple," said Damola during their biweekly dam meeting. He sprung up suddenly from his chair and began pacing as the other members watched him closely. "We'll march through the campus chanting the names of the students who were killed in 1978," he said. "And we'll make signs demanding fair wages for teachers and funding for our schoolbooks."

"But how can we be sure the administration won't react the way they did the last time . . . ?"

Aisha asked. Her voice trailed off, but of course, everyone knew what she was referring to. The vice chancellor had set paramilitary troops on students— seven of them died. The violence triggered protests at universities across the country. Not that Funmi had been aware of what was going on at the time. She had been too young and had never been one to pay attention to the news.

"They won't do anything," Damola said matter-of-factly. "It will be peaceful."

"How do you know?" Aisha asked.

"Why would they make the same mistake twice? All the negative publicity they got afterward. And what are we doing? Are we carrying guns?"

Aisha slowly shook her head.

"Then that settles it," he said.

Later, when Damola and Funmi were in his car, sticky with each other's sweat, he asked her what she thought about his plan.

"Well, you know I can't go," she said. "These shifts at the hospital are no joke."

"Yes, it's true."

"You're not nervous?"

"Why should I be nervous?"

"Come on, Damola. You're so close to graduating. Won't your parents be upset? And what happens if things get violent?"

"Then they get violent. But why should they?"

"Oh, Damola, be serious now. Don't be naïve."

"Naïve?" Damola suddenly sat up; Funmi's back dug into his steering wheel. She climbed over to the passenger's side while Damola cranked the driver's seat to its upright position.

"I upset you?" she asked.

"I'm not naïve," Damola said quietly. "If there's violence, there's violence. It's an unfortunate consequence of fighting for what is right. Our demands aren't radical."

"Of course not," Funmi said.

"Okay then. I understand if you can't come," he said.

She nodded. She wouldn't come.

FUNMI'S SHIFT WAS PARTICULARLY grueling the day of the protest. She had spent the night in Damola's car and trudged back to campus in the early dawn, luckily escaping the prying eyes of the night security guard who manned the gate that led into the women's dormitory. She lay in bed for an hour before she had to get up to bathe and change into her uniform. Cursing after she missed the first bus, she set out on foot toward the hospital, a thirty-minute walk that left her white tights stained with orange dust. Her nursing supervisor eyed Funmi suspiciously but said nothing. Then commenced a long day of trailing the senior nurses as they went from room to room. She took copious notes, made beds and washed hospital linens until her hands were dry and cracked.

At 4 p.m. sharp, she stood outside the hospital waiting for Damola to arrive. He told her that he would pick her up after the protest, which should have been over by now. It was supposed to have begun at 11 a.m., starting in the sculpture garden and then would make its way past the botanic garden and the drama village. Damola had even suggested going inside the lecture halls and dormitories, which seemed like asking for trouble, but what did Funmi know? All she knew was that Damola was supposed to come at four o'clock.

When fifteen minutes had passed, she took a danfo in the direction of the campus. Maybe in the excitement of the action, he had forgotten. She had exited the vehicle and was just rounding the turn that led to the main gate when she heard it. The faint pop of gunfire. And then screaming. She spun on her heels, unsure of where to turn. But then the mob of people running toward her made it clear. Trained from the various religious skirmishes that happened over the years not to question a mob, she ran back toward the hospital like she had never run in her life, the fear and the panic propelling her tired body forward.

She went straight to Aunty Buki's house and knocked on the door frantically. Aunty Buki opened the door, surprised to see her niece. Then she saw the commotion outside. "I'm not sure what's going on, Aunty. Please, I need to use your phone," said Funmi.

"Yes, of course," Aunty Buki said. She beckoned Funmi in and locked the front door behind her. The sounds of screaming were fainter here inside the brick house. With shaking hands, Funmi dialed Damola's dormitory number. There was no answer. Her heart began to beat wildly. With mounting fear, she tried Zainab at her father's house.

"Zainab, Zainab, are you on campus? What's going on? What's happening?"

"I'm not on campus," Zainab said. "But stay clear. The police are there, there was some shooting earlier. I'm not sure of all the details. Have you heard from Damola?"

"No," Funmi said quietly, and she hung up so she could try Damola's dormitory again. The line to the dormitory had been disconnected. Aunty Buki, in an attempt to be useful, set a cup of tea down in front of Funmi. Funmi nodded gratefully, but she knew she couldn't keep anything down right now. Her stomach was in violent knots. Something was wrong, something was clearly very wrong. She closed her eyes and willed Damola to call her, to appear on her doorstep apologetically with a bottle of groundnut as a gesture of goodwill.

. . .

OUSMANE CALLED FUNMI LATER that night to tell her what she already knew. He was gone. Over the next few days, the story would emerge. The students had begun their protests as Damola said they would, in the sculpture garden and the botanic garden. They had then made their way through the lecture halls and then controversially through the female dormitories, where men were strictly forbidden. They gathered in one of the common rooms, and for their trouble, the university sent the Mobile Police their way, men who were army trained and bloodthirsty, always looking for ways to humiliate yeye university students with their uppity airs and penchant for causing disturbances. The university said a volatile student threw something at the police, sparking the shooting frenzy. But this seemed unlikely because the protest had been peaceful and held in one of the common areas—not outside. How could students have acquired rocks to throw?

No matter how the uprising started, by the end of it at least twenty students were dead (the official reports said eight, but this simply wasn't true), their bodies slumped over in common rooms and dormitory hallways. Scores more were raped. The violence sparked a series of riots throughout the state. Students at the polytechnic attempted to burn down a police barracks. All of Kaduna was up in arms—outraged over the wasted lives. There was later an official investigation and a futile apology from the vice chancellor, who subsequently stepped down.

The burial was in Jos. She went with Aisha and Ousmane and the other students of their group. Ousmane drove Damola's car there—a tense five-hour drive. They met Damola's parents for the first and last time. They had no idea who she was of course, beyond a member of a group they had never approved of. Funmi had been surprised at how small and mild-mannered his parents were, how shrunken. And yet she could see the striking resemblance between Damola and his mother, right down to those honey-brown eyes, which were now constantly shining with tears. She saw the parents at the homegoing service, but they did not attend the actual burial because according to Yorùbá tradition, it is not right for a parent to see where their child is buried. Such a death upends the natural order of life.

CHAPTER 25

Zainab

November 1987

ZAINAB HAD BEEN A WIFE FOR SIX MONTHS, ONE week, and three days. It was a title she was still getting accustomed to. Occasionally, she would be rinsing rice or hanging clothes to dry in the courtyard and her eyes would alight on the ring on her right hand and she would stare at the hand as if it did not belong to her. Even now, as she stood in their kitchen, molding the mounds of dan wake she planned to boil, she would stop occasionally to admire the flash of gold on her ring finger. Already, this hand had been used for purposes hitherto unknown to her. It had guided Ahmed into her on their first night as husband and wife, even as—especially as—it hurt. It had smoothed Ahmed's furrowed brow as he graded student exams at their dining room table. And, now, lately, it reached for her stomach, soft but not yet full, budding with new life.

She was preparing lunch for Funmi, who was spending the weekend in Zaria. While Zainab had kept her promise about not doing her youth service after graduation, Funmi and Enitan had been conscripted—Funmi not too far away, in Bauchi, about a five-hour drive from Zaria, while Enitan had been stationed in a village in Edo State in the southwest part of the country, teaching maths at a school. While they still made sure to talk to each other when they could, once a week on Sundays, Zainab felt Enitan's absence profoundly.

Funmi had called to say that she had a free weekend coming up and would be spending it in Kaduna, and so Zainab invited her over for lunch. Ahmed was in Kano for the week, visiting extended family. It was the first time Zainab had been properly alone since she had married. She had gotten up early, thinking that maybe she would write, but she had sat at the dining room table, pen in hand, drawing concentric circles as she thought of baby names she would not be allowed to call her child. The firstborn was always named after the paternal grandfather if he was a boy, and after the maternal grandmother if she was a girl.

Zainab had just finished setting the table when Funmi knocked on the door.

"Coming," Zainab called out as she opened the door.

"It smells good in here," Funmi said by way

of greeting, stepping inside the flat, her combat boots kicking up a maelstrom of dust, which Zainab made a mental note to clean later. Funmi stomped into the living room, then the kitchen, then craned her neck to see down the hallway, Zainab trailing her. She had moved into Ahmed's flat when they married, but they were planning on finding a bigger place soon. This was not a space designed for a growing family. Zainab gestured Funmi over to the dining room table. "Can I offer you a soft drink?"

"Yes, Fanta, please," Funmi said. Zainab came back from the kitchen with an open bottle and a glass. Funmi put the glass on the table and took the bottle from Zainab. She drank long and lustily. Zainab watched, amused.

"Did you run here?"

Funmi sucked her teeth, then belched for good measure.

"Goodness gracious," Zainab said, sitting down at the table.

"Ahn-ahn? I can't burp among friends? Na wa o."

Zainab rolled her eyes. "How was the drive?"

"It was fine. I took the bus." Funmi looked again at the bottle and then finished it. She placed it back on the table, where Zainab was certain a water stain would grow.

"You know Damola used to say we were like Coke and Fanta."

"Oh, really?" Zainab said. She was surprised. Funmi didn't talk about Damola often.

Those first few months after his murder had been brutal for all of them, no exception for Zainab. Though they had drifted apart since their romantic relationship had ended, she still thought of him fondly and had been gutted to hear of his death. But she recognized that her grief did not compare to Funmi's. Zainab had expected impulsive weeping, hysteria, anger, eruptions. Instead, Funmi became very quiet, which in some ways unnerved Zainab more. She did not smile, did not laugh, had no sassy retorts. She lost weight. The old Funmi only began to make appearances during their last year of university. She had teased Enitan for crying on their graduation day and had bragged about how she would demolish all the other corpers during the physical fitness portion of their orientation.

"I don't even remember why he brought it up. I think he used to say that's what he thought when he saw us together on campus," continued Funmi. "But now whenever I drink Fanta I think of him." She laughed then, a short, bitter thing. "Isn't that stupid?"

"I don't think it's stupid at all," said Zainab softly. They were quiet until Funmi asked where the food was. Zainab went to the kitchen and brought out the dan wake and boiled eggs, the tuwo shinkafa with miyan taushe. She placed a bowl of warm water in front of Funmi so she could rinse her hands. She watched with satisfaction as Funmi began eating hungrily.

"They don't feed you in Bauchi?"

Funmi rolled her eyes, her hand slick with palm oil.

"So what's up?" Zainab asked a moment later. "Have you heard from that guy? What was his name? The one who said he wanted to marry you?"

"Yinka," Funmi replied, her mouth full of soup. She had been doing her clinical shift at the hospital when the March 1987 religious riots had begun; Enitan and Zainab had already taken refuge in Zainab's father's compound. Holding his mysteriously acquired Russian handgun, Zainab's father had strolled the perimeter of the courtyard while smoke from burning buildings—churches mostly—hung in the air like thick, unmoving clouds. Zaria would continue to smell like fire for many days afterward; the university's grand chapel would have to be rebuilt. That was the result of a wave of cheap and senseless violence that was permeating the region more and more, with tensions between fundamentalist Muslims and Christians reaching a fever pitch as so many young, unemployed men with too much energy were happy to wield their power in destructive ways.

While Zainab and Enitan had fretted over what was happening outside, Funmi had apparently met some young army commander who lived in Lagos and had been sent to Kaduna to help stanch the violence and had gotten his hand cut and was waiting for treatment at the hospital. "He said he wants to marry me," Funmi had told them wryly some weeks later when Funmi had visited Enitan and Zainab at Zainab's compound. Enitan and Zainab had joked about him afterward, every so often reminding Funmi about her husband. But then Funmi had surprised them by saying that he had called Aunty Buki's house a few times. So there was some interest there, perhaps.

"And has Enitan told you about her oyinbo friend?" Zainab asked.

"Charles?" Funmi laughed and sucked the meat off a piece of bone. "Of course not."

They both began chuckling. It was exciting for Enitan that she had potentially met someone, though Zainab doubted it would go far. Enitan hadn't been very revealing on the phone; she had just mentioned that the only other teacher at the school besides her fellow corper was an American man a few years older than them. Instantly, Zainab had begun to tease Enitan about it. "You like him, abi?" she would ask, and she could hear Enitan squirming over the phone, she swore it. But Enitan would never give a satisfactory answer.

"We should go and visit her as a surprise," Funmi said.

"Yes!" Zainab had never been to Edo. Her hand reached instinctively for her belly. There was time to plan a trip, plenty of time.

"And how's Prof?" Funmi asked.

Zainab smiled. "He's wonderful."

"In bed as well or—"

"For goodness' sake!"

"What? I can't be curious?" Funmi winked and laughed wickedly.

"Actually . . ." Zainab began, but then she felt shy. She knew it was so early. But she wanted to share the news. "I'm pregnant."

Funmi shifted in her seat. Her eyes had unexpectedly clouded over. "Congratulations," she said. "How many weeks?"

"Six. It's still very, very early. But I've been dying to tell someone. You're the only one who knows besides Ahmed, of course."

"You haven't told Enitan?"

"Not yet. I was going to wait until our next phone call."

"Well, I'm flattered," said Funmi, though she did not sound flattered. When she seemed to register that Zainab was not thrilled about her lack of excitement, Funmi said again in a more cheerful tone, "Seriously speaking, congratulations! You will be a wonderful mother."

"Thank you." Zainab smiled at Funmi. Funmi smiled back, though it was tight-lipped and pained.

"There's no need to lie," Zainab said, growing irritated. "If you have something to say, just say it."

"Ahn-ahn! I said I was happy for you."

"But you clearly seem upset!"

"Not everything is about you!" Funmi got up.

"What is it, then?"

"Abeg, no waste time," she muttered, heading toward the front door.

"Why are you leaving?"

Funmi spun on her heels to face Zainab, her eyes lit with fury.

"You know I was pregnant once? With Damola's child. Aisha helped me get rid of it. It was the right decision. But I can be upset. So leave me alone!"

"Oh, Funmi, I'm so sorry. I didn't know." She put her hand on Funmi's shoulder.

Funmi shrugged the hand off and her face closed in on itself. "It's in the past." She paused. "I didn't want to tell you because I didn't know how you would react. It happened more than three years ago now. Enitan went with me."

Zainab nodded. She was calculating the timeline of when this would have occurred. She felt embarrassed suddenly.

"Please, Funmi, don't go. Sit down and finish eating."

Funmi stared at Zainab for a long time.

"All right," she finally said, and she let Zainab lead her back to the dining room table.

CHAPTER 26

Enitan

January 1988

I HAVE A SURPRISE FOR YOU."

Enitan felt her cheeks grow hot at the sound of Charles's voice.

She smiled in his general direction, still finding it difficult to look him directly in the eyes. They always held a look of sustained interest that made her squirm under the intensity of his steady gaze. He had caught her arm as she was walking past him toward the other classroom, pulling her close enough to him that his chin grazed her hair. "Come to my place tonight," he whispered. She hurried away from him, mortified that the other students might see them and suspect something. The girls were already entirely too inquisitive, asking her why she wasn't married yet and giggling to themselves about Mister Charles.

All day, as she made students recite their

multiplication tables and gave them short assignments on the little chalkboards purchased by the missionaries, she remembered the electric current that had run through her body when he had pulled her toward him. She had never been that close to a man before. He had smelled like powder detergent and red clay. His houseboy must have just done his laundry.

The six months she had spent in this village, a three-hour drive from Benin City, had not been easy ones. She found it difficult to get along with her fellow corper, Ruth, an Igbo girl from Anambra State who was engaged and spent every waking moment, so it seemed, figuring out how to communicate with her boyfriend who was stationed somewhere in Jos. Enitan's mother had been so thrilled to learn that she was going to be in Edo State, and not too far from Benin City where there were many Cele churches. Both Ruth and Enitan taught at the three-room schoolhouse built by English missionaries back in the 1920s. Enitan taught maths, Ruth taught science, and Charles, an American Peace Corps volunteer, taught English. She noticed him immediately; he was the first white man she had ever really been in close contact with. He made a point of talking to her, just pleasantries at first. Where was she from? Where had she gone to school? He had been interested in the fact that she had gone to the university in Zaria; he wanted to know more about the northern part of the country. He had asked her what food she missed most from there and she had told him about kilishi.

She found his attention bewildering and flattering. She ignored Ruth's curt summation: "It's because you're the only single girl here." No, there was evidently something about her that he liked. And she liked how he perceived her—as this smart, alluring, competent, and thoughtful woman.

That night as soon as it was dark, and she was assured that Ruth was still at the schoolhouse talking to her boyfriend on the school's landline, Enitan grabbed her flashlight and went over to Charles's place. She knew where he lived, because all oyinbo people who cycled through the village were habituated in the one building with an indoor toilet. That too had been built by missionaries.

The door was slightly open and a prism of weak kerosene light hit the step that led into the house. She pushed open the door. "Mosquitoes will get in," she announced as she entered.

"What was that?" Charles said, coming toward her, holding wrapped newspaper in his hands. It was hard to see his face in the dull light; he was mainly just a hulking shadow, but she was sweating now anyway, knowing that he was looking at her.

"The door, you should not leave it open. Mosquitoes will come in."

"Come here," he said, moving closer to her.

She could smell it suddenly, that familiar peppery smell.

"Is that kilishi?" she asked, unable to mask her excitement at the thought.

Charles nodded. "I told you I had a surprise."

They unwrapped the newspaper in the kitchen, not bothering to get plates. He pulled a bottle of bitter lemon (for her) and Vitamalt (for him) out of his cooler. She had been surprised when he told her how much he loved malt. It was not a drink oyinbo people tended to love, even Enitan herself did not care for it much. He did not have a bottle opener so Enitan opened both bottles using her back teeth. Charles had stared at her after she'd handed his bottle back to him, a look of astonishment mixed with admiration on his face. "I think I'm in love," he told her, putting his hand over his heart. Enitan laughed nervously. She knew he was joking, but her pulse had quickened when he said it.

They sat at his kitchen table and Charles told her about his childhood. He had grown up the youngest of three, and the only boy, born to a lawyer father and a homemaker mother with family money that disappeared after a series of disastrous business decisions his father made with his wife's money. That set the central tension in motion: his mother resented his father; his father was ashamed. They finally divorced when his older sisters went off to college; before then his mother simply stewed while his father drank and made a fool out of himself, as Charles put it. Charles tried to find escape where he could.

That escape turned out to be in books. Adventure books mostly when he was growing up; he loved Jack London and the Hardy Boys and Sherlock Holmes mystery novels. They offered him a respite from the tight-lipped, repressed dysfunction of his family life; his older sisters coped by doing cocaine and speed at parties they took the train into the city to attend.

Both sisters would finally sober up after their father's stage four cancer diagnosis. One transferred to a state school where she got an accounting degree, married a classmate, and was now pregnant with her second child; the other had gone back to get her postbaccalaureate, was in med school now, and engaged.

While his sisters were beautiful in a distinctly New England way (ruddy-cheeked, slim apple-shaped figures), Charles was an awkward adolescent, with flaming-red hair and pale skin. He didn't have much luck with girls, but he had won a few writing competitions, which validated his early reading obsession. An English teacher put him on Hemingway and it was then that he really fell in love with the writer's life. In fact, it was "The Snows of Kilimanjaro" that had first put the idea of Africa in his mind. That Hemingway had, at best, only a marginal relationship with the people who inhabited the continent, that so much of his bravado around hunting wild game was predicated on the idea that the humans who lived in these places were only useful as minor figures, the boys who gather brush for poor doomed Harry, sliding in and out of the main white characters' domestic drama, well, Charles didn't know any better at the time.

Like so many white boys, he confessed to Enitan, blushing, though Enitan had never read Hemingway, had heard of him only vaguely—he became obsessed with the mythos of Hemingway and the Africa that he loved, with those animals and that landscape, Africa as a battlefield, Africa as a stage for white men to display their masculine prowess. He loved **Heart of Darkness** too, with an intensity that he still couldn't shake, a lot of colonial literature as well, and the depraved, bleak settings depicted by writers like J. M. Coetzee. In university, he finally expanded his repertoire, encountered Chinua Achebe for the first time, read Africanist critiques of Hemingway and the like. But that tendency to romanticize Africa was in his blood. **Out of Africa** was his mother's favorite movie—had Enitan seen it? It had come out a few years ago, it was based on a book. His mother had seen it in theaters five times. She would watch the VHS incessantly after his father's death; she loved the scene everyone loves, where Robert Redford washes Meryl Streep's hair. Enitan told him she had never seen this movie. And Charles had been momentarily taken aback at that admission, but then of course he corrected himself, why would **she** see the film, what story could it possibly have to offer the average Nigerian? Is it a love story? Enitan asked him, seeking clarification. Yes, Charles said. There are love stories here, she told him. Sure, sure, Charles said, but the point he was trying to make was that Western art about Africa fixated on the wildlife, on the imagined darkness on the continent, and much of Charles's early obsessions with Africa were admittedly part of this bent.

The first time they slept together had been in the middle of a Saturday afternoon. Charles had dismissed the houseboy he had been given for the day. He had never become entirely comfortable with the concept of someone else doing his cooking, his cleaning, washing his clothes, even though his family had once had money. "It just feels shitty, Eni," he said. And Enitan had wondered at that phrase; she had never heard "shit" used or described in that way before. Enitan had come over and Charles had suggested that they make puff puff. He loved the name; he thought it was adorable. Every time she said it, he would laugh. "Amazing all the names various cultures have for fried dough. The French have beignets. We have donuts. And in Nigeria, you have puff puff!"

"We have donuts too," Enitan told him. (She would miss jam donuts in particular; the American version was too sweet.) Enitan's mother had given Enitan a recipe for puff puff, but even though Enitan had tried it out many times, she had never been able to make good-looking puff puff. Something always went wrong when she tried to fry them. Sometimes the oil wasn't hot enough, so the puff puff soaked up too much of it. Other times she was unable to duplicate the perfectly shaped golden-brown spheres her mother could make. Enitan warned Charles that she was not a good cook and Charles had said they could be bad cooks together. They had just set aside the dough, wrapping cling film over the bowl and placing it outside on the verandah so the dough could rise.

"We will have to wait an hour," Enitan said.

"I can think of something we can do for an hour," Charles had replied. He had kissed her then, gently, first on the cheek and then on the lips. She froze, self-conscious, completely caught off guard. He had no way of knowing this was her first kiss. He pulled away from her. "You are so unbelievably sexy," he told her, and she laughed because it was objectively an absurd assertion to make. She had never been sexy and she would never be sexy. But how thrilling to hear herself described that way, regardless. She hadn't realized how much she desired to be desired, hadn't dared to think that this was a possibility for her. He kissed her again, hungrily this time, probing open her mouth with his tongue; her hands wrapped around his neck, noting the hair that was there. He carried her into his bedroom, just a twin mattress, his shoes on a raffia cloth by the door, his clothes hanging on a rod that had been newly installed. He laid her down. She did not tell him that she had never done anything like this before, had never kissed anyone, had never had anyone put his mouth **there,** as he did, or enter her the way the way he did, or kiss her gently afterward the way he did. And suddenly her world was open to new possibilities.

THE DAY ENITAN LEFT Nigeria, she contracted diarrhea. She and Charles were taking a late flight, one that left Lagos just before midnight, with a layover in London and then another flight from there to New York. It would be Enitan's first time on a plane. Her first time ever leaving the country. She had gotten her passport and visa just two months before. The school's driver, Samuel, had driven her to Lagos for the interviews. It had all gone so smoothly, such a marked contrast from the usual horror stories of curt embassy employees who—based on what they had eaten that morning or how well they had slept—would perfunctorily crush years of preparation, disintegrating hopes and dreams with one red-ink stamp: DENIED. That Enitan had been able to secure both her passport and visa so quickly made her feel anxious—she was waiting for the other shoe to drop.

Samuel drove them to Lagos for their trip. He was a highly religious man and had already communicated his reservations to Enitan wordlessly, with expressions of disapproval he did not bother disguising when he dropped them off at the hotel they planned to stay in for two days before they left Nigeria for good. Charles wanted to spend some time in Lagos so they could sightsee. Enitan was less enthused. She did not want to sit in traffic all day and the city overwhelmed her. "Think of it as our pre-honeymoon," Charles told her. He was giddy in the way he must have been as a young boy, looking at her as they drove, though she pretended not to notice, her face mashed against the window. "I'm so lucky," he whispered, taking her hand and kissing it. Enitan noticed Samuel's icy glare in the rearview mirror. He dropped his gaze when he saw her looking at him and she moved her hand away. It was Charles's last year in the Peace Corps when they had met; whatever they had been doing was not supposed to have lasted this long, was not supposed to have had this much meaning. What was the point if he was going back to the U.S. before the year ended?

But then he asked her to marry him, so casually

that at first Enitan hadn't thought he was serious. She laughed and looked at him, his skin still slick with sweat, the bed damp from lovemaking, the smell of roadside fire filtering in through the open window. She had told him that he needed to get the screen fixed; he kept telling her he would and yet the mesh screen would lean against the wall under the window for the rest of his time in Nigeria—creating ideal conditions for mosquitoes to fly in unimpeded. (And sure enough, three weeks after they landed in New York, Enitan got malaria, and though she insisted to the unbelieving doctors that this was what she had, they placed her in an isolation unit anyway, believing she had meningitis. In between fevered dreams, she watched young doctors, medical residents, she assumed, gawk at her through glass as the attending physician described her symptoms. That would be the first but certainly not the last time she realized the value of her words and her nursing degree in America—practically worthless.)

"Get married? Don't be a cliché," she said to Charles.

"A cliché in what sense?"

"Asking me to marry you after we've just fucked." She relished saying that word. It was a deliberate act of rebellion that her mother was not present to witness, but she felt an illicit thrill regardless. Charles always found it funny when she said it; he'd repeat it in a crude approximation of her Nigerian accent. "Fock," he'd say, and he'd laugh, kissing her forehead when she playfully frowned.

He laughed again that night as well, and then pulled her close to him, throwing his long limbs over her own, his feet like ice against her (his body was always cold; it was remarkable even in the humidity). He covered her with kisses: at her temple, on her nose, her lips. She liked it when he did this too, when he held her so tightly, she could hardly breathe, when his full weight was on top of her. It anchored her. She reveled in the security it gave her—that feeling of someone pinning her to the earth, to the mattress, it was a physical embodiment of what it meant to be grounded.

"I'm serious," he murmured into her hair, and then he pulled her apart from him again so he could look at her face. "I'm serious," he said once more. "Marry me." And she had looked at him then.

She thought of the stories he had told her of his childhood in Connecticut; she had struggled to say the word and she had asked him to spell it for her and he had written the state's name on a piece of paper. This was before they had even so much as kissed, when he seemed to always be finding ways to keep talking to her at the schoolhouse. He had written **Connecticut** in blue ink on a torn piece of paper and she had later saved that paper, had examined it in the corper's hostel. Even in the dark when she could no longer read what he had scrawled on there, she would look at it, trying to imagine a young, unhappy Charles.

When he graduated university, he took to heart the advice of an early mentor, who told him to volunteer or teach abroad, to do something that would get him out of New England, to actually work before considering grad school or publishing the short story collection he had written as his thesis. And so he applied for the Peace Corps, knowing only that he wanted to be somewhere on the continent. His mother was awfully frightened about the decision; she had downsized, sold the house, and moved to a part of Connecticut where there were more "Afro-Americans," and though she would never say this outright, they frightened her. That Charles was volunteering to go right to their ancestral homeland made her frantic. "Only think how shocked she'll be when she meets you," Charles had told Enitan with satisfaction, and Enitan had said nothing then, even though it made her uneasy. After all, she knew what it was like to want to thwart a mother. She had done the same thing.

She had visited her mother for the last time, shortly before Charles proposed, and as she had drearily come to expect, the visit had not gone well. Sharon berated her for not calling more often and insisted that she go to church with her. When Enitan refused, Sharon began praying out loud in front of her, a habit she had picked up that Enitan found especially annoying. Passive-aggressive entreaties for God to help her with her child, to bring out the demon of disobedience that lived within her. Enitan had cut the trip short and taken a bus back to Edo a day later. Her ears still rang from her mother's insults. "Ṣé, you don't love your mother anymore? You're ashamed ehn? All this university education has gone to your head? You know I went to university too? I read mathematics—I was going to study abroad in London." It was the closest hint Enitan had ever gotten about her father's identity.

"What happened?" Enitan asked her.

"What happened?" she was shouting now, but it didn't matter, her mother's face clenched in on itself. She didn't need to say anything. Enitan could fill in the blank herself. She was born and she had ruined her mother's life and the early, all-consuming, oppressive love Sharon had for her daughter had curdled into something sour, harder-edged. Now Enitan was a failure, up and only until she was willing to do exactly as her mother desired.

"Fuck this," Enitan had muttered under her breath, zipping up the carry-on she had barely unpacked and marching off to the bus station.

When Charles left the States for Nigeria, it was a fuck-you of his own sort to his mother, his sisters, his unhappy New England life. He arrived in Lagos with a stunning amount of ignorance about the nation. He had done some preliminary reading but not nearly enough. He was taken aback at how unlikely he was to see an elephant roaming down the street. He quickly learned that there were no mountains in this country, not really, not magnificent ones like in Kenya. But then there were the people whom he met, the students with their zeal for learning and their curiosity and their determination even amid all the poverty. It was inspiring, it was moving, it made him look at all the benefits of his own childhood all the more harshly. His four-year-old niece was so spoiled compared to the children here. Children back home had so much material advantage and still they complained, they were uninterested in their schoolwork, they didn't seem to understand how desperate kids their own age were to learn. In Nigeria, education was everything, everything—parents would do anything to secure a good education for their children and there was something so pure, so noble in their efforts.

He loved the country, would want to return perhaps, but now he had a novel to write and, using his share of his father's life insurance money, he planned to live in New York, renting a cheap apartment in Brooklyn and working on his novel during the day, maybe bartending at night—it wouldn't be financially necessary, at least not for a year or so, the payout was large enough, but bartending would be a good way to meet interesting people to populate his novel and short stories. Enitan could live with him; she'd love New York; it was a fascinating place. Had she ever dreamed of going to America?

And Enitan had had to confess that no, she did not think much about America. It was a blank space in her imagination, a place where white people lived and where the TV shows were made. Before her mother had sold off the TV, they would watch **The Beverly Hillbillies** when it came on air, and at Zainab's house they watched the cartoons and some of the movies, **Jaws** and **Alien** on VHS. America was a place where disaster always seemed to be happening; their movies were always violent; someone was always bleeding to death or covered in blood, missing eyes and arms and limbs.

When Charles asked her to marry him, when he confirmed that he was serious, she began to wonder about America again; she began to think about the country with curiosity, recalling the stories Charles told her about New York, about skyscrapers and escalators, fields of green in Central Park—it appealed to her, it did. And then there was the tantalizing option of escape—she wasn't sure what she would do after her months as a corper were over; there were no nursing jobs in this village, which had no hospital, and she was not married like Zainab. It would not be easy to find work, not with all the austerity measures the government had been forced to impose as a condition of the loans the IMF and the World Bank had offered, conditions that would plunge the nation into a prolonged recession.

Zainab had expressed her disapproval the last time Enitan had spoken to her three months before she would leave Nigeria. She called both Funmi and Zainab weekly on Sunday afternoons in the school office.

The last time they had spoken, Zainab had announced her pregnancy. She was certain of it; they had not even been trying but it had happened sha. She had horrible morning sickness but hoped she would have a girl. Enitan had been briefly startled at the news, thinking of how quickly Zainab seemed to be hurtling toward the traditional markers of adulthood at only nineteen.

"And how are you?" Zainab asked Enitan after Enitan had congratulated her.

"I'm fine," Enitan said. She hesitated for a moment, unsure of how to broach the topic of Charles's proposal, unsure if she should even broach the topic at all. There was a tone that Zainab tended to take when Enitan talked about Charles. It wasn't quite accurate to call it condescension, but it was a kindred attitude, as if the past few months of marriage had suddenly conferred upon Zainab a wisdom and knowingness about the world Enitan was not privy to. The tone irritated Enitan. Zainab was not the only person having sex now.

"How is Charles?"

She heard it then, in the blithe, almost-dismissive way Zainab said his name.

"He's asked me to marry him."

"**Marry** him? What? How long have you two even been talking? You are sure he is serious?"

"Of course he is serious."

There was silence on the line for a moment, just the sound of the static-filled connection.

"Hello?" Enitan asked.

"I'm still on the line."

"And so? What do you think?"

"I think it's a horrible idea. Have you really thought this through? Where will you live? Have you talked to your mum?"

Now it was Enitan's turn to be silent. The questions offended her, even though she had naturally contemplated them.

"You can't really trust these oyinbo men, Enitan. My father always says they are fickle. They change their minds at any opportunity. What if you marry him and he leaves you? What will you do then?" Zainab began to relay in detail the story of one of her husband's associates at the university who had married an oyinbo man against her family's wishes, how her family had cut her off completely. Enitan stopped listening. She was surprised at the degree of her anger, how quickly it had increased. Zainab didn't understand. She and Funmi had always had luck with boys: all the letters Zainab had fielded, all the double takes Funmi attracted. Boys were always following them around like lovesick puppies—until Charles, none of them had been interested in Enitan.

After Zainab finished speaking Enitan said, "Okay," and hung up. She didn't call Funmi that weekend. She didn't want to deal with the possibility of more advice, more questions that didn't square with the decision she realized she had already made. On Monday afternoon, while her junior students were eating lunch in the courtyard, she got a call from Funmi. There was no preamble or introduction.

"Zainab says the oyinbo man asked you to marry him?"

"Hello to you too."

"So are you going to marry him?" Funmi asked.

Enitan was silent.

"I suppose you must do what you have to do," said Funmi as if Enitan had answered. "I suppose I would do the same thing," Funmi added, and then she said, "I know you have to go. Goodbye." She hung up the phone before Enitan could say anything further.

THEY BOUGHT SUYA FOR their last supper, as Charles dramatically (and somewhat blasphemously, Enitan thought) put it. If she had known then just how much she would miss Nigerian food in the coming years, she would have forced them to go to a buka as well and to gorge themselves on pounded yam and efo. And then consume polythene bags full of oranges and starfruit, guava and mango. How she would miss oranges in particular; she would never adjust to the gaping discrepancy between appearance and taste in America. In New York, the oranges were big and round, so healthy looking, and yet when you bit into a wedge, the flavor did not explode across the tongue the way it was supposed to. How she would long to go to the market not far from her mother's house in Abeokuta to buy an orange for fifty naira from the row of fruit sellers, solemnly peeling orange skins that fell at their feet in perfectly shaped spirals.

Before they ate suya they had gone to the beach and walked for a long time, watching young men ride horses, their hoofs whipping up tiny whirls of sand. Enitan had dabbed her toes in the water though she was petrified of the ocean; the idea of swimming in it terrified her and it was not clean. After the beach they had gone to the hotel and asked the concierge to buy them good suya. Enitan had insisted he would have a better handle on what suya was safe to consume. But when she felt the rumblings in her stomach later on, as they packed their things and sat down in the car that would take them to the airport, she wondered if he had chosen wrong.

"You okay?" Charles asked her, as she concentrated on keeping the contents of her stomach inside her body amid every sudden bump or lurch on the road to the airport, the city strangely still and silent because it was so late. She only nodded, grasped his hands. She had told him about Zainab and Funmi, and he had asked her if she wanted to see them before she left; they could fly to Kaduna, he would pay for the tickets. She said no. If she was going to do this thing, she would have to do it now. She worried that seeing them would make her reconsider.

When she and Charles boarded the plane, and it was clear that she was going to be sitting by the window, she realized with mortification that she would have to be getting up to use the toilet throughout the flight, but it was too late now. They sank back in their seats, her stomach flip-flopped, the plane began to accelerate, Enitan gripped Charles's hand with a force she did not know she was capable of, and then suddenly they were in the air and she could see Lagos below her, specks of lights amid great stretches of blackness before them, and Enitan kept thinking about how she was on her way to America and she had not told Funmi or Zainab and she wondered now if this pain she was feeling in the pit of her stomach was a symptom of that loss.

CHAPTER 27

Funmi

IT HAD BEEN FUNMI'S IDEA FOR THEM TO GO to Lagos. She had heard Zainab on the phone, how listless she had sounded, devoid of all emotion. You can try again, Funmi thought impatiently. You are young. But a loss was a loss; a wanted baby had not materialized, though all the evidence had been there; the belly had grown, the hips had widened. Zainab was devastated. So when Yinka had offered to fly Funmi down to Lagos to visit him, she was suddenly willing to test the degree of his interest in her. "Can I bring a friend?" she had asked him from the Nitel phone booth where she would go each Sunday to check messages on Aunty Buki's landline while in Bauchi.

"Of course," Yinka had said smoothly, not a trace of hesitation to be heard. Quickly, arrangements were made. Funmi would meet Zainab in Kaduna. Ahmed would drive them to the airport and they would both take their first airplane ever to visit Lagos, where Yinka would put them up in his guesthouse. Zainab rallied admirably, Funmi thought. When they arrived at the airport, Yinka's driver was waiting for them, and he whisked them away to Ikoyi. Yinka took them out for dinner that evening, a ritzy restaurant where the women wore sleek, elegant dresses and lipstick, and the men dress shirts that they sweated through. Yinka was attentive to Zainab, expressing his condolences for her loss, asking her questions about Ahmed's studies and her own playwriting—surprising Funmi with his fastidiousness. In the car ride back, she told Zainab that she would have the guest room to herself that night.

All week, they lounged. They went horseback riding at Bar Beach, which had been scary and also exhilarating. On Wednesday, Funmi began to feel restless. It felt strange to be enjoying these luxuries without Enitan there.

"Remember when we said we were going to visit her? This is the time to do it," Funmi told Zainab.

"How will we get there?"

"Yinka now."

He was a piece of swallow in her hands—flexible, amenable. They had never been to Benin City either. The drive took five hours as they made their way on awful roads, cratered by heavy rainfall. They spent the night in Benin City and then made the three-hour drive to the village the next morning.

Funmi instructed the driver to pull up to the schoolhouse. It was just around lunchtime, and students sat on their haunches outside in their dusty school uniforms, eating from giant communal bowls of rice. They eyed Funmi and Zainab with curiosity as they got out of the car and walked up the steps that led to the schoolhouse, not sure which of the three rooms they should enter.

"Can I help you?" asked a young woman wearing a long-sleeved dress, her hair hidden under a purple hijab, her Hausa accent unmistakable.

"We're looking for Enitan Adesina. She's a corper stationed here," said Funmi.

"Enitan?" said the woman hesitantly. "Oh, she must be the old corper. She left."

"Left?" Both Funmi and Zainab said this at the same time.

"But she had some months remaining," said Funmi. "Where did she go?"

"Miss Adesina?" This was a student now, a teenage girl with close-cropped hair, sitting in a huddle of other girls on cement bricks.

"Miss Adesina is in America."

"What?"

"Yes o. She and Mister Charles," said another student. The other girls giggled conspiratorially when she said that.

"What?" Funmi said again.

"Please, do you have a landline?" Zainab asked. "We have got to make a phone call."

"The phone is only to be used for emergencies," said the new corper slowly, but Funmi cut her a ferocious look. "Please, only for a moment," Zainab added. The corper reluctantly led them to the school office. Zainab took out her address book from her purse and found Aunty Sharon's number. She dialed and Aunty Sharon picked up immediately.

"So you have finally saw fit to call your own mother!" Sharon shouted, loudly enough that Funmi could hear everything she was saying clearly.

"No, Aunty, it's me, Zainab."

Sharon's tone shifted, but only slightly, Funmi thought, considering the circumstances. "Have you heard from her? Has she told you where she is?"

"No, that is what we're trying to figure out. We're at her school. We were going to surprise her . . ."

"She's gone!" interrupted Sharon indignantly, shouting so loudly Zainab momentarily had to pull the phone away from her ear.

"Hold on," said Zainab. "Aunty, gone where?"

"New York! She called me from the airport to say she was going and then called me again yesterday to say she landed. Can you just imagine? What kind of wickedness is this? To leave the country without even consulting me first? To marry and not even tell your own mother? I have been praying to God every night asking for His wisdom, seeking His counsel. Why He would permit such a thing I do not know."

Zainab was too stunned to continue listening. She handed the phone wordlessly to Funmi.

Funmi placed the phone to her ear. Aunty Sharon was in the middle of a speech or a prayer, it was difficult to tell.

"That the Devil would possess my daughter . . ." Funmi tuned Aunty Sharon out. So Enitan had gone and married this oyinbo man without telling them. She wondered about the urgency Enitan must have felt that she had taken flight so quickly. Zainab was fuming.

"Unbelievable," Zainab said.

Funmi shrugged. "She had to do what she had to do."

"What she had to do? What she had to do?" Zainab repeated, her anger growing by the minute. "We haven't even met the man! We know nothing about him!" She was shouting now; some curious students had tiptoed toward the window and were leaning in to see who was speaking with such wrath.

Funmi watched Zainab scream and rage for several minutes. She thought it was good for her, to get out that misdirected fury. Was it Enitan she was really angry at or the baby that had died inside her? And why did Funmi suddenly have a feeling of preternatural calm, a sense that they would hear from Enitan one way or the other?

. . .

A MONTH LATER, SHE received the first letter with a photograph enclosed. **Funmi, I would have told you sooner.** Funmi tossed the letter aside and stared at the photograph instead. It was Enitan all right, in a simple white dress, smiling bashfully at the camera, a tall white man with red hair smiling beside her. This was the man she had left them for. Funmi had stared at that photograph for a long time. When Zainab called her, she knew she had received a letter too.

As Zainab asked over and over again how Enitan could just abandon them like that, how she could just flee, Funmi thought of Damola and she said nothing. She said "yes" when she needed to. She sensed that for Zainab something had been broken, but she also knew that this wound, whatever it was, would surely heal in time.

Zainab did not speak to Enitan for two years. Ahmed collected Enitan's letters, which were always written in Enitan's pretty, looping cursive. The letters themselves started off handwritten but then began to be typed, suggesting that the writer had acquired new skills in this America. It was Funmi who finally persuaded Zainab to reconcile, after visiting Enitan when she and Yinka went on their honeymoon, a lavish three-city whirlwind tour that featured a stop in New York.

Part III

Lagos, December 2015

CHAPTER 28

Enitan

THE RECEPTION HALL WAS MERCIFULLY DARK, in stark contrast to the unsparing sunlight outside. Votive candles surrounded tall vases of flowers on each table. Silk curtains lined the walls and a projector beamed **D & D** in ostentatious cursive script behind the stage. A purple love seat with tufted cushions stood center stage while a mountain of token gifts for the dowry: baskets of fruit—oranges, banana, mango, and pawpaw—tubers of yam, and giant sacks of rice were perched in one corner. Another projector emblazoned **D & D** on the dance floor and spotlights doused the hall in shades of lilac and purple. Tucked away to the side of the stage was a towering cake with a slightly terrifying sugar rendering of the bride and groom in their traditional clothing. And in the shadows, standing near the gifts, was a bored-looking security guard, his AK-47 casually slung over his shoulder.

"Are you sure this isn't the wedding?" Remi

whispered to Enitan as she, Zainab, and Enitan tried to find their table.

"Traditionally the engagement ceremony **is** the wedding," Enitan said. "Ah, there we are." Flatteringly, it seemed, they had been seated quite close to the stage. They claimed their chairs. There weren't a lot of other people in the reception hall yet, but all three had grown tired of standing in the hot sun, not knowing anyone.

"Did you have an engagement ceremony, Aunty Zainab?" Remi asked.

Zainab shook her head. She and Enitan made eye contact, both remembering the contracted blowout Ahmed's request for her hand in marriage had sparked. "Not like this."

"What about you, Mom?"

Enitan was grateful that Remi appeared to have put their altercation at the airport behind her.

"We didn't have an engagement ceremony, Remi. You've seen the pictures. Just the court wedding and a small reception."

"So how did Nigerian weddings get so big?" Remi asked. She took out her phone and snapped a photo of the menu. It was hard to read since the lighting was so dim, but if you squinted you could make out the options printed in flamboyant cursive: jollof rice or fried rice with chicken, beef, or fish stew, semo or eba with egusi. Nothing vegetarian. A waiter holding a wine bottle in each hand, clad in full English waistcoat attire, approached their table.

"Red or white?"

"Red," Remi and Enitan said at the same time. Enitan looked at her daughter. She knew she shouldn't be surprised. Charles wouldn't have been, and Remi was nineteen and in college. Drinking was inevitable, but still here she was, being surprised.

"I'll have red too," Zainab said.

Now Enitan looked at Zainab. She couldn't remember ever seeing Zainab drink.

When the waiter had gone, Remi held up her glass.

"Cheers," she said. Enitan and Zainab laughed. They cheered and clinked their glasses. Zainab took a sip of her wine and grimaced.

"You don't like it?" Enitan asked.

"You know I'm a good Muslim girl. But I thought I'd join in just this once to taste it."

"And?"

Zainab made another face and they all laughed.

"I had wine for the first time on our wedding day," said Enitan. "After the courthouse ceremony."

"Wow, Mom, really? I didn't know that."

Enitan nodded. She had taken a few sips of the Star beer Charles would sometimes buy from vendors when they were both living in the village, but other than that no wine. Not even palm wine. Her mother had strictly forbidden it and Enitan hated the smell anyway.

Gradually, people began to enter the hall in twos and foursomes. Ogas strolled in, their bellies hidden by accommodating agbada. Aunties followed in resplendent gèlès, holding sequined and beaded and brocaded bags. A few young mothers carried wide-eyed babies in their Sunday best. Preening twentysomething women in tight sleeveless dresses highlighting slim waists and round bosoms walked unsteadily on imposing heels, their gèlès framing their faces like halos. In the courtyard, Enitan had stared mesmerized and slightly dismayed at their makeup: the gold point at the nose and against the cheekbones, the long, velvety fake eyelashes, the harsh lip liners, the same dramatically arched eyebrows. This was the style these days, was it? Wow. Though, admittedly, Enitan had never been one for much makeup anyway; in university she had been afraid that wearing foundation would only aggravate her acne.

"Good afternoon," said a woman wearing a light blue lace buba and iro. She pulled out her chair and sat down at their table. A younger woman wearing a low-cut black dress, who looked like the woman's daughter, sat down beside her. "Good afternoon, ma," she said in a crisp English accent, first to Enitan and then to Zainab.

"Good afternoon," Enitan and Zainab chorused.

"Hello," said Remi politely in the general direction of the two women.

Enitan nudged Remi's knee with her own under the table. "Next time, say 'Good afternoon, ma,' and make sure you greet the older woman first," Enitan whispered under her breath. It had been a long time since Enitan had been around Nigerians of this ilk—rich and therefore arrogant as a result. She had to prepare herself for their judgment.

A couple who looked to be in their fifties ambled over, the woman sporting a sequined pink buba and iro, her intimidating bosom on full display. The man behind her was much shorter; he held her purse.

"Good afternoon," said the woman imperiously as she sat down on the chair her husband pulled out for her.

They all exchanged "good afternoons," Remi adding a "ma" at the end of hers.

A group of smartly dressed young men wearing fitted tunics and trousers, talking drums slack on their shoulders, walked up to the stage. The recorded praise and worship music that had been playing quietly faded. The ceremony was about to start. A middle-aged woman, wearing a glittering yellow gèlè that matched her dress, strode onto the stage holding a microphone. "Ladies and gentlemen, ladies and gentlemen," she said. A murmur went throughout the room. The band began to play in a sudden, eruptive roar.

"Ladies and gentlemen!" shouted the MC, or alága ìjókòó if Enitan wanted to be technical, her voice straining to be heard over the music. She tilted her head back, holding on to her gèlè with one hand so it wouldn't fall. "I said, layyyydeees and gentlemen. Get on your feet! The Akingbola family, the family of the bride, are arriving. Please, greet them!"

The drummers began to pick up the pace—their sticks transforming into a mesmerizing blur of movement. A spotlight suddenly flooded the other end of the giant ballroom. The doors flung open.

"Mo rí re, mo rí re, mo rí re gba," sang the bandleader. Funmi stepped into the hall, looking regal in her rose-gold aso-ebi, her gèlè at an immaculate angle on her head. The guests erupted into whoops of encouragement as Funmi began to dance her way down the hall, Yinka walking behind her, both of them flanked by a looming rose-gold mass of Yinka's extended family.

Zainab looked at Enitan. Enitan nodded her head, already knowing what she was thinking. They should be dancing alongside Funmi. It was only right. Ignoring the involuntary somersault her stomach did, Enitan rose when Zainab stood.

"Where are you going?" Remi began to ask, but Enitan grabbed her hand, interrupting her. "Come on," she said. Zainab strode confidently onto the pathway, bopping her shoulders to the music. Funmi's face broke into a wide smile as Enitan followed. Thankfully, the spotlight was bright enough that the rest of the ballroom was cast in shadow. As long as Enitan couldn't see people's faces, she would be fine. She shuffled from side to side, even as her stomach flip-flopped. She could hear the guests cheering. When she got close to Funmi, she put her arms around her. "You look beautiful," she shouted above the music. Funmi beamed. "I am so glad you are here! I was going to ask you to enter with us!" She extended her arm so Zainab could join their circle and they danced together, laughing. Remi held her phone up in the air, presumably recording them; all Enitan could see of her was the white fluorescent glow from the flash.

"Ẹ kú iṣẹ́ oo!" said the alága ìjókòó encouragingly to Funmi as Funmi dabbed her forehead with a tissue she had extracted from her ostrich feather purse once they had all reached the front of the hall and Enitan, Remi, and Zainab had returned to their table. "She has done well," said the alága ìjókòó, turning now to the rest of the guests. "Me too, I can dance o!" she said, a mischievous look on her face. "You don't believe me?" she exclaimed in mock consternation.

"Band, play me something!" The band broke into a rousing instrumental number and the alága ìjókòó began to dance onstage—a bouncy, energetic shuffle of her shoulders.

The guests laughed appreciatively, though notably everyone at Enitan's own table was quiet.

Now that Enitan and Zainab had gone up to dance with Funmi, the other guests at the table seemed to have determined that they were of some importance. Enitan had noted the way the woman in pink had looked her up and down when Enitan had sat back down in her chair. She was watching Remi closely too.

The woman was about to open her mouth to speak when a strident, straining alto from the other side of the room began to sing: "Today o, I will lift up my voice in praise!" Once again, the spotlight hit the double doors that led into the hall. A woman clad in royal blue and carrying a microphone continued to sing as she danced into the ballroom, the band accompanying her.

"The groom's family is entering. That's their alága ìdúró," Enitan whispered to Remi, preempting inevitable questions.

"What's that?"

"She's like the spokesperson for the groom's side of the family."

Dele's family began to enter the hall, dancing—a magnificent swarm of silver-clad men, women, and children.

Enitan could spot the mother immediately, wearing a smug, beneficent look on her face, as people surrounded her. Enitan noted the slight shimmy she did with her shoulders, the way she readjusted her ìborùn, as if she were royalty. This was the hope, the dream, the goal of course. See how much money we have. See how much God has blessed us.

People rose in their seats, clapping, taking out iPads and phones to capture the proceedings the professional videographers were already filming. A few women took naira bills from their purses and surrounded the mother, lightly tossing the bills in her face and on her shoulders. She bopped beatifically in place, closing her eyes and pretending as if she didn't notice what they were doing. Two younger women, clones of their mother, scrambled to pick up the bills. Two money changers, wearing all black and carrying thick wads of dollar bills, circled the perimeter. An oga, his gold watch twinkling on his thick wrist, flagged the money changers down.

"What's happening?" Remi asked, mildly alarmed.

Zainab chuckled.

"They are spraying the family. It is like a blessing," Enitan said. She wasn't sure how else to explain it. This spraying of money was a tradition, but it hadn't always been so extravagant. Funmi would send videos to their WhatsApp group of big-bellied ogas at high-society weddings solemnly throwing hundred-dollar notes at the bride and groom from a thick brick of bills in their hands as if the money were confetti. It was all far too ostentatious for Enitan's taste.

"It's enough, it's enough!" the alága ìjókòó shouted into the microphone from the stage. "Save your money-o! The bride hasn't even commot," she said, and her chiding drew some gentle laughter.

The alága ìdúró led the Baloguns to the front of the hall. "Ẹ káàsàán, Mummy and Daddy!" she said, once the music had died down. She kneeled in front of Funmi and Yinka. "Good afternoon, Mummy and Daddy. We the Balogun family greet you." She turned to the assemblage of various Balogun family members and stage-whispered: "Men, remove your cap and prostrate! Women, kneel!"

The guests laughed and some clapped. Before Remi could turn to ask her once again what was happening, Enitan whispered, "The groom's family is paying respect to the bride's family."

A waiter stopped by their table and placed small plates of chin chin around them. Zainab sighed. "No real food yet," she murmured to Enitan. It was going to be a long night.

After the alága ìdúró had led another rousing Yorùbá number, a young girl, who couldn't have been older than seventeen, emerged from the scrum of silver-attired Baloguns, holding an elaborately designed gold plate. The alága ìdúró handed the microphone to her.

"What's going on?" Remi whispered.

"A young female relative from the groom's side of the family is going to read the family's marriage proposal," Enitan whispered back.

Remi shuddered. "That sounds mortifying."

The girl began to read in a tremulous voice. "On behalf of the entire Balogun family, we humbly request your approval of the lifelong union between our dear son, Ayodele Esupofo Balogun, and your exquisite daughter, Destiny Ifeoluwa Akingbola," she said. "We believe that their love for each other is genuine and profound. With God's help, they shall live in connub . . ." Here she paused delicately, mouthed the word to herself, and then repeated it in a stronger voice, "Connubial bliss for the rest of their days. Therefore, we formally seek your consent for our son and your daughter's hand in marriage. We know that what God has joined together no man can tear asunder. We kindly await your reply," she finished reading.

"As you are here celebrating your cousin's wedding, so we shall celebrate your own wedding in Jesus' name!" exclaimed the alága ìdúró, waving her microphone like a military baton. A chorus of "Amen!"s broke out from the Balogun side of the family, particularly from one woman who must have been the young girl's mother. The talking drummers started back up again as the girl's relatives surrounded her. She danced awkwardly to the music as aunties began placing naira bills on her forehead.

Enitan shook her head. Remi picked at the bowl of chin chin.

"Mom, how long is this going to be?" she whispered.

Zainab overheard and smiled. "You didn't prepare her?" she asked Enitan. "We probably won't get out until midnight." She and Enitan chuckled quietly. The woman in pink eyed them. Once again, she was about to speak when a deafeningly loud Afrobeats track began to play.

"I know this song!" Remi said excitedly, and she began humming along tunelessly. The lights dimmed and a spotlight shone on the large double doors that led into the hall. A cadre of young men, all wearing sunglasses and fitted tunics and trousers, made their entrance, marching in time to the music to the cheers of the guests.

Dele was in the center wearing a purple agbada; around his neck hung several bright coral beads. He beamed as the men began to do a choreographed dance, one that drew exclamations and whoops and titters from the young female guests. Some of the men began throwing dollar bills in the air, spraying themselves as if they were in a rap music video as they made their way to the front of the hall. "Na wa o," Zainab whispered to Enitan. One of the groomsmen held Dele's fila as Dele dropped to the floor suddenly and began to wriggle his body like an insect; the screaming from the young women increased tenfold. Enitan could only watch in helpless amusement. The dancing continued for several more minutes, until finally, thankfully, it came to an end when the men had reached the front of the stage. The alága ìdúró gestured for the music to stop. "Now is the time to greet Mummy and Daddy," she said, holding her microphone like a scepter. Dele got down on his knees.

"Ahn-ahn? Is that how you greet your mummy and daddy? Prostrate yourself, my friend!" she exclaimed amid laughter from the other guests.

The alága ìdúró began to sing in Yorùbá; Dele and his parents stood up and danced.

Growing weary at the sight of more dancing and spraying, Enitan turned back to the table.

The woman in pink now made her move.

"Please, how do you know the bride's family?" she asked Enitan.

"We went to school with the mother of the bride," said Enitan.

"Yes," said Zainab.

"Do you live in Nigeria? I detect an American accent," said the woman in pink, who did not acknowledge Zainab's response.

"No, we live in New York," Enitan said, frowning slightly. She was beginning to sense where this conversation was going.

"New York? We were there just this past summer. We stayed on which side was it again, George?" The woman in pink turned to her husband, who had been dozing slightly.

"Ehn?" he grunted.

"When we went to visit Temi in New York, where

did we stay? It was near Columbia University, where our youngest son goes to school."

"The Upper West Side," Remi said drearily.

The woman in pink looked at Remi with interest.

"Do you go to Columbia as well?"

"No," Remi said.

"Oh," the woman said, not bothering to hide her disappointment.

Enitan suddenly felt compelled to tell the woman that Remi had in fact turned down Columbia. She didn't say anything of course, but she was embarrassed at how strong her inclination was to impress her.

"My son is studying chemistry at Columbia University; he is going to go to medical school afterward," said the woman. "What are you reading in school?" she asked Remi.

Enitan turned to look at Remi. She was curious about the answer, actually; Remi had changed her major many times.

"I'm a gender studies major," Remi said.

"All these young kids these days, they never want to study anything practical," said the woman in blue, who had evidently been listening but hadn't felt compelled to speak until now. She laughed softly to herself.

"You can read anything you want in university and still get a practical second degree," Enitan said, defensively she realized. The daughter of the woman in blue was staring avidly at her hands, which were placed in her lap; they glistened with a fresh coat of white nail polish.

"I wish you could talk some sense into this one," the woman in blue said to the woman in pink, craning her head toward her daughter. "This one is reading literature. For what?"

Zainab sat up in her chair. She and Enitan exchanged looks.

"How do you know the bride and groom?" Enitan asked hastily. Anything to get away from this wretched subject. Also, there had to be a reason why such heinous people were seated so close to the stage.

The woman in pink narrowed her eyes and rolled her shoulders back. "I am Yinka's eldest stepsister," she announced. Her face was closed to follow-ups. At that moment, Enitan felt sorry for her. She wasn't wearing rose gold, so clearly she had not been included in any of the wedding planning. And she was not sitting with the rest of the Akingbolas, in the seats reserved for the elders. That she had been placed at a table fairly close to the stage would have to suffice.

"My late husband served in the army with Yinka back in the eighties," said the woman in pink solemnly. "It was very nice of him to invite us," she added. The table settled into an awkward silence mercifully broken by the frenzied playing of the band.

Finally, Destiny was entering the hall. The spotlight landed on the doors once again and a murmur of excitement went through the crowd.

"Ahhhhhhhh bi é ṣé!" sang the alága ìjókòó. "Ẹ ṣé oo!" responded the guests in a resounding chorus. They all rose to their feet as the bridesmaids began to dance in. Phone cameras flashed all around them like lightning bugs. It was hard to make out Destiny amid the throng of women, but when the bridesmaids had reached the front of the hall, Enitan could finally see her. She was wearing all purple; her ìborùn was studded with fake pearls as was her gèlè. A lilac veil covered her sequined gèlè as was custom. It was impossible to see her face.

CHAPTER 29

Zainab

WHO IS IN THE GARDEN?" THE ALÁGA ÌJÓKÒÓ
sang out.

"A little fine girl!" the bridesmaids chorused.
Zainab stood to get a better look at Destiny.

"I said, who is in the garden?" The alága ìjókòó
sang again with an unnecessary amount of aggression, Zainab thought.

"A little fine girl!"

Zainab nudged Enitan. They should be up there.
And so Zainab clawed her way through the swarms
of people who had quickly migrated over to the
main attraction, iPads aloft like signs at a concert.
Destiny was in the middle of the scrum, veiled,
holding an extravagantly feathered purse as dollar
bills floated over her, her head bowed as she moved
in time to the music.

Zainab reached out and grabbed Destiny's hand.
Destiny looked up. "You look beautiful," mouthed
Zainab. Destiny nodded and almost went down

into a kneel, but one of the bridesmaids grabbed her other hand and pulled her up as the percussionists ratcheted up their drumming. Zainab turned to see Enitan telling Remi to help pick up the money that had fallen to the floor. The dancing continued for several more minutes, until at last the alága ìjókòó began waving her microphone in the air.

"Thank you o! Thank you, friends of the bride!" she exclaimed. Zainab lingered near the front of the stage; she wasn't ready to go back to the table just yet. Enitan tapped her arm and sidled up next to her.

The alága ìjókòó pulled Destiny forward so she was standing in front of Funmi and Yinka, who sat upright, no doubt beaming. "Destiny, your mummy and daddy are now going to cover you in prayer," the alága ìjókòó said. "Kneel down in front of them," she instructed. Destiny obediently got down on her knees and bowed her head. Funmi and Yinka laid their hands on her shoulders and the prayers began, long, fervent murmurs, exhortations of Jesus' name, and requests that His blood cover them all. Zainab bowed her head and peeked at Enitan, whose head was also bowed. Their eyes met then and they both suppressed the barest of snickers. Funmi was praying fervently, shaking Destiny's shoulder vigorously with her braceleted forearm. Yinka's head was bowed and he nodded ever so slightly. Zainab had never seen this side of Funmi before. What newfound godly devotion a wedding could provoke! The alága ìjókòó also began to pray in Yorùbá and the hall filled with "Amin!"s. Zainab joined in when she sensed the end of a sentence, distinguished by a sudden and deafening increase in volume and speed, those warm, round tones rising rising rising. Zainab said her "Amin" and snuck a look at Dele, who was already seated on the dais. He was fiddling with his fila, which he had taken off for the prayers.

"In Jesus' mighty, mighty name," the alága ìjókòó finally said, raising her head. "Amen!" replied the wedding guests. Zainab saw Funmi take out her handkerchief and wipe tears from her eyes. The alága ìjókòó began to sing and the musicians played, a slower tune this time as Yinka and Funmi pulled Destiny up to sit on their laps for photos. Funmi had taken Destiny's veil off, and Zainab could now see Destiny's face fully for the first time.

She had been transformed into any number of the women who adorned the lifestyle magazines at any salon worth its salt: her eyelids doused in gold eyeshadow, her eyebrows drawn into dramatic onyx lines, her cheekbones newly prominent courtesy of some magical whittling makeup brush, her lips a fetching plum red. But Zainab could see the remnants of tears that Destiny had furtively tried to wipe as she smiled gamely for the cameras, sitting on her parents' laps as if she were four years old.

The percussion began to pick up again. Destiny and Funmi both rose, Funmi with Destiny's veil in her hands. She said something to Destiny and Destiny nodded as Funmi placed the veil over both of their heads. They began to dance as the alága ìjókòó sang and the photographers snapped. Zainab wondered what Funmi was saying as Funmi steered Destiny, turning her slowly around and around as the alága ìjókòó sang in that grating, tuneless soprano of hers. Zainab went to sit back down at the table. Enitan and Remi had already returned. It looked as if the waiters had set down new dinner plates. Food at last.

Zainab palmed a handful of chin chin and leaned back in her chair. Enitan patted Zainab's forearm. "Pẹ̀lẹ̀," Enitan said, a hint of mirth in her eyes, and Zainab laughed. She knew enough Yorùbá to recognize the slight sarcasm in Enitan's "sorry."

Funmi and Destiny had stopped dancing and Funmi had extricated herself from under the veil. The alága ìjókòó had taken Destiny's hand and was singing and waving to the Akingbolas simultaneously.

"What's going on?" Remi asked Enitan.

"Destiny is saying goodbye to her family as she now goes to meet the Baloguns," Enitan whispered. Remi looked like she was about to reply, but a waiter set down a plate of jollof rice in front of her and she became quiet. The sight of food after such a long afternoon had that effect.

The alágas were talking over each other in loud Yorùbá as Destiny stood in front of her mother- and father-in-law, her hands demurely at her sides. The alágas began to sing.

A waiter set down a plate of jollof rice with chicken stew for Zainab. She had asked for eba with efo riro, but she would take whatever was offered to her. She was hungry.

"Destiny Ifeoluwa, you are welcome in this house!" exclaimed the alága ìdúró. "And now you are going to meet your new mummy and daddy!" she said. Destiny kneeled in front of the Balogun parents and the prayers began again.

"Who is in the garden?" the alága ìjókòó sang in a reprise, and the friends of the bride surrounded Destiny. They danced another turn before Destiny was led to the steps of the stage alone. Her veil had been taken off and someone had given her Dele's fila.

"Oya, oya!" The alága ìdúró ushered Destiny as the percussion began again. "Dance to your husband now!" she instructed, and the wedding guests laughed and Destiny smiled tightly as she moved haltingly from side to side, holding the fila in one hand, her face focused, it seemed, on not tripping over her dress. Dele nodded along from the dais absentmindedly; he was chewing gum, which Zainab found shocking, his sunglasses still on his face. Destiny reached the stage and the photographers swarmed them again. She placed the fila on his head. The alága ìdúró crept up behind her and whispered something. Destiny adjusted the fila so it sat on the right side of his head. The alágas began barking commands at Dele as the band members (diligent band!) continued to beat their talking drums. Dele got up and Destiny sat down. Then Destiny stood up and Dele sat down. Finally they were both standing and Dele began scattering dollar bills over Destiny as she shuffled uncomfortably from side to side, the alágas seeing who could out-sing the other in their microphones.

"Jesus," Remi muttered under her breath, and Enitan shot her a warning look.

Zainab could only sigh and lean back in her chair, giving herself a moment to digest the food. She looked over at Funmi, who was seated so her back was toward them. All Zainab could see was how upright she was in her chair. Yinka's head meanwhile was bowed. Surreptitiously texting someone on his BlackBerry, no doubt.

"The Baloguns have brought you so many gifts!" exclaimed the alága ìdúró, looking at Destiny. "Hundreds and thousands of gifts for you!" she added theatrically. "Now go and pick one gift, the one gift that is the most important gift of all!"

Destiny walked unsteadily over to the tower of presents on display at the corner of the stage. The gift she chose had already been selected for her of course, a thick Bible-shaped present covered in gold wrapping paper. She brought it over to where Dele and the alága ìdúró were standing.

"This gift," said the alága ìdúró, turning to the wedding guests, most of whom were still tucking into their meals, "is the most important gift of all!" Then turning to Destiny and Dele, she said, "It is your manual. Your guide throughout this life of trials and tribulations. The Holy Bible!"

Destiny held the book awkwardly in her hands.

"Unwrap it now!" said the alága ìjókòó impatiently from where she was standing offstage, on the runner that divided the bride's family and the groom's family from each other.

Destiny handed the Bible to Dele to unwrap.

"I see something o!" said the alága ìdúró in a stage whisper. "I see something on the Bible! You see it too, abi?" she asked the alága ìjókòó, who nodded. "I see it o!" the alága ìdúró said. "Untangle the tangle," she began to sing as Dele unwrapped the package sheepishly.

"Do you know what it is?" Zainab asked Remi, turning toward her.

Remi shook her head.

"The ring," Enitan answered for her.

As Dele tried to open the box, the alága ìjókòó took Destiny by the hand. "This is your last moment as a single lady. Wave to everybody with your hand like this." She made Destiny stick her hand in the air as the alága ìjókòó begun to sing, "You're a single lady, you're a single lady."

"Oh my God, is that Beyoncé?" Remi asked, and she groaned. The young British woman at their table giggled. Destiny, looking quite embarrassed, submitted to the alága ìjókòó's prodding as she showed her naked hand to the assemblage of Akingbola family members. Poor dear. Though Zainab had to admit that the manicure had turned out quite nicely.

Once Destiny had returned to the front of the hall, after a confusing lull in which the alágas had shouted commandments at each other, Dele adjusted his agbada a few more times and then proceeded to pick Destiny up off the floor. The hall erupted into the loudest cheers of the night—there was always something about that display of brute strength that seemed to excite otherwise distracted wedding guests. "Show your bride!" the alága ìdúró shrieked into the mic and Dele, looking proud of himself, swung Destiny easily in his arms as she held on to his shoulders, her face a tight rictus of discomfort that would have been hard to pick up on had Zainab not known her so well.

"It's almost over," Zainab told Destiny under her breath, knowing full well she could not hear her.

· · ·

THE CEREMONY FINALLY ENDED a little past midnight. Zainab and Enitan had long since sat down, their elbows on the table, their aching feet sliding out of their low heels.

"Ladies and gentlemen, ladies and gentlemen!" One of the groomsmen stood onstage, cupping his hands for amplification. "The final bus is departing in fifteen minutes."

"Fifteen!" Enitan and Zainab said at the same time.

"These events are for the young," Enitan said.

"Yes o! I cannot believe we will be doing this again tomorrow," Zainab said, and she yawned and leaned back into her chair. Resting her head against cool, freshly laundered pillows would feel amazing right about now.

She and Enitan had gone to sit in the lobby for a while just to get away from the loud music. The automated glass doors that led into the hotel opened occasionally, letting in humid night air and inebriated hotel guests. A young white couple sauntered in, giggling. Zainab eyed the woman; she still found it jarring to see white women in Nigeria—it's not as if Nigeria was exactly a tourist-friendly country. This couple sounded American, judging from their loudness. The woman was wearing a long olive-green dress and white Converse trainers. Her face was red.

She locked eyes with Zainab and Zainab turned away quickly, feeling embarrassed. To her horror, though, the woman was now walking toward them, dragging her companion by the arm.

"I just wanted to say that you both look absolutely beautiful," she said, her words slurring. "Like goddesses."

"Thank you," Enitan and Zainab replied in unison.

"I wanna take a picture with you ladies." She tugged on her companion's arm.

"Todd, take a picture of us."

He looked slightly embarrassed.

"Babe, come on, they don't want to take a picture with you."

"Would you mind taking a photo with me?" The woman spoke over her partner, looking directly at Zainab.

This was embarrassing for everyone involved, Zainab thought.

She smiled. "No pictures at this time. We've been taking pictures all day," she added.

The woman looked crestfallen. Her partner's face turned scarlet.

"Come on," he murmured, and he led her away from them toward the elevator.

When they were out of hearing distance, Enitan sucked her teeth.

"Can you just imagine if the roles were reversed?" Zainab said.

"They would call the police!"

At this, they both started laughing.

Back at their table in the hall, Zainab chuckled, thinking again of that woman. Enitan asked her why she was laughing. "That oyinbo woman." And then Enitan began laughing too. They were suddenly in another laughing fit, tears coming to their eyes, when Remi came to their table, holding her gèlè in her arms. She had sweated off most of her makeup through spirited dancing. Her face was flushed and her baby hairs were dark against her forehead, slick with perspiration. She had a worrying look on her face.

"What is it?" Enitan asked.

Remi drew closer to their table and said in a quiet voice, "I think you should both come with me."

Both Zainab and Enitan looked at each other.

"It's Destiny," Remi added.

Zainab raised an eyebrow. They stood and followed Remi's lead.

The hall had largely emptied out. A small group of bridesmaids and groomsmen were huddled in the far corner. A few were talking excitedly. "Let's go to Escape!" one of them said. Others were on their phones, their faces awash in a white glow that made Zainab's eyes ache reflexively. Most of the women had taken off their heels and were wearing flip-flops. They had come prepared. Smart.

Waiters were making their way through each

table, slowly clearing plates in a subtle attempt to get stragglers to leave. Spilled drinks made the dance floor slick, and Zainab's shoes felt sticky as she walked past. She yelped at what she thought was a caterpillar of some kind. When it didn't move, she looked closer and realized it was an eyelash. They reached the lobby.

Soft piano music was playing. She was vaguely aware that the song was an instrumental version of a pop tune she recognized—something that was popular in the '80s. Remi led them down a flight of stairs. On this floor there were boarded-up gift stores that sold key chains in the shape of djembe drums, wood sculptures, and Yorùbá masks you could find for lower prices and higher quality at the actual market. A headless mannequin wore a green I LOVE LAGOS T-shirt. They were trying sha. The faint smell of cigarette smoke lingered in the air.

The farther they walked down the hall, the stronger the smell of cigarette smoke became, until they came to a sudden stop. Destiny was sitting on the floor at the far end of the hallway, her back against the wall, her gèlè on her lap, a cigarette snug between her middle and forefinger, a glass of something brown in her other hand. The lighting was bad here. It was fluorescent and created shadows on Destiny's face that made her look older than she was.

"I came downstairs to find an open restroom," Remi explained quietly. "And I saw her down here.

We talked a little bit. She doesn't want to get married. We have to find a way to tell Aunty Funmi."

Zainab and Enitan looked at each other after Remi had spoken, a long, pregnant look. Destiny hadn't seen them. She put the cigarette to her lips and inhaled.

"Let me go and speak to her first," said Zainab.

Enitan nodded. "I'll be here," she added.

It took some doing, some gathering up of her skirt and shifting of her body, but Zainab managed to sit down beside Destiny. She took the cigarette from Destiny's fingers and placed it in Destiny's glass, where it sizzled momentarily before going out.

"You know better than to do that."

Destiny looked briefly like a child again—that same bashful creature who would emerge when summoned to greet Aunty Zainab, always with her four fingers in her mouth—a shy, cautious little girl.

"So," Zainab said. She was Destiny's godmother. She had been there for the christening at the church. As the pastor poured the water over Destiny's head, Destiny had gazed up at him with a placid look on her face. No tears, no wailing. Funmi had complained over the years about this quality of Destiny's, her inability to disobey. Zainab had laughed about it. What kind of mother wants unruly children, girls especially? Outspoken girls were a liability here. But wasn't it inevitable, that moment of rebellion? It would come sooner or later.

"What is the matter?"

"I can't do this," Destiny said. "Please don't tell my mum."

Zainab was silent. She could not say she was surprised. She had had a premonition after all, especially after that voicemail. But Funmi had been determined. Maybe she would be happy now that there had finally been a moment of resistance, though the timing of course was most unfortunate.

Zainab searched for her words. She could not do what she normally did in such situations, when a daughter-in-law asked her for teething tips, for example, or for how to get the baby to sleep through the night. In those scenarios she remembered what it was like to be a young mother—the exhaustion, the anxiety, the fear. It was easy then to be gracious and sympathetic. But this dilemma was not one Zainab was familiar with. She'd had the opposite problem after all. She had been desperate to marry Ahmed, but her father was staunchly against it. "What do you want to do?" Zainab finally asked.

Destiny didn't reply. They sat in silence for a while, listening to the tinny pop music, to the sounds of the cleaning crew, the squeak of shoes against newly mopped floors.

"I tried to talk to her and she just wouldn't listen!" Destiny said slowly after a long silence. She sighed, exasperated. "It just feels like everything is happening so quickly and I'm not in control of anything anymore, if I ever was. All my life I have done what my parents have required of me," Destiny added. "And now I just feel—" She stopped herself. "It's too late to change anything," she said with resignation.

"It's not too late," said Zainab. "Though I wish you had talked to me first. I'm worried about you, darling. And you know that if you had had any doubts we could have talked through them. We still can," Zainab added, not wanting to make Destiny feel worse. "But I do think we need to get your mother. It is not right that she should not be present for this conversation."

"She doesn't understand. She'll only make things worse. She never listens to me. She'll tell me to get over it, that marriage requires sacrifice, that I'm deluding myself with fairy tales."

Zainab sighed. That did sound like Funmi.

"I'm not happy, Aunty," Destiny said abruptly, holding Zainab's gaze for the first time. "I'm not happy at all. I can't remember the last time I was, but I feel like I can't say these things. Who cares about being happy in a country where so many people are really, really suffering? Happiness is for Americans, that's what Daddy always says. They are always seeking it out because they have the time and money to do so. God, even saying this out loud, I feel like I sound exactly like the white girls in my first year at uni worrying about what they chose to read in school, going on about how they want to do something fulfilling. I had a roommate who said she was depressed her first year. She couldn't get out of bed to go to classes. I was disgusted at the time: she just seemed so lazy. I wanted to scream at her: You know how many Nigerians are desperate to be in your position? To have the option of going to university and you're just squandering it away, lying in bed all day watching **EastEnders** and smoking constantly. She was the one who got me on these." She gestured at the floating cigarette. "The thing is, now I understand her. I understand her completely. I see my life stretched out before me—finishing school, working in the NHS, marrying Dele, having kids. I see the options and I don't know if I want any of them. You see this?" She turned her right arm so the inside of her wrist was showing. There were scars there, faded now but scars nevertheless—the work of a knife or a razor blade.

"I'm afraid, Aunty," said Destiny. "I don't know what to do."

CHAPTER 30

Funmi

UNMI WAS FINALLY SITTING. IT FELT GOOD to take her shoes off; the carpet under her feet was soft and recuperative. She had done what she had set out to do. She had danced. She had sprayed her daughter and future son-in-law with crisp fifty-dollar bills, had been publicly flirted with by the much younger Afrobeats star to the charm of the crowd, Yinka barely registering him at all, as was to be expected. She had bid farewell to the guests she needed to personally thank for attending the ceremony, the senators and the oba and Yinka's most senior business associates and the older Nollywood actress who had patiently tolerated requests for selfies all night. The hall was essentially abandoned now. The house lights, bright and unflinching, were on, and the cleaning crew was slowly working their way through each table.

Yinka had quietly retired long before. "Can you ride the last coach if necessary?" he asked her, and if it had been another occasion, she would have started an argument with him, but she wanted to wait until the very last minute to leave the venue anyway so she did not mind. This was the reward of her labor, the fruition of months of planning. Yes, this was only the engagement; the church wedding would be tomorrow, but still she could enjoy the adrenaline rush of a job well done. The first major hurdle was over. Her momentary bout of panic, that things would not go through, had abated. As she and Destiny had danced together under Destiny's veil, Funmi had asked her, wasn't she happy, wasn't this good? And Destiny had nodded, tears filling her eyes, overwhelmed with emotion.

"Madam." It was Sunday.

"Faithful Sunday. Reliable Sunday. How far now?"

Sunday nodded in greeting. "Madam, the coach is here."

"All right."

She shifted slowly in her seat, adjusted her gèlè. She would have taken it off but she had no idea what her hair looked like under it and wanted to wait until she was home to find out. She stood up slowly and put her heels back on. A small group of bridesmaids and groomsmen were still huddling in one corner.

No one else was left in the hall; she had seen Zainab, Enitan, and Remi get up about fifteen minutes ago, probably to go to the bathroom. Zainab and Enitan had really tried, sha. Troupers through and through. She had felt the full weight of their friendship, the way it had continued to endure, despite everything.

She had just finally stood up, when she saw Remi heading toward her, walking with the quick, urgent movements of someone on a mission.

Funmi had been delighted with Remi; she had danced quite a bit at the ceremony. Well, dancing was perhaps not the right word for Remi's movements. There was no sense of rhythm to them. She had been among the first group of young people to start dancing once the ceremony was over, and the videographers had loved her, surrounding her as she danced with reckless frenzy—arms out and hips shaking. It was a good thing she had done; she had succeeded in melting the frostiness that always initially descended on events like this, the young people not wanting to seem too eager to dance, the girls especially, watching each other with judgmental, appraising eyes.

But when Remi began to dance and some young men began to dance also, the iciness lifted, especially as the alcohol flowed freely, and soon enough, everyone was dancing without inhibition. The dancing even got competitive with whoops and cheers of encouragement and then of course the mother-in-law, that incorrigible woman, had to keep getting up to dance as if she were the bride, very embarrassing. A swell of young people had surrounded her as she tried to follow the choreography of a young man, his feet moving with an elasticity that seemed to defy the laws of gravity. "Ah ahn! Mummy has moves o!" one guy shouted, holding his phone aloft so he could capture the scene.

"Remi, well done," Funmi said.

"Thank you, Aunty."

"You should go and get your mother and Aunty Zainab. The last coach is here."

"Aunty Zainab said I should come and get you. That you need to go and talk to Destiny."

"She's still here?" Funmi said, surprised. She had bid good night to both Dele and Destiny about forty-five minutes ago. Dele was supposed to go with some groomsmen to the hotel they had booked for his last night of singledom. And Destiny was supposed to have changed and gone out with the bridesmaids.

"Take me to where she is, but I hope she knows we don't have much time. The coach is leaving shortly."

"Yes, Aunty," said Remi. Funmi followed Remi out of the ballroom and into the lobby. Now that she had had some time to sit, the air-conditioning made her shiver.

"Congratulations, ma," the receptionist called out to Funmi as she followed Remi toward a narrow staircase at the end of the lobby. Funmi nodded her thanks. As they went down the stairs, she could smell cigarette smoke.

She thought smoking was banned indoors at this hotel; that had been a factor in choosing it. Zainab was walking toward her. When they were within arm's length, Zainab grabbed Funmi's hands. "Please, Funmi," she said quietly, "listen to what your daughter has to say."

Feeling too confused to come up with a more cogent response, Funmi simply nodded. She could see now that Destiny was sitting on the floor a few feet away from them. Funmi winced at the sight of her, at the beautiful custom-made gown now on the floor, the dark sweat patches under her arms. Sitting next to Destiny was a glass full of some brown liquid, whiskey if Funmi had to hazard a guess. And was that a cigarette floating in the glass?

"Why are you sitting on the floor like this?" Funmi tried to keep her voice down, but she was angry.

Destiny didn't say anything. She just looked down at the floor.

Funmi was genuinely bewildered now. She spun around seeking help and saw that Zainab and Enitan were now right behind her.

"What is she doing? What is the meaning of this?" Funmi asked them, as Enitan and Zainab flanked her on either side.

"She doesn't want to get married," Zainab said.

"What?" Funmi's limbs felt heavy.

"Take some deep breaths," Enitan said.

"Why is she doing this to me?" Funmi moaned.

Her nightmare was coming true. She felt faint, she really did. She sank to the floor, a slow descent as Zainab and Enitan tried to pull her up and Funmi resisted. What would she say to all the guests tomorrow? How would Yinka react? The indignity of the whole situation. The humiliation. She thought bitterly of Nike George, of the triumphant look she would be sure to have on her face when she heard the news. How would they even send the information out? Would she be forced to call every guest? Would they all be checking their email tomorrow morning? Jesus. Jesus. Jesus.

"You've got to relax," said Zainab quietly. "You just need to talk to her. She needs her mother."

"At least she is talking to you now and it is not the wedding day yet," Enitan added. This was supposed to be comforting, but it only made Funmi feel worse.

"Nothing is final. It is not the end of the world. Just please, listen to her and try to be reasonable," Zainab said. Reasonable, kẹ. Funmi scoffed.

"We are here for you, Funmi. We are here for you and you know that we love you and support you no matter what," said Enitan. They tried to get Funmi back on her feet, but she refused to move. She wanted to lie on the cold tiled floor. She didn't care if it made her look like a fool. Her daughter had already embarrassed her enough.

CHAPTER 31

ZAINAB AND ENITAN MANAGED TO GET FUNMI in a more lucid state by helping her to a white plastic chair at the end of the hall, probably meant for the night guard, who was nowhere to be found. Destiny approached them tentatively, as if her mother were a vengeful wasp waiting to sting her at any turn. She was back to the timid Destiny who was so familiar to them, newly cowed, awed at her ability to practically incapacitate her mother over this news.

As Enitan strained to keep Funmi upright, she locked eyes with Zainab, who was murmuring under her breath, "It's all right Funmi, relax, relax." Enitan tried to get Funmi to stand up but Funmi refused. She had, in fact, taken the gèlè off her head, revealing surprisingly thinning hair smelling vaguely of Sulfur 8 and sweat.

"Funmi, Funmi, please calm down," Enitan said. She looked at Destiny, who was watching them balefully. Remi had returned; Enitan could see her by the staircase, unsure of where she should be.

"Funmi, darling," Enitan said.

"I'm sorry, Mummy," Destiny said, walking toward them. She said it again more firmly. "Mummy, I'm sorry."

Funmi scowled.

"No, actually," Destiny said, clearing her throat, her back straightening. "I'm not sorry. Well, I am, but mostly I am not."

"Kí ló ń sọ?" Funmi muttered. What is she saying?

Destiny looked up at Zainab, as if she was gathering strength. Funmi thought back to the conversation Zainab had tried to have with her earlier that day. They had been plotting against her.

"I'm sorry that it's taken me so long to say this. But I don't want to get married, at least not right now. And I know that in your own way you think you're doing this for me, but you're not. I don't know who you're doing this for."

"What are you saying? How can you—"

But Zainab interrupted her. "Funmi, listen," she said with a force that did momentarily mute Funmi. "Listen," she said again more slowly.

"I've been going along with all your decisions for all my life. I just can't take it anymore. I want to live my own life!" Destiny's voice broke a little. "I tried to tell you sooner; I really did, but you wouldn't listen!"

Then she began to cry steadily.

Funmi was confused. She did not know how to react to this burst of emotion, to this new tone from her daughter—one of defiance, of hurt and despair. Zainab put her arms around Destiny as Destiny sobbed. Funmi sat there, watching. She knew that she should go and comfort her daughter, but she also knew that she could not move.

"Funmi," Enitan said.

"Remember what you said to me, Funmi?" Enitan asked. "Remember what you said to me when you found out about Charles?"

Remi had come toward them now, no doubt curious to hear what Enitan had to say about her father.

"You told me I had to do what I had to do?"

Funmi scowled. "You know that is not—"

Enitan interrupted. "How is it not? When Zainab married Ahmed? When I left?"

Destiny had stopped crying. She drew back from Zainab and held her mother's gaze, her face wet with tears and mucus.

"Why didn't you tell me sooner?" Funmi asked Destiny.

"I tried, Mummy, you **know** I did."

Funmi was quiet. She was remembering the

conversation she had had with Destiny in the bathroom and the look on Destiny's face, how contorted it was with frustration and anger. Yes, that had been Destiny's attempt to reach out and Funmi had chosen to ignore her completely. She felt a current of shame then—and remorse.

"You've never listened to me. You've never let me do what I want to do. When I wanted to study photography, you and Daddy just shut it down completely. I tell you that I'm unhappy and you ignore me, tell me to pray about it, tell me how lucky I am—"

"But you are—"

"I know I am!" Destiny said, her volume escalating. "And that makes me feel worse! You want me to be exactly how you were, how you are! But we're two different people!"

"You can't say that I have not tried," Funmi said quietly, feeling tears coming to her own eyes unexpectedly. "With the wedding I tried to keep you involved. I kept asking you what do you want, what do you want . . ." She closed her eyes and the tears began to fall then.

"I know I should have said something sooner," said Destiny, her tone softening. "It just felt like everything happened so quickly, like we were on a conveyor belt and I couldn't get off . . ." She stopped talking and there was an awkward silence that hung in the air between all of them.

"You know your mother was one of the most headstrong girls I ever met in university," Zainab said suddenly to Destiny. "You know she went and took my boyfriend?"

"Really?" Remi asked from over at the staircase. Enitan laughed. Destiny smiled slightly.

"Now is the time you decide to bring this up?" Funmi asked.

"My point being," said Zainab, continuing on as if she hadn't heard, "Destiny, you come from what the English call hardy stock."

"What the Yorùbá call olorikukun. Literally, stubborn," added Enitan.

"I don't know what you two are talking about," said Funmi.

"Your mother may not realize it now, Destiny," continued Zainab. "But I know that there is a part of her that is very proud of you. Because you are standing up for yourself."

"Thank you, Aunty," Destiny said softly and gratefully. She turned to look at her mother.

They were all watching Funmi now, waiting to see what she would say. She closed her eyes. She was thinking of the day Destiny had been born, how at first she did not cry and the doctor had thwacked her on her bum and then she had begun to delicately mewl. How when Funmi had held Destiny close to her chest, she had been alarmed at the terror she had felt in that moment. She had no idea what she was doing. Her own mother was long since dead, a collage of halcyon memories. She thought of all the times she had tried and failed to understand her daughter, to bridge this gap that seemed to have always existed between the two of them.

She suddenly felt a wave of exhaustion crash over her. Tomorrow, she decided, she would deal with the repercussions of Destiny's decision, with her own discomfort and gnawing shame. Tonight, she just needed to sleep—a long, deep sleep. She picked up her gèlè from the floor and stood. She placed her hand on Destiny's shoulder. "Okay," she said. Even as she said it, she was not entirely sure what she meant, what she was agreeing to, what she was admitting. All she knew was that they were at a turning point now; they could not go back to how things were. "The coach is here," Funmi said. "Let us go home."

Acknowledgments

My heartfelt gratitude goes to PJ Mark, Jordan Pavlin, Claire Conrad, Sara Nisha Adams, and the rest of the teams at Janklow, Knopf, and Hodder Studios for all of their support and enthusiasm for this novel. To Karolina Waclawiak and Jami Attenberg, thanks so much for your crucial early encouragement. To Yinka Elujoba, Kovie Biakolo, Colin Cage, Bim Adewunmi, Tolani Akinola, and Dami Obaro: I'm so grateful for your helpful feedback on my rough (!) drafts. And I'm especially grateful to the women whose decades-long friendship loosely inspired this novel: Aunty Yetty, Aunty Bunmi, and my mother.

A NOTE ABOUT THE AUTHOR

Tomi Obaro is an editor at BuzzFeed News. She lives in Brooklyn.

tomiobaro.com
Twitter.com/TomiObaro